MW00939320
Enjoy the Journ
Brenda Beem

Evernight Teen ®

www.evernightteen.com

ISBN: 978-1-77233-574-3

Cover Artist: Sour Cherry Designs

Jacket Design: Jay Aheer

Editor: JC Chute

BRENDA BEEM

DEDICATION

To Justin, Jenna, Jon and Brittney,
You make me proud.

ACKNOWLEDGEMENTS

My writing partner, Dennis, and my writing group, Writers in the Rain, are my creative pillars. They are my touchstones for ideas, feedback, and they encourage me by sharing their writing journeys. I appreciate every moment I spend with Fabio Buena, Martina Elise Dalton, Eileen Riccio, Suma Subramaniam, Angela Orlowski-Peart, and Dennis Robertson. I can't imagine what my novels would look like without them.

I've loved hearing from other writers, bloggers, family, and friends who read Knockdown. Your many forms of positive feedback spurred me to keep writing. Mary Avzaradel, the bookmarks you made were awesome. Cathy and David Durning, I am still blown away by the special way you supported my novel. Gail Wohlford, thank you for reading my rough drafts and praising them when I was full of doubts. Ridge Reading Group and Barbee Mill Readers, you encouraged me with your discussions. My sisters in P.E.O, I appreciate your promotion of Knockdown. It was gratifying to see book after book go to a good cause. Allie Urban, your edits were perfect.

Gary, without your backing and your love of sailing, I would not have created what I have. Claude and Ines, thank you for your praise. Jon and Brittney, I am thrilled that you included my novel in your wedding. Jenna, thanks for showcasing Knockdown at your Acupuncture Clinic. Justin, your help with formatting saved me. Barbara, thanks for reading my novel to your class.

Evernight Teen, I am grateful you chose to publish Knockdown and Beached. You have been incredible to work with. Jane Chute, your edits and insights are amazing. Many thanks to the Evernight Teen staff for all you've done to turn my stories into novels.

BEACHED

Knockdown, 2

Brenda Beem

Chapter One

I closed my eyes and swam in the cool water, my strokes long and clean. I imagined I was back in my high school pool and let my body take over, allowing it do what it had trained for years to do.

My boyfriend, Takumi, called to me and I raised my head and treaded water. The salt from the bay burned my eyes as I watched my friends swimming back to *Whistler*, our sailboat.

The bay we'd anchored in was calm. The sea would have glistened if the sun had been shining. But I hadn't seen the sun for weeks. Not since volcanoes erupted and plumes of cascading ash triggered a new Ice Age.

To escape a tsunami and the icy weather, my brother and I had sailed our family's boat down the West Coast from Seattle, to this little bay on an island near the California shore. Our young crew had been celebrating by diving off the boat and playing in the water.

"*Toni*," Takumi yelled again and pointed toward the shore.

A rowboat with three men was gliding towards us. My heart raced as I lengthened my stroke and sprinted to *Whistler*. Takumi pulled me up onto the swim platform. I hurried below, threw on my least dirty clothes, and rushed on deck.

Our four-year-old crewmember, Makala, chased Boots, a little wiener dog around with a towel. Boots escaped and shook from head to long, narrow tail. Doggy droplets flew across the stern of the boat.

Zoë, my brother's girlfriend, squealed when spray hit her in the face. Jervis, a friend of Dylan's and the biggest guy on the boat, grabbed Makala and carried her below deck. Her protests echoed off the water.

I joined my brother Dylan at the rail. Takumi stood behind me. Jervis returned without Makala, and perched on the back of a cockpit bench.

When the rowboat was about a hundred feet away, the scruffy guy rowing bellowed, "Get your captain. We need to speak to him."

Dylan and I locked eyes. He was eighteen. I was sixteen. We'd survived a tsunami and a thousand miles of rough seas. We'd been threatened by the Coast Guard, a motorcycle gang, and an Ice Age.

Dylan and I were the captains.

Takumi touched my shoulder. "I'll go below and get the spear gun."

"Bring up the pistol, too," I whispered and checked to see if our crew was ready.

Angelina—Makala's older sister—rested with her back against the mast. Angelina could shoot, better than any of us, but she'd been wounded and was now feverish.

Nick, Dylan's friend from school, tied his long damp hair in a ponytail. He'd become Angelina's boyfriend, and hovered over her. Worry lines etched his face.

Boots heard the splash of the oars and began barking. I wished he were as big as he seemed to think he was.

Dylan reached over and squeezed my hand. I swallowed the lump in my throat. Dylan *never* held my hand. Our brother Cole was the one who'd always comforted me, but he'd died saving Makala's life. I pushed his memory aside. I had to deal with these men first.

Dylan hid the gun Takumi handed him behind his back. "Okay!" He called out when the rowboat was about a hundred feet away. "That's close enough."

One of the three men tried to stand, but fell back onto his seat when the boat rocked. He wore what looked to be hospital scrubs. "What do you mean?" he called out. "You… you told one of our people that there was a sick person on… on board. I'm here to… to check him out. No diseased person will be allowed on our island."

"He's a she. And she has a gunshot wound, not a disease. Do you have antibiotics? The wound's infected," I said.

The man rowing—a burly guy, with a scar running down his cheek—pulled the oars in. He placed his hand on the shoulder of the man who'd been talking.

A fat bald man sitting in the bow sneered. "The doctor has lots of medicine, but it will cost you."

"Cost us?" I glanced at Angelina and Nick.

The burly scar-faced man began rowing again.

"What kind of doctor are you?" Jervis yelled.

The man in scrubs stammered, "I'm a… dermatologist. Medicine is in… short supply. You understand. Lots of—"

"Fine. Whatever you want, if we have it, we'll give it to you," Nick shouted.

Scarface smiled. "Good. We want the sailboat."

"*What*?" I cried.

"Stop rowing. Now!" Dylan yelled.

Baldy leaned over and came up with a gun. He pointed it at Dylan and grinned.

Dylan swung Angelina's pistol around and aimed back. Takumi pushed me behind him and raised his spear gun. Surprise showed on the men's faces.

"*Whistler*'s not on the table," Dylan growled.

Boots barked in agreement.

"We want to talk to the adult in charge here," Baldy sneered.

"That would be me and my sister," Dylan replied.

Scarface and Baldy laughed.

"You're just a bunch of kids. Make it easy on yourself. Put the gun down and let us onboard." Baldy snorted.

Jervis came back on deck with a second spear gun and stood next to Takumi, mirroring the way Takumi held his gun. Makala kept whimpering below deck.

The rowboat guys stopped smiling.

Dylan held the gun steady. "Look. We don't want a fight. We just want help for our friend."

The doctor argued with the scruffy guys. "Just let me look at—"

Scarface shoved him down into the bottom of the boat.

"Let's go." Baldy kept the gun aimed at Dylan as the rowboat spun in a circle. "No trade. No doctor."

"Stop them!" Nick yelled at Dylan. "Do something. Get the doctor back here."

"Nick, we can't give them the boat." I shook my head slowly.

"But…" Nick stared at Angelina.

"Wait!" Zoë emerged from the cabin below.

Scarface stopped rowing.

She held a bottle of tequila and a bottle of rum in the air, and sauntered slowly to where we stood. "We have liquor. We can trade you antibiotics for booze."

Zoë never stopped surprising me.

The burly guys smiled. "That's more like it." Baldy looked over at his friend.

"Okay. One bottle for every pill, and another bottle for the doctor's examination," Scarface said.

The doctor hung his head.

"Deal," Dylan said. "But you aren't coming onboard *Whistler*."

I stepped around Takumi. "Nick and Dylan, row Angelina out to meet the doctor in our dinghy. Doctor, check her out and see that she isn't sick."

The doctor sighed. "I can do…do that. But if what you say is…is true, I need her to come to my medical tent. I will need to clean and bandage her wound and…and monitor her, to see how the antibiotic is working."

"Angelina?" I looked at her.

She turned to Nick. "I'll go with the doctor. But Makala stays here."

Nick helped Angelina to her feet. She swayed with the gentle rocking of the boat. "Jervis, remember your promise."

Jervis shook his head.

"Angelina, don't go talking about dying, again. You're already getting better," I said. "Actually, we should all get checked out while the doctor's here. Then we can visit you at his clinic."

The doctor nodded. "I…I'll take everyone who wants to go on shore's temperature. No fever means you can come to the island."

"Good," Zoë said. "Because I'm going with Angelina. Check me out first."

"What?" Dylan roared. "No you're not."

"Yes, I am." Zoë moved to the stern and began unfastening the lifelines. "Angelina's my patient. Besides, I can't wait to get off this boat."

"Zoë!" Dylan grabbed her arm. "Those men have a gun."

She raised one eyebrow at him, shook his hand loose, and climbed down to the swim step.

Both Dylan and Baldy lowered their weapons. Takumi held the spear gun at his side.

Jervis went below deck and returned with Makala. She ran and clung to her sister.

One by one, Nick rowed us across to the boat with the three men. The doctor leaned across our dinghy with his battery-operated thermometer. Taking our temperatures took only seconds.

Dylan and Takumi kept their weapons close by throughout the doctor's process. Everyone tested was found to be fever-free.

Finally, it was Angelina's turn. It hurt me to see how thin she'd grown. Her large brown eyes took up most of her face. The gunshot wound had taken a lot out of her.

"Okay. Payment first," Scarface said. That's seven examinations so far…and now, the injured girl. You owe us eight bottles of booze."

"Eight!" Dylan cried. You said…"

"We said one for each person examined and one for every pill. The doctor examined seven of you already." Baldy pulled his gun back out and placed it across his lap.

"All he did was take our temperature," I cried.

"*You son of a—!*" Dylan yelled.

Zoë held the bottles of alcohol high and waved them. I could see the glint in the eyes of the big guys. "How about this," she said. "The temperature thingy is only worth a beer. We'll give you eight bottles of beer for taking our temperatures, the bottle of tequila for examining Angelina, and the bottle of rum for an antibiotic when she gets to shore."

Baldy shook his head. Scarface dropped the oars in the boat, and moved closer to his friend. They whispered, glanced at us, and finally laughed.

Scarface moved back to the center bench. "Okay. Since you're new here, we'll take it easy on you. But don't expect us to be so generous next time."

I couldn't believe what jerks these guys were. I put my hands on my hips. "Who are you guys?"

"We're the island's—sheriffs." Baldy looked at Scarface and chuckled.

"Yeah! Sheriffs. I like that." Scarface smiled.

The doctor ignored them. "I…I need to check the girl out."

"Okay. I'll get the beers. Here, catch!" Zoë turned and tossed the large bottles she'd been holding at the rowboat.

Scarface caught one, but Baldy missed. The bottle bounced off the bottom of the boat and almost ended up in the water.

Zoë stopped in front of Angelina. "While you *sheriffs* check out the quality of our stuff, I'll help the doctor with Angelina. He can ride to shore in our dinghy."

Scarface and Baldy were too busy opening the bottles to answer.

"I'm going too," both Nick and Jervis cried.

"No, Jervis," Angelina whispered. "You have to stay with Makala."

"But…" Jervis glared at Nick.

"No-o-o!" Makala wrapped her arms around her sister's leg. Angelina yelped with pain.

I peeled the four-year-old off her sister. "We'll visit in the morning after the doctor fixes her up, okay?"

"Sissy!" Makala kicked and flailed her fists at me.

"Ouch! That hurts!" I rubbed my shin.

"Makala. Stop!" Angelina scolded. "Remember when Mom was in the hospital? We went to visit her every day? That's where I'm going, to the island hospital." Angelina gestured at the shore.

"Take me with you!" Makala whined.

"You need to stay here, with Boots." Angelina moaned as Nick helped her into the dinghy. "Visit me in the morning."

"Promise?" Makala held up her pinky finger.

"Promise." Angelina held up hers.

Zoë climbed in behind Angelina. Nick began rowing. When they came alongside the little rowboat, the doctor awkwardly climbed on board the dinghy. Scarface and Baldy were slugging down their bottles, only pausing long enough to count the beers Zoë dropped into their boat.

The doctor frowned when he took Angelina's temperature and showed the results to both girls. Zoë sighed and helped remove Angelina's bandage. Still, the doctor shook his head. Zoë argued and gestured. Finally, the doctor wrapped her wound back up and nodded. Nick continued rowing Zoë, Angelina, and the doctor to the camp on shore. I wondered what Angelina had said to convince him to help her.

I moved around the boat, hanging wet towels over the rails, and carrying soap and bottles of body wash back to the head. Makala wouldn't stop crying and Jervis finally carried her back down to the cabin below.

Dylan stopped me. "I'll stay on deck and keep watch. But If I hear a scream or gunshot, I'm going after Zoë."

"Zoë will be fine. She can take care of herself." I left to see if Jervis needed help.

Makala was cradled in Jervis's lap when I found them. They were both almost asleep.

I felt suddenly exhausted. None of us had slept for more than a few hours at a time for days. I came back on deck with blankets and Takumi and I snuggled next to the fire we'd built in the barbecue we'd found and installed in the cockpit. I fell asleep listening to the sheriffs get drunk as they floated around the bay.

Makala's cries woke me. It was pitch dark and Takumi was gone.

"Sissy!" Makala yelled. "Sissy!"

Chapter Two

Thick clouds covered the moon and stars. I shivered. My hair was still damp from my swim and my eyes struggled to focus in the dark. I found Dylan and Takumi standing together in the stern. They both held their weapons.

A small boat glided across the still waters of the bay towards us. I worried Baldy and Scarface were returning, but this boat seemed larger than the one they'd been in. Jervis and Makala joined me on deck. Jervis shined a flashlight across the water.

"Sissy?" Makala cried. "Is it Sissy?"

Zoë's high-pitched voice called out from across the water, "Jeez, Makala. Stop yelling."

As the boat grew closer I could tell there were only two people in our dinghy. Nick was rowing.

"Makala, Angelina's okay." Nick swung the dinghy around to face us. "The doctor and his daughter are taking good care of her. We'll tell you all about it when we get onboard."

"The doctor has a daughter?" I echoed and relaxed a little. I hadn't liked the idea of Angelina alone on shore with those creeps. I scanned the bay and tried to find the tiny rowboat the drunks had been partying in, but they were gone.

Makala sniffled.

"We'll visit Angelina first thing in the morning," Takumi told Makala. He laid the spear gun down and snapped a lid on a bin filled with of fresh fish and seaweed. While I'd slept, he'd been catching our dinner.

Makala pouted.

Before she could protest again, Jervis handed her the flashlight. "Aim it down on the swim step." Jervis showed her what he meant.

Dylan ran to the stern and helped Zoë out of the boat while Nick tied it up to *Whistler*.

Zoë covered her eyes. "Makala! You're blinding me."

Jervis pulled Makala onto his lap and turned the flashlight up at the clouds.

A small fire still blazed in the barbecue we'd built in the cockpit. I fanned my hair as close to the flames as I dared.

"So, what's it like on the island?" I asked as soon as Nick had the dinghy secured.

"Muddy. Dirty." Zoë wrinkled her nose.

My shoulders slumped. We'd finally made it to the island we were seeking. We all needed to feel land beneath our feet. Even with the creepy guys around, I'd been excited to go ashore and explore.

"But Angelina's getting help?" Takumi stood at the cockpit opening, wiping his hands.

Zoë thought for a moment. "Yeah! The medical dude seems to be a real doctor. He even built a little two-bed hut, made out of some of the wreckage. He and his daughter, Kat, keep it clean. I saw a number of bottles of antibiotics, some simple equipment, and sterile bandages."

"Sounds good." Relief flooded over me and I glanced at Makala. She'd been listening to every word.

Nick hurried below.

Zoë joined us around the fire pit. "It isn't a hospital. Not even close. No x-rays or anything, but it's better than nothing. The doctor and Kat sleep close by in their own tents. The clinic beds are just a couple of sleeping bags on the ground."

"What did the doctor say about Angelina?" Jervis asked.

Zoë warmed her hands over the fire. "He said we brought her to him just in time. I told him the infection had actually been worse, that we made our own antibiotics. He didn't believe our tea stuff really helped, but then, he didn't see her when her fever was high."

Jervis scowled. "He didn't think my penicillin tea idea worked?"

Zoë shrugged. "It doesn't matter. He cleaned the wound, put on a fresh bandage, and started her on a z-pack antibiotic. She was already looking better when I left."

"Thank God!" I sighed.

Makala closed her eyes and sucked her thumb. Takumi put the last piece of wood on the fire.

Dylan wrapped his arm around Zoë and whispered, "Did he have what you needed to test for…?"

She shook her head.

I pretended I hadn't heard while I tried to imagine life aboard the boat with a pregnant Zoë.

"I'm starving." Zoë raised her head. "What time is it? All they had to eat was hard-boiled seagull eggs. Do you guys know how small they are?" She stared at me. "Do you?"

I shook my head and pulled out my cell. Every time I looked at my phone, my heart fluttered with hope. Maybe there would be a text from my parents. For two weeks we'd been without cell service. No one knew where their families were or if they were even still alive.

The usual, "no service" message appeared on the screen.

I stared at the wallpaper photo of my family. My twin brothers, Cole and Dylan, were kneeling with me in the sand on Alki Beach, a favorite Seattle spot. Dad stood behind us with his arm draped around Mom. We'd been so happy.

I sighed and shoved my phone back into my pocket. "It's ten o'clock," I told Zoë, then heard a thump and turned. Nick was adjusting his backpack as he untied one of the kayaks.

"What are you doing?" Dylan asked.

Nick held the light plastic kayak over his head and carried it toward the stern. "I'm going back to stay with Angelina. You'll need the dinghy to go ashore in the morning and I didn't want to leave it unattended on the beach all night. We can't trust anyone."

He dropped the kayak into the water and tied it to the swim step. "The jerky guys who came with the doctor arrived on the island just a few days ago. That's their wrecked sailboat." I could barely make out the top of a mast in the shallow water close to shore. "Everyone I met is scared of them. One man told me that just before the tsunami, guards opened up the prisons, and let everyone go free. He's sure the creeps are released convicts."

Jervis bolted upright in his seat. "You went off and left Angelina alone with *convicts*?"

Nick glanced back at the shore. "I waited until they were asleep. They were so drunk they fell into their tents and started snoring. Listen!"

We faced the beach and concentrated. The island was about four hundred feet away, but it was amazing how clearly sound traveled across the water. In between the splashes of the gentle waves on the shore, we could hear the uneven snorts and snores of the drunks.

"What if they wake up?" Jervis held Makala on his lap.

"I'll be back before they do." Nick jumped down to the swim step, climbed into the kayak, and shoved off.

We watched him paddle across the bay.

"Why did Nick say we couldn't trust anyone?" Dylan asked Zoë.

She gazed across the bay at the beach. "The boats and kayaks on shore are beat up. I'm sure the *Whistler* looks like heaven to everyone. Even our dinghy is in better shape than anything I saw."

"Really? I didn't think about *Whistler* being such a target." Dylan's eyes narrowed.

Zoë shrugged. "Some people seemed nice. I talked to a few who were curious and desperate for news. Nick was right, though. They are all scared of the convict guys."

I stirred the fire. "How many people did you see?"

"Let me think. There were three couples, two families with kids, and about six guys that seemed to be by themselves. That doesn't include the two drunks. Some people might have been out exploring, though. All the campsites are up on the hill above the beach. Mostly they have small tents. Wood is scarce, so they share a fire made out of the wreckage they find."

She stood and walked to the rail. "A young woman told me that they take turns hiking to other beaches to find wood. She let me know that if anything burnable shows up on this beach, it's theirs."

"Humph! She sounds real nice." Jervis spoke softly as he rocked the thumb-sucking Makala.

The fire crackled and a board splintered. Nick disappeared into the darkness.

Zoë pointed to the east side of the beach. "A freshwater stream is right over there."

Dylan followed her gesture. "Good. We'll use the plastic bins to haul water back to *Whistler*."

Zoë sat back down, leaned over, and stirred the fire. Sparks flew in the air and we scrambled to make sure they didn't land on anything that might burn or melt. Then we listened to the sounds from the island.

I stood, walked to the side of the boat, and then back to my seat. It wasn't fair. We'd had enough to deal with. Why couldn't the island be the safe haven it was supposed to be?

I focused on the snores coming from the shore. The few times they stopped, I held my breath, and waited for the heavy breathing to continue. I exhaled when it did.

Takumi announced that dinner was ready. He'd prepared a crab, fish, and seaweed mixture that he suggested we roll up in leftover pancakes. The salty taste of seaweed was beginning to grow on me. Even Makala didn't complain about "green food" anymore.

Zoë sucked the meat from a crab leg, and I wondered when she'd stopped being a vegetarian.

I finally laid my plate down and yawned. The fire was dying and we were out of wood. I pulled the hood of my sweatshirt up over my head.

"Go to bed. I'll sleep on deck," Dylan said.

"No. We take turns guarding the boat," I told Dylan.

Zoë headed for their cabin. "The convicts were lucky they made it to shore, as drunk as they were. They aren't going anywhere tonight. I'm going to bed."

"I'll keep Boots up top with me. He'll warn me if anyone comes near the boat." Dylan lined a couple of seats cushions up, and lay down.

"Dylan's right." Takumi picked up Boots. The little dog's tail wagged and he licked Takumi's face. "Boots is a pretty good little watchdog."

Makala had fallen asleep in Jervis's arms and he carried her to bed.

When I came out of the ship's head, Makala was asleep on the couch where Nick usually slept. Jervis lay on his mattress in the middle of the floor, reading by flashlight.

"Goodnight," he mumbled, and went back to his novel.

I tiptoed across the room to the girl's cabin. Takumi was there, waiting for me. I stood in the doorway and shivered. Takumi pulled back the covers and I hurried to him. His body slowly warmed mine.

"You are so beautiful." Takumi traced the outline of my cheek with his finger.

I reached to push his long hair away from his face. It bounced back over his dark eyes. "You're not so bad yourself," I grinned.

He moved his lips to mine. "I want to be with you, Toni."

Our lips came together. I got a whiff of his berry-scented body and smiled.

"What?" he asked.

"You smell like strawberry body wash." I grinned.

He buried his nose in my hair. "You smell like fruit too."

"Is that good?"

"Perfect!" Takumi stared into my eyes. "You know I would never do anything to hurt you. Trust me?"

My grin faded. "With my life."

Our kisses deepened. I let myself go and became lost in his embrace. When we pulled apart, we both gasped, craving more. But in this dangerous new world, we'd agreed that we couldn't risk my getting pregnant.

I stared at the ceiling and sucked in air.

Takumi cradled me in his arms.

I rested my head on his shoulder and closed my eyes.

****

Boots' barking woke me. Daylight streamed through the hatch above. Dylan and Zoë's cabin door slammed open and Takumi and I leapt apart. We hurriedly added layers to the clothes we'd slept in, and started out the cabin door.

Takumi stopped me. "I do love you," he said, and pulled me around to face him.

I flashed back on the first time I'd seen him standing alone at the Marina. I remembered the way he held me during the tsunami. He'd been there for me when Cole died, and every day since.

I stared into his exotic eyes. "I love you, too," I whispered.

Chapter Three

The cloudy sky seemed brighter somehow that morning. I had to shade my eyes as I searched the deck. Boots crouched on the bow, yipping non-stop.

Dylan stretched out on the cockpit bench. "So. You going to tell me you were playing cards again last night?"

Takumi stepped in front of me. "I told you. I would never put Toni in danger."

I'd had enough. "Dylan, let it go. Takumi and I are together. Get over it." I stepped to the rail. "Why's Boots barking?"

The little dog was obsessed with something in the water. He growled and barked again.

Dylan's eyes were bloodshot. "Damn dog. He barks every time a seagull flies over or a seal swims by. Great guard dog, that one."

Takumi and I laughed. I pulled Takumi with me, toward the bow and Boots.

"You're just going to walk away?" Dylan snarled.

"Yep," I replied and bent down to pet Boots. "What's wrong, boy?" I asked. His muscles were tense, and every bark shook him from his head to his tail. He was focused on something in the water. I looked down. A fin in the sea below us circled the ship.

"Shark!" I jumped back, tripped on a cleat, and fell onto the railing.

"Sharks?" Takumi steadied me.

A fin in the water below us raced toward the stern. We were safe on the boat, but I trembled to think that we'd been swimming here the day before.

Takumi smirked.

"You like sharks?" I asked.

"Actually, shark tastes pretty good," he said. "But that's not a shark."

As if on cue, the creature in the water leapt in the air. It was a dolphin. A *large* dolphin, which stood on its tail fin, squealed, and then scooted backwards.

"Someone get Makala," I yelled.

Jervis hurried up on deck with Makala in his arms. "What? What's going on?"

Makala rubbed her eyes and whimpered for her sister. Boots continued to yip and bark.

"Boots, stop it." I nodded at ripples where the dolphin had gone under. "Makala, watch!" The dolphin flew out of the water, just in front of us. Makala's face lit up, and all the signs of a sad little girl disappeared.

Dylan and Zoë joined us on the bow. Two more gray dolphins came and frolicked with the first. Boots went crazy. I picked him up and tried to calm him down, but he fought to be free. Makala laughed and danced around the deck as the dolphins squeaked and played on and under the water.

It was magical. I used valuable battery power on my phone and took a picture. The dolphins passed by the boat at least five times, always squealing and performing at our side. I think they enjoyed teasing Boots as much as entertaining Makala.

Then, as quickly as they'd arrived, they dove beneath our boat and left the bay.

Boots finally stopped making a fuss.

"Time to go see your sister," I said cheerfully before Makala's whining started again.

* ***

Dylan offered to stay with Zoë and guard the boat.

"No, I'm going ashore. She's my patient," Zoë argued.

I finished tying Makala's shoes and joined in the discussion. "You've already been on shore. Dylan hasn't. But he's offering to stay anyway. He needs back-up."

Zoë stomped to her cabin and slammed the door.

Makala tugged on the bottom of my jacket. "Sissy and I brought flowers to Mommy in the hospital. Can I bring some now?"

"Sorry, sweetie. We don't have any flowers and there probably aren't any on the island yet. It might be too cold. But it would be nice to bring her something." I glanced around the boat.

"She likes coffee," Jervis said as he came out of the head. "So does Nick. Do we have any left?"

I'd never become a fan of the bitter stuff, but my parents drank gallons of it. When we'd left Seattle there'd been a large bag of coffee grounds onboard. I didn't know how much was left.

Takumi checked the cupboard and pulled out an almost empty package hidden all the way in the back. "It's decaf. But that's better than nothing. There's just enough to make one pot. Makala, maybe you can find a picture of a flower in one of the magazines and make a get well card?"

Makala ran to what was left of the magazines.

"Good idea. I'll help." Jervis searched the desk for pens and markers.

I dug around in a deep storage space until I found a thermos. While I was rinsing it out with a small amount of boiled seawater, an idea popped in my head. I carried the thermos to Zoë's cabin and pounded on her door.

"Go away," She snarled.

"Open up. I need your help," I insisted.

The door opened a crack and Zoë peeked out. "What now?"

I pushed my way into her room. "I want to put something in the coffee to knock the convicts out. What do you have?"

Zoë thought for a moment, then rummaged through her stash from a mega yacht we'd found on our journey. "They're big guys, but these sleeping pills are pretty strong. Do you want to kill them?"

"No!" My voice croaked with shock. "Just knock them out."

She poured the entire bottle of sleeping pills into the thermos. "Just don't let any one person drink the whole thing. Want me to take it to shore for you?"

"I got it," I said, and left.

Zoë followed me and argued that she should be the one to go ashore.

I kept saying no as we loaded the dinghy with empty bins to collect water, paper cups, the thermos, a full bottle of gin, and a half-empty bottle of rum. The few bottles of alcohol we had left were less than full.

Dylan, Zoë, and I discussed our plan. We agreed that if Angelina were strong enough, we'd bring her back to *Whistler* with the medications, and sail to another bay. Jervis argued that it wasn't safe for Makala to go ashore. He didn't want her near the guy who had a gun.

"They'll know we are up to something if you don't bring Makala," Zoë insisted.

I told Jervis and Dylan about the drugged coffee.

Jervis eyebrows knitted together with concern. "Okay then … but at the first sign of trouble, I'm getting her out of there. And I'm not waiting for the rest of you. Got it?"

Zoë shrugged. “Those guys are so excited to get the booze. They won’t give you any trouble.”

Jervis picked up Makala’s lifejacket. “I still say Makala should stay here.”

Boots barked as we rowed to shore. It was early, and I’d hoped to land on the island unnoticed, but with all the noise he was making, there was no chance of that. We took turns rowing and I studied our new home as we approached. Although it was off the coast of California, it didn’t have palm trees. I was so disappointed. Instead, a few clusters of straggly pines dotted the cliffs above the beach. Ten pilings stood upright in the bay. They were all that was left of a wharf. The beach that had looked sandy was really coarse gravel. A high cliff-like bank rose above the sea. It was dotted with the colorful tents I’d seen from the boat. Up close, I saw that around these tents were elaborate campsites, with clotheslines and makeshift places to sit.

I sighed. We’d found shelter and fresh water. And it was a big island. If we didn’t feel good about staying here, we could go to another part of the island. We’d just have to find a way to leave a message for my parents. This was the bay where Dad had suggested we meet.

A small group of campers greeted us as we came ashore. Takumi threw them a line and two young guys pulled the dinghy up on the beach. My legs almost buckled when I climbed out of the boat. It had been so long since I’d been on land. Tears of joy welled in my eyes, and Takumi helped me to a log. I could still feel the rocking of the boat.

“We made it,” he whispered. We watched Jervis tie the boat to a huge boulder then sit Makala down on the beach. “We made it!”

"Where are you guys from?" a very tall guy with a dark beard asked.

"Seattle," Jervis answered.

"Wow. You sailed a long way." An older man studied our sailboat.

"It's been an adventure." I took Takumi's hand and wished with all my heart that Cole were here with us. He would have loved knowing we'd made it. "Thanks for your help," I told the island guy.

"Do you plan to stay here?" a thin guy made a face as he lifted the bottles of alcohol out of the boat and handed them to me.

Takumi and I looked at one another.

"Our friend is with the doctor. She's injured, but as soon as she's better, we'll be on our way," I replied.

"That's too bad," the older man said. I wasn't sure if he was talking about Angelina being hurt or our leaving.

We were all anxious to see Angelina and Nick. Takumi led as we hurried off in the direction the campers told us to go. A little ways up the hill I spied a little girl with curly red hair and a woman watching us. When Makala saw the girl, she ran ahead to greet her.

"Hi!" Makala said gleefully.

The girl hid behind her mother.

"Her name is Sophia. She's a little shy," the mother said.

"I'm shy too." Makala bounced on the balls of her feet and pointed to Boots, who could still be heard barking. "That's my dog. His name is Boots. Does your little girl have a dog?"

Sophia peeked out from behind her mother and shook her head.

"That's okay," Makala said. "You can play with mine. We found him in a tree."

The little red-haired girl took a step toward Makala and held out a dirty baby doll. It was missing one arm. "I have a Susy."

Makala's eyes got big. "Can I hold her?"

Soon Makala was cradling the doll and chattering away with her new friend. I hated to pull her away, but reminded her that Angelina was waiting.

Sophia's mother grabbed my arm. "We're not safe here." She stared out at the bay. "Please. Take us with you when you leave."

I didn't know what to say. I stared helplessly at Takumi.

"We'll check with the others when we get back." Takumi pulled me away. I hated the choices this new world forced on us.

The woman grabbed Takumi's arm. "Thank you. My husband doesn't get along with the convicts and I've been so afraid. Please, tell your friends. Make them understand. We have to leave here."

She described the way to the doctor's hut. I'd only taken a few steps when Sophia's mom stopped me again. "My husband is searching for wood and something to eat. We can be ready to go the minute he gets back."

I forced a smile and kept walking. We followed the path up the steep bank. When we came to a lookout spot, we checked back on our dinghy. The guys who had helped us ashore were still hanging around it.

I could see why Nick didn't want to leave our dinghy on the beach overnight. It was a miracle that anyone made it to the island in the kayaks and rowboats that were scattered around on the beach.

"I'm going to go back and guard the dinghy," Takumi whispered, then let go of my hand. "I'll check out where to get water."

I'd planned on taking Takumi aside and telling him about the coffee, but there hadn't been a good time. And now it was too late. I sighed. Maybe it was for the best. Takumi would have insisted that he be the one to pass the drugged coffee out to the convicts. I was sure if the plan was going to work, I had to be the one to do it.

But as we hiked the steep hill, I kept glancing back. I didn't like leaving Takumi behind.

"Come on, Toni. The sooner we get there, the sooner we can leave." Jervis nudged me forward.

I quickened my pace and wished Zoë had put two bottles of sleeping pills in the coffee instead of one.

The doctor's camp was a little ways off, by itself. We hiked along the edge of a steep bank. Jervis and I made sure Makala didn't slip and fall.

Faces appeared at the tent flaps as we passed by. It was strange how eerily quiet the settlement was, for having so many people. At first I thought it was because it was early morning. Then I realized … the drunken snores had stopped.

Chapter Four

Baldy stood at the entrance of the plastic tarp-covered building. He didn't seem hung over at all.

"Heard you were coming." He laughed. Boots' yips still echoed in the bay.

"He's our guard dog." I felt the corners of my mouth quiver.

Baldy laughed again.

I hated his laugh.

"Come in. Your friend's doing better." He held up the flap but stayed outside.

Angelina did look better. Much better. The color was back in her face and she was sitting up. Makala ran to her.

On a campstool beside Angelina sat a girl about my age. Her hair was short with purple-tipped spikes. She had more earrings in her ears than I could count, and tattoos snaked down the back of her neck.

She grinned at Makala and Angelina's noisy reunion. "I'm Kat," she said.

I smiled back at her. "I'm Toni. Thanks for taking care of Angelina."

Nick was spread out on top of a sleeping bag on the ground. He got up as we entered. His eyes were red and he didn't look like he'd slept much.

Scarface appeared at the opening and barged in. "Aww! Isn't that sweet?" He stared at Makala and Angelina.

I felt chilled. I didn't care for Baldy, but for some reason, Scarface terrified me to the core.

Jervis stood at the foot of Angelina's sleeping bag. There wasn't much room.

Kat moved out of the way so Jervis and I could get closer to Angelina. She glared at Scarface and finally left the hut.

"I'm fine, thanks, Kitty Kat," Scarface called after her.

Kat flinched as she dropped the flap behind her. My skin crawled.

"How are you doing?" Jervis ignored the con and tried to balance on the tiny stool Kat had been sitting on.

Angelina rubbed Makala's back. "Lots better." She kissed her sister's forehead.

Scarface moved closer to me.

Nick stepped between us. "Be careful. They're planning something," he whispered.

Scarface shoved Nick aside. "Never liked guys with ponytails."

Nick glared back in silence.

Jervis moved beside Angelina. "Ready to go back to the boat?"

She threw back the sleeping bag and nodded. Makala stared wide-eyed at Scarface.

"What's that?" He stared at the thermos.

I turned to Angelina. "Takumi made you a pot of coffee. And Makala has something for you, too."

Makala held up a large flower cutout. "Jervis and me made you a get well card. Toni helped me write the message. It says, 'get well soon,' right, Toni?"

"Makala, it's beautiful. And coffee?" Angelina read the message on the card. "That sounds…" Her eyebrows knitted together. "Wonderful." She stared up at me with concern.

I tried for an innocent smile on my face.

Angelina laid the card face down on her sleeping bag. “The card is beautiful, Makala.” She hugged her sister. “Thank you so much. And Toni, I can’t wait to have a cup of coffee.”

I opened the thermos, poured a cup, and began to pass it over to her.

“Smells wonderful.” Angelina reached out her hand.

Scarface leapt across the tiny space, grabbed the cup from me, and gulped it down in two swallows. I gasped. The coffee was hot. I’d never seen anyone down a scalding cup of coffee so fast.

He handed the cup back to me for a refill. Angelina appeared as shocked as I felt.

Makala scooted off the sleeping bag and hid behind Angelina.

No one said a word for a long awkward moment.

“Makala, did you tell your sister what we saw this morning?” I finally asked.

Angelina glanced nervously at Scarface, and then smiled at Makala. “Tell me.”

Makala whispered. “Do’fins! Big do’fins! They did tricks.”

“Really! You are so lucky.” Angelina looked at Jervis and nodded.

Jervis stood. “Makala, I left something on the boat. I want you to come with me.” He turned to Scarface. “We’ll be right back.” Jervis grabbed Makala and quickly moved to the tent door.

I held my breath, waiting for Scarface to stop him. But he didn’t. Scarface almost seemed pleased to see Jervis leave. Jervis was huge. Could Scarface be intimidated by him?

"What is it, 'ervis? What did we leave?" Makala asked. The tent flap fell behind them.

"A surprise." Jervis' voice was growing faint. He was moving away, fast.

"Okay then." I scowled, feeling suddenly worried that Jervis's leaving was a mistake. "Nick and Angelina, why don't we go back to the boat, too?" I opened the thermos again and offered another cup to Scarface. "Over there's your payment." I gestured at the corner where the two bottles stood.

Scarface downed the coffee, then moved to the bottles. He held them up to the light, one at a time. "Looks like this one is a little short."

"Yeah, but Dad said it was his best stuff. That should make it all right."

"Don't you tell me what to think, girlie! The deal was for a full bottle for every pill and treatment." Spit flew from Scarface's mouth. With Jervis gone, he seemed to act even tougher.

Nick moved beside me. "Don't yell at Toni."

Scarface hesitated for a moment, then shoved Nick. Nick struggled to get up. Scarface pulled out a gun and aimed it at Nick.

"Whoa. Everyone relax." I stood with the open thermos in my hands. "We can work this out."

I took my time pouring a third cup of coffee, partially to let everyone calm down, but mostly because my hands were shaking. Scarface drank it down just as fast as he had the others. I handed half a cup to Angelina, then poured another. Nick reached up for it.

Angelina's eyes widened. Nick hadn't read the card.

Scarface seized the coffee from me before Nick had a chance to take it.

"Hey, knock it off." I tried not to let the relief I felt show in my voice. "Didn't you ever learn to share?"

Scarface gulped that cup too. "Yeah, I know all about sharing. Now pour a cup for my buddy."

Baldy must have been listening, because the flap opened. "Everything okay, boss?"

Scarface handed him the cup of coffee. "Yeah. These kids think they can cheat us. Look what they brought. A half-bottle." Scarface held the bottle in question high in the air.

Baldy sipped the coffee and shook his head. "Sounds like they're reneging on the deal. Sounds like we gotta change the agreement."

"We have more bottles on the boat. After we get Angelina settled, I'll bring three back to you."

"You think I'm stupid?" Scarface yelled. The spray hit my face. "You think I don't know that the minute you're all back on that boat, you'll sail off into the sunset…? No way."

I wiped the spit away. "I'll bring back the bottles. I keep my promises. We need Angelina back on the boat. Makala misses her sister."

"That so?" Scarface laid the bottle down. "Here's the new plan. Sissy guy here goes back to your boat and tells everyone to come ashore. It's *our* boat now."

"No!" I screamed. I couldn't let this happen. We'd gone through too much.

Scarface turned the gun on me. "You got no choice. I'll stay here and guard you girls. As soon as my friend tells me everyone's off the boat, and we have your weapons, I'll release you. If you don't do as I say, or if anyone interferes with my buddy, I'll start shooting. You have one hour."

Nick's fingers formed a fist. "Bastard. You…"

I blocked Nick's path. "Just do what he says. We don't want anybody to get hurt."

Scarface grinned. Baldy laughed.

I stared at Nick. "Please. Just go."

"Yeah, stud. Do what your captain here says." Baldy chuckled and took another sip of coffee.

Nick moved slowly to the opening, turning to stare back at Angelina every few feet.

Scarface held the gun inches from my head. "You got one hour," he told Nick.

Baldy followed behind them carrying his almost full cup of coffee. I collapsed on the sleeping bag Nick had been on. The open thermos fell, spilling the last of the coffee on the dirt floor.

Chapter Five

The spilled coffee soaked into the dirt floor and became mud.

"Why'd you do that?" Scarface stared at the puddle. "You wasted it."

Angelina held up her cup. "Don't yell at Toni. Here, take mine."

Scarface seized the cup from Angelina. I hoped three and a half cups of the sleeping potion would be enough.

I tried not to stare, but it was hard. I kept watching for signs the pills were taking effect. He pulled the campstool over to the corner of the clinic, sat down, and aimed the gun at me. I just wanted him to pass out, and quickly, before Baldy came back.

Time slowed.

Scarface rubbed his chin and chuckled. "I planned to take Kat with me, just for company." He laughed again. "But maybe I should take you too. You're a little scrawny for my taste, but you seem smart, and you know the boat."

"No way!" My rage turned to terror. I imagined wrapping my fingers around his filthy neck and kicking him where it hurt.

Scarface cocked the gun.

"Do it!" I screamed. "I'd rather die than go with you."

The flap flew open. The doctor entered followed closely by his daughter. "What's g…going on?" he asked.

"Kat. Run!" I yelled.

Kat turned and started to flee.

Scarface jumped up, knocked me down with his fist, and fired the gun. I lay on the ground and held my hands over my ears. When I looked up, light streamed through a hole in the blue tarp roof.

"Get back here, Kitty Kat, or I'll shoot one of the girls," Scarface bellowed.

Kat slowly re-entered the tiny clinic. Her lips trembled.

My heart pounded in my ears. I took a deep breath. Our only hope now was the drugs.

We needed time. Time for the drugs to take effect. I stared at the opening. If Takumi, Nick, or Jervis heard the shot, they might get desperate and attack Baldy. I had to warn them, make them wait.

"I have to go to the bathroom." I rose to my feet.

Scarface gestured to a bucket in the corner and sneered. "You ain't going nowhere."

"Wh…what are you doing?" The doctor placed his hands on his hips.

"They're taking our boat." I cradled my head in my hands. "And he's threatening to make Kat and me go with him."

The doctor swiveled to face Scarface. "You, you, said you wouldn't hurt... anyone. You said you just wanted the sail boat."

"You *knew*?" I raised my head and glared at the doctor. "You knew they were going to steal our boat and you didn't say anything?"

"S...sorry. They promised no ... no one would be hurt. They said they would leave the island."

Scarface giggled. "I'm no' gonna hurt th' girls. We're just gonna have a little *fun*."

I shivered with revulsion, then realized he was slurring his words. "You're a jerk."

Kat kneeled beside Angelina and closed her eyes. A tear ran down her cheek. She must have seen this coming.

I said in a calm voice, "Angelina, did you show Kat the pretty card Makala made?"

Kat wiped her eyes, read the note, then stared at me.

I shook my head just a little, hoping she wouldn't give anything away.

Kat handed the card to her father. "Look at the get well card. It's lovely."

Scarface bolted from the stool. "I wanna see tha' card. You are up ta some t'ing." He started to sway. His face scrunched in puzzlement as he took a step forward. Then, without warning, he collapsed, landing part way on top of me.

I forced myself not to scream and rolled out from under him. The doctor, Kat, Angelina, and Makala were frozen with shock.

"The gun. Where's the gun?" I whispered.

We searched around the dirt floor and sleeping bags, but couldn't find it anywhere. Scarface had to be lying on top of it. The coffee-sodden mud soaked into my pants when I kneeled and tried to roll the huge man over. He groaned. I struggled to keep him raised up but I couldn't both hold him and search for the gun. Desperate, I asked the doctor for help.

He reached far under where Scarface had been lying and pulled out the gun. I laid Scarface back carefully so he wouldn't wake up. Without a word, I grabbed the gun from the doctor's shaking hand.

"I don't trust you." I aimed the gun at the doctor. "Now, help me tie the creep up."

Angelina threw back the covers. "Toni, hand me the gun."

I passed Angelina the pistol. She examined the bullet chamber, then glanced up at me. "It's loaded."

Kat joined in the hunt for something to tie Scarface up with. The doctor found a couple of long ace bandages. I yanked the tie strings off the sleeping bags.

"Come on, hurry!" I handed two of the ties to Kat. She secured Scarface's feet. "Doc, use a bandage as a gag." I tied Scarface's hands behind his back. He moaned, but didn't wake up.

The doctor had just finished gagging him with an ace bandage when we heard a dog bark.

Scarface squirmed, but his eyes stayed closed. Angelina kept the gun aimed at him.

Baldy and our crew were coming back. I stared down at the sleeping form. If the boys had given in to his demands, Baldy would have the pistol from the boat. We had to get that gun before he discovered Scarface was tied up.

Boots' yip sounded almost outside.

"Boss!" Baldy called out. "Everything okay?"

Boots ran inside and jumped on Angelina. Scarface's eye's fluttered open, then closed. I pulled a blanket off Nick's bed and threw it over him.

"Hurry! Stand behind the flap. Smash him with the stool," I told the doctor in a soft voice.

"Toni!" Takumi's worried voice made my heart beat even faster.

The flap opened. "Boss?" Baldy's face appeared in the opening. The doctor crashed the stool over his head. The boat's pistol flew from his fingers as he stumbled into the clinic. I dove for the gun.

Takumi, Nick, Dylan, and Jervis rushed in behind him. Before Baldy could regain his footing, the guys had him pinned to the ground. Takumi straddled Baldy's chest and punched him in the face. Nick rolled him onto his back and held his hands together. Kat walked over and kicked him in the side.

Dylan handed Nick a roll of duct tape and raced over to me. "Are you okay?"

The boat's gun shook in my hand. Dylan took it from me and turned it on Baldy. Angelina was still aiming Scarface's gun at the bundle on the floor.

We'd done it. The plan had worked. But I couldn't stop shaking.

"I need to get out of here." I felt like throwing up.

When Nick and Takumi were done wrapping Baldy's ankles and wrists with duct tape, Takumi helped me out of the tiny hut.

Chapter Six

Zoë sat waiting on a log outside the medical hut.

"What happened?" She stood. "Is Dylan okay?"

I told her the short version.

"Looks like my plan worked." She lifted the flap and went inside.

"Her plan?" I mumbled.

Takumi gripped my shoulder to stop me from saying something I would regret. I gulped in gallons of fresh air and focused. It was over. Everyone on *Whistler* was safe. That's all that really mattered.

Angelina and Nick came out. Angelina leaned on Nick, but seemed so much better than just the day before, even after all the drama. Boots took off and raced around, exploring the grasses, bushes, and trees that had survived the tsunami.

"The cons are all tied up," Nick said.

I gave Angelina a hug. "You okay?" I asked.

She rubbed my back, just like she did her sister's. "Thanks to you." She glanced around. "Jervis, where's Makala?"

Jervis looked like he wanted to whisk Angelina to safety too, but didn't move. "I took her to her friend's tent to play. She's safe with Sophia."

Angelina smiled. "Thank you. I'm so glad you got her out of there."

Jervis glared at me. He'd been right. We should have left her on the boat. I took off on a path to the beach, putting as much distance as I could between myself and the cons. Takumi remained at my side.

A ways up ahead we came to a pile of sleeping bags, a couple of small tents, flashlights, buckets, and fishing gear scattered about in the dirt.

"This is our stuff. We were allowed to take one armload," Takumi whispered.

This would have been all we had left to survive with if the cons had gotten their way. I was so engrossed in staring at the small pile, I didn't notice the young man who sat on a log a few feet away.

His arm movement startled me. He was calmly whittling a long spear that already seemed sharp. He stood as we approached.

"Everything okay?" he asked.

I grimaced. Nothing was okay. My brother Cole died trying to get to this island. My parents were supposed to be here, but weren't. The safe refuge we'd been hoping to find had been anything *but* safe.

"Yeah!" I said. "Everything's fine. The two cons are tied up in the doctor's hut. Are you good with that?"

The guy shrugged. "I'm Jeremy. If you're Toni, my wife and my daughter, Sophia, met you earlier. The little girl who came with you is playing at my place right now. My wife said you told her we could leave the island with you."

I cleared my throat and bent over to pick up a cooking pot and my backpack while I sought the right words to answer his question.

Jeremy sighed. "Earlier, I watched your group hike up the hill. When they dropped everything and ran for the hut, I said to myself, "Jeremy, you should just stay here and keep an eye on their things. They don't realize that stuff disappears if you're not careful."

Angelina raised her eyebrows and handed Takumi Scarface's gun. As soon she and Nick had their arms full, they headed down to the beach.

Takumi and I took a seat on Jeremy's log.

"Thanks for keeping an eye on our stuff," Takumi said. "Our group is deciding what to do with the cons. Maybe you and some of the other island campers should help make the decision."

Jeremy stared at the hut, lost in thought. Finally he closed his pocketknife and began walking away.

"Where are you going?" I asked.

"The convicts hurt and stole from some of the people here. It is only fair that everyone has a say in what becomes of them. I'll tell the others." He strode a few feet, then swiveled to face us. "Are you going let my family sail away with you?"

I took a deep breath. "We're not sure what we're going to do, but we don't have enough room for everyone on the boat as it is."

"I see." Jeremy's shoulders drooped as he climbed up and over the hill behind us.

Part of me wanted to cry, but more of me wanted to hit something. Takumi must have felt my frustration. He bent down, picked up a handful of dirt, and turned his palm up and let the wind blow the dirt away, particle by particle.

Slowly, the handful evaporated. He bent and picked up another.

I watched the breeze blow and scatter the dirt across the hill. Somehow it was calming. When he picked up a third handful I asked, "What are you doing?"

He focused on the dust he was creating. "Do you know how many times I wondered if I'd ever feel land again? It is a miracle we made it here."

"We almost didn't," I said as I put my gear down.

He let the third handful slowly float. "But we did. We're lucky. There's a doctor here, no disease, water, land, and a sea full of food. Besides, there's no bad guy anywhere that can stand up to you."

"Stand up to *me*? You've got to be kidding." I picked up my own dirt clump and threw it at him.

"Hey! I'm the good guy." Takumi chuckled and brushed the dust off his jacket. "What you did was brave. Jervis told me about your drugged coffee plan. I just wish you'd been the one to tell me. I wouldn't have gone back to the dinghy."

I grimaced. "Makala was always close by and I couldn't trust her not to tell. I'm sorry. I should have tried harder to find a way to tell you what was going on."

Takumi bent to pick up another clump of dirt, then changed his mind. "Yes, you should have. But it all worked out. And now, those guys will be gone, one way or another. We can explore the island just like we talked about. We can set up our own campsite. Maybe we'll even find a fresh water lake or pond to swim in."

A real fresh water bath! I rubbed the dirt off my fingers and looked around. Really looked. Across the bay stood a clump of trees. How they'd survived, I didn't know. Beyond that, lay land and more land. A whole island to get to know… somewhere in the middle of the island, the travel book said there was an old homestead and buildings. And somewhere close by, my parents could be waiting.

Takumi was right. We should hike inland and see what the tsunami left. I leaned against him. "I love camping."

Takumi smiled and my heart did flips.

We picked up a load of our gear and began our climb down to the beach. Nick and the girls were a short ways up ahead. *Whistler* gently floated in the calm bay, beautiful with her blue hull and tall mast. From a distance the pieces of duct tape and dents in the hull couldn't be seen. The sea beyond the bay was dark. The steep cliffs and high banks protected our little boat, the beach, and the campers.

I saw movement along the far edge of the bank behind us and watched. A group of men and women were headed toward the medical hut. I was glad they'd be able to take part in the trial. All of a sudden, three of the men broke away from the main group, and started down toward the beach.

Both the dinghy and *Whistler* were unprotected.

"I have Angelina's gun," Takumi said and bolted.

I hurried after him. At the shore, we watched a guy take hold of the line that was tied to our dinghy. The other two men were bent over a couple of badly beaten-up kayaks.

"Hold it right there!" Takumi pulled out the gun as we raced across the gravelly beach.

The three guys dropped the lines and held up their hands.

"Dude!" the tall bearded guy who held our dinghy line cried. "What's your problem?"

"You're taking our boat. That's a problem. Now move away," I said.

The guys who were near the kayaks shook their heads and pulled the kayaks up to higher ground. Then they waded over to a small rowboat and drug it up on the shore too.

The bearded guy holding our dinghy stood with his hands in the air. "It's gonna be an extra high tide today." He pointed at the large boulder our line was tied to. "That rock will be underwater in about an hour and then, poof." He demonstrated with his fingers. "Your line and dinghy will just float away. But if that's what you want?"

Takumi lowered the gun. My cheeks burned. These guys were trying to save our boat, not steal it.

"We, we didn't know," I said.

"You didn't ask," one of the guys near the kayaks said.

"Sorry." Takumi checked the safety and put the gun in his waistband. "We didn't get a very warm welcome when we arrived yesterday."

"Yeah." The bearded guy with our dinghy glanced up at the hill where the medical hut was. "Those convict dudes messed things up here, big time. Before they arrived, we mostly worked together. Kinda like one big family."

"Well, they won't be a problem anymore," Takumi said.

"Right. Now you're threatening us with a gun."

He was right. We'd never have thought to pull a gun on someone two weeks ago. I'd never even held a real gun back then. Now it was our first thought.

"Let's try this again." I reached out my hand. "I'm Toni. This is Takumi. Thanks for trying to protect our dinghy."

The bearded guy hesitated for a moment, then shook my hand. "You're welcome. I'm Ned, that's Banks and Brad."

We shook hands all around. Takumi helped pull our dinghy up on the beach.

"We heard a gunshot." Ned looked up the cliff to the doctor's hut. "Anyone get hurt?"

I told them about Scarface wanting to kidnap Kat and shooting a hole in the roof to make her come back. Then I explained how I'd drugged the coffee. As I spoke, the three men folded their arms and frowned, clearly not appreciating how clever I'd been.

The more I talked, the more uncomfortable I became. What was their problem? My cheeks burned. My plan worked. The escaped cons were tied up. They should be happy.

"What are you guys going to do with them?" Banks or maybe it was Brad asked.

"We don't know. I think your people and ours are deciding," Takumi said.

"Live by the sword, die by the sword," Ned said. His friends nodded.

Really? My mouth hung open. Were we supposed to just let them steal our boat? Were Kat and I just supposed to sail away with the creeps? What was wrong with these guys?

"Look. We didn't come here to make problems. We've only protected what's ours." Takumi's eyebrows cinched.

The guys looked at one another. "We voted that no guns would be allowed on the island."

I gritted my teeth. "Yeah? And how well did that work out, when the convicts showed up with a gun?"

One of the "B" guys rolled his eyes.

Takumi quickly pulled me into his arms. "Take a deep breath before you say anything," he whispered in my ear.

"What's the point?" I answered, loud enough for them to hear.

From out of nowhere Boots appeared and barked at us as if he hadn't seen Takumi or me in ages. I finally picked him up, got my nose licked, and put him back down. He raced back to Nick, Angelina, and Makala who were a short ways down the beach. Makala threw a stick a few feet away from her. Boots picked it up and dragged it along the water's edge.

The guys we'd tried to talk to moved off to study a long wooden piling. It was stuck upright on the beach. Jervis and Kat were slowly making their way down the path from the doctor's camp. The trial of sorts was finished.

"What's the verdict?" I asked when they joined us.

Ned, Banks, and Brad moved to stand close behind us.

Kat threw a rock into the bay. "I wanted them to…" she noticed Makala and paused. "I think Dylan's going to sail them to another island and leave them."

"Right!" one of the B's said in a snippy tone. "As soon as the boat's out of sight, he'll just throw them overboard."

These guys were too much. "Knock it off!" I yelled. "If my brother says he'll take them to an island, he will."

"One of us should go along to make sure," Ned said. The B's agreed.

Takumi held me back and called out, "He'll probably let you go if you want. It's about four hours to the closest island. That's four hours over and another four back. And that's if there is good wind." He turned around and stared into my eyes. "I'm going to stay here and search for a good place to make camp."

I grinned. Hiking, walking, anything on shore sounded wonderful. There was no way I wanted to get back on that boat and I never wanted to see the creepy cons again. But if I stayed, Dylan and *Whistler* would leave without me. There were so many dangers out on the ocean. What if there was an accident? What if they were attacked by pirates? What if there was another tsunami and the boat wasn't secured?

Takumi was my boyfriend. I loved him. But Dylan was my family. *Whistler* was my home.

How could I choose between them?

Chapter Seven

Mid-afternoon approached. In the distance, we could see streaks of rain. Rain would make the sailing trip even harder for *Whistler*. The air had a slight chill to it and I shivered.

Takumi wrapped me in his arms. "You don't have to see those creeps ever again."

He thought I was freaked about seeing Scarface and Baldy. He hugged me so tight I had trouble breathing.

"I'm okay, Takumi." I stepped away, ignoring the confusion on his face.

Nick and Angelina joined us on the edge of the dinghy. Makala gave up on sticks and began tossing pebbles at the water. Kat tried to show her how to skip rocks, but Makala's rocks never quite made it far enough to splash into the sea. Makala grew frustrated, but Boots wagged his tail, and happily chased after the bouncing rocks.

"If Dylan ends up taking the convicts to another island, what are you guys going to do?" I asked Nick, Angelina, and Jervis.

Angelina held her injured shoulder. "The doctor said Makala and I could stay in the medical hut until our campsite is ready. Makala is so excited. She can't wait to play with her new friend."

"I'm going to find us a perfect campsite and get a good night's sleep. Just think. No cons. No rocking." Nick kissed Angelina's forehead.

"For the next few days you're going to feel like you're rocking, no matter what you do. It takes time to get rid of sea legs." I smiled.

Jervis glanced at Angelina and Nick, who sat cuddled together. "I told Dylan I'd go with him."

Kat raised her eyebrows at Jervis's reaction. The three pacifist guys were having a deep discussion while they lounged on an upside-down rowboat a few yards away. Boots drug a stick almost as long as he was up the beach. Makala called and chased after him. He growled and stayed just out of her reach.

"What about you two? Stay on the island or boat?" Nick asked Takumi and me.

"I vote *island*!" Takumi said.

"Dylan will need help if he's going to sail and guard the cons." I glanced at Takumi. He looked disappointed.

We watched the last of our crew, Dylan and Zoë, head our way. The island people had to be guarding the cons. I peered down at *Whistler*. If only she could make my decision for me.

"What did you decide?" I asked when they finally arrived.

Dylan held hands with Zoë. "Lots of campers showed up. Some wanted to make a prison and keep the convicts tied up until things get back to normal. Kat wanted to kill them."

Kat shrugged.

Dylan continued. "In the end, we offered to sail them to the closest island, Santa Rosa, and leave them without a boat."

"What do you mean, *we*?" I asked, although I already knew the answer.

"Jervis offered to help. I figured you and Takumi would want to come too. Nick can stay and watch over the girls."

"Are any of the island people going with you?" I gestured at Ned and the B's.

"No, why risk it?" Dylan followed my gaze. "They might try to ambush the boat."

I shook my head. "We talked to those three. I don't think they'd swat a fly if it was biting them. I think you should take at least one islander with you if we're going to stay here."

Dylan tipped his head. "'I should take'? Does that mean you're not coming with me?"

Before I could think of an answer, Zoë shoved her hand in my face.

"You haven't seen my ring. Dylan just asked me to marry him. Isn't it beautiful? I'm so excited. Can you believe it? We're going to be sisters."

Blood rushed from my head to my feet. I grabbed Takumi to keep from fainting. Zoë was talking, but I couldn't follow her words. All I could do was stare at the huge sapphire and diamond ring she must have taken from the yacht in Grays Harbor. It took me a few moments to realize she'd stopped speaking. Everyone was staring at me.

I forced a smile on my face. "Congratulations!"

Makala pulled Zoë's hand down so she could see the ring. "Sissy, did you hear? A wedding! Will we have lots of food? And dancing? Can I wear a pretty dress?"

Zoë grinned from ear to ear. "Makala, you can be the flower girl."

Makala's face lit up. "Flower girl! Sissy, did you hear… I'm going to be the flower girl." Her smile faded. "What's a flower girl?"

Zoë turned to me. "We're not going to have a big wedding here on the island. But one of the campers is an attorney. He said he could write up a wedding contract and do the service for us. Oh! And I have an important question to ask you." She paused. "Toni, will you be my maid-of-honor? I know, I know, you normally wouldn't be my first choice, but all my friends are still in Seattle. When we get home, my parents will want to have a huge wedding at their club. You don't have to be the maid-of-honor then—just for the wedding here. So will you?"

My jaw dropped. Fifteen minutes ago, I'd been fighting for my life. Now, Zoë wanted me to be her… her what? Substitute maid-of-honor? The corners of Takumi's mouth twitched. He was struggling not to crack up.

That did it. I burst out laughing.

Zoë took a step back. Tears welled in her eyes.

"Toni!" Dylan grabbed my arm.

Takumi spun around to hide his laugh, but his shoulders still shook. I tried not to look at him. I bit the side of my cheek to stop from giggling.

"Zoë, I'm sorry!" I gasped for air. "It's not you. I'm, I'm messed up from the whole ordeal." I tried to hug her. She was stiff and didn't hug me back. "I'd love to. Now let me see that gorgeous ring again."

Zoë wiped her eyes and held up her ring.

"What did you have in mind for the wedding?" I laced Takumi's fingers in mine behind my back.

It took Zoë a few more seconds to recover, but then for the next ten minutes or so, she told us her wedding plans in minute detail. I tried to pay attention and squeezed Takumi's hand, hard, to keep us both from cracking up again.

When Zoë finally slowed down, Dylan stood. "We need to get the cons on the boat and get going. Coming or not?" he asked me.

I cleared my throat. "Dylan, I love you. I always will. But you're going to have your own family now. I need to stay here with Takumi. We'll search for the perfect place to anchor *Whistler* and build our camp." I turned to the boat. "And while you're bringing the creeps down, we'll row out and get some more supplies for while you're gone."

"I can't leave you here alone. Mom and Dad would…" Dylan started to argue.

"She won't be alone." Takumi stood close beside me.

Dejected, Dylan pointed at Ned and the 'B-named' guys on the beach. "Fine! I'll ask if they'll come along and help."

He was still strolling over to the islanders when we launched the dinghy. Takumi, Nick, Angelina, and I rowed as fast as we could back to *Whistler*. Jervis stayed to watch Makala. I shoved as many jackets, towels, and clothes as I could into pillowcases. Angelina gathered her large pack and stuffed it with clothes. Nick and Takumi packed the foodstuffs and half of the pans, plates and silverware. I hunted for sleeping bags and tents, but they were already onshore, so I took pillows and blankets instead.

"What about stuff for Jervis?" I asked Nick as he packed bathroom items.

"He's going with Dylan and Zoë to the island."

"I know. But after. Is he going to make a camp on shore, or stay on the boat?" I carried a load to the dinghy and hurried back to the cabin.

Nick handed me a bag with toothbrushes and toothpaste. "He wants to search for his mom and sisters. I heard him ask Dylan to drop him off in Santa Barbara on the way back."

"No!" I froze and stared at Nick.

"Dylan told him to wait until cell service is back. He promised he would."

Angelina had been quiet. She walked over to the radio. "Do you think there is enough battery power left?" She flipped the breakers and the cabin filled with the sound of static.

The radio was still working. I raced to find my charger cord and plugged my cell in.

"This is Angelina, come in, over," she said and waited. There was no response. She changed the frequency, and repeated her call. Still no response.

On the third try, we heard a woman's voice. It was the President. Relief flowed over me. She was still alive. We still had a government.

"...And we are waiting for our scientists to determine how long this cold spell will last. The northern states are frozen over. The ice has begun to stop the flow of many of the major rivers that provide water for the south. Despite previous promises, Mexico has closed its borders to all except those who have Mexican passports, or those vouched for and sponsored by a Mexican citizen."

I turned the volume up on the radio. The President sighed. Her sigh gave me goose bumps.

"Yet all is not lost. I'm happy to report that our service men and women alongside many cell phone providers have resurrected or repaired thousands of miles of cell towers. Southern families, churches, and local organizations are providing shelter for refugees. Food from warehouses all over the country is being shipped and trucked to provide for our people.

"I pray every day for the survival of each and every one of you. Our scientists are searching for ways to correct this unnatural weather pattern. Some predict we will return to a new normal after five years. Others insist it may take hundreds."

"Five or hundreds of years? That's a big spread." I moaned.

"Shush!" Angelina put her finger to her mouth.

The President continued. "I encourage everyone to work together to provide shelter, food, and water to those in need. I've ordered the military to re-establish law and order in our southern cities and refugee camps. Crimes should be reported and criminals will be punished.

"I assure you the government of the United States is strong and working hard to provide for its people. I am still your President. Please share this message with those who have not heard it. God Bless!"

The radio grew static. A male voice came on. "This has been a message from the President of the United States broadcasting on the Emergency Broadcast System. This message will repeat in sixty seconds."

Angelina checked her cell. "Still no service. Can we listen from the beginning?"

I unplugged my cell, checked the time, and turned it off. "No, we should get back. Dylan will run out of daylight if he doesn't get started soon." I grabbed a heavy down comforter and four pillows off the couch, threw the gear in the dinghy, and climbed aboard.

Takumi handed his goods down to me and paused. "Give me a second." He hurried into the cabin and returned to the dinghy with our two sets of snorkeling equipment and one of the spear guns. "I'd like to spear some fish, or maybe find a lobster or two."

I grinned at the thought of fresh lobster. "Then we should take the kayaks. Dylan can have the dinghy with them, and we'll still have water transportation."

We discussed paddling the kayaks back, but in the end, towed them behind the dinghy.

Dylan, Jervis, Zoë, the cons, and a few men from the island were waiting on the shore when we got back. Dylan held a gun on the bad guys. Scarface was still knocked out and slept on the gravel with his arms tied behind him. Baldy sat on the beach, his arms and legs wrapped tight in duct tape.

Angelina relayed the message from the President to the group. Dylan took out his cell and checked it.

"Still no service?" A guy I hadn't seen before asked Dylan.

"Nope," Dylan said.

"At least yours has a charge. Mine's been dead for a week," another said.

"We're going to need to put some water in the water tanks before we go." Dylan reached for one of the plastic bins. I grabbed the other and followed him.

"Getting married, huh?" I asked as I washed my face and hands in the fresh water stream. "You're only eighteen, you know. What about college?"

Dylan waded into the stream with his bin. "Those old dreams are gone. I love Zoë, and besides, she's having my baby."

"Are you going to wait until we find Mom and Dad?" I rolled up my pant legs.

"No, Zoë wants to be married when we meet them. She doesn't want to be the pregnant girlfriend."

"Okay. Well, if you're happy, I'm happy for you." I carried my bin into the stream.

Dylan hauled his full bin out of the water and groaned as he carried it to the beach. "Wait and let me carry yours. Heavy!"

When both bins were on shore I waited for Dylan to catch his breath. "Let's row the dinghy over here. Easier than carrying them down the beach."

"Good idea," Dylan turned and yelled. But we were too far for anyone to hear.

"I'll tell them," I said and turned to leave.

Dylan stopped me. "Zoë has never had many girlfriends. I'd appreciate you being a little nicer to her."

"Me? You don't think I'm nice enough to her?"

Dylan glared. "She's pregnant. Give her a break."

I forced myself not to roll my eyes and nodded. "You're right. I'll do my best." The crew had sorted out the gear from the boat and some of it was going back. The three islanders only brought one small bag each, but when the water bins were loaded, the dinghy was full.

"I don't feel good about this." Dylan stared at me.

"About what?" I asked.

"About leaving you here." He moved toward me.

I threw my arms around his neck and squeezed. Giving Dylan a hug wasn't something I'd done, not for years, but it felt right.

"Be safe," I whispered and kissed his cheek. Then I turned to Zoë and forced a smile. "You too, future sister-in-law."

Chapter Eight

Despite my brave words, I couldn't stand on the beach and watch *Whistler* sail away. Instead, I grabbed a load of gear and headed back up the steep embankment to the campsites. Takumi promised he'd follow right behind me as soon as he got the kayaks secured.

Nick and Angelina wanted to stay on the beach, and let Makala play. They mentioned going in the water. Kat said the place where we'd gathered fresh water was a great place to swim. The creek emptied silt along the shore, and the silt made an almost sandy beach.

Boots' barking and the sounds of merriment followed me as I worked my way up the hill. I tried not to be annoyed at the fun they were having, but the load I carried was heavy. I wiped the sweat from my forehead and wondered: what was taking Takumi so long?

I stopped at what was left of the pile of gear our crew had abandoned earlier and unloaded. As I began sorting it into piles that would make campsites, I took inventory. We had two small tents. Each tent could sleep two people at the most, three if one of them was as small as Makala. We were short at least one tent. I placed the tents off to the side and divided up the gear as equally as I could.

While I wondered which pile to put a fishing pole and tackle box in, I heard laughter coming up the trail. I couldn't place the laugh. A few moments later, I heard Kat's voice and then she giggled. Takumi said something I couldn't make out, and then there was that strange laugh again, deep and throaty.

Could the deep belly laugh I heard have been from Takumi? I tried to think of a time he'd laughed out loud, totally unrestrained. I couldn't. We'd been too busy trying to survive to find time to let go. And on the boat, when we did have fun, we had to be quiet. Someone was always sleeping.

It shouldn't have, but it bothered me that he could laugh like that with Kat. They'd just met. It didn't make it any easier to know she was beautiful in a gothic, mysterious way.

I was still holding the pole when Kat and Takumi appeared over the edge of the embankment. Takumi was loaded down with gear. Kat's arms were full of pillows. I showed them where to dump the stuff.

Kat waved at me, whispered something in Takumi's ear, and took off toward her campsite. Takumi chuckled. His eyes seemed to sparkle. When he leaned down to kiss my cheek, I stepped back. The sparkle left his eyes.

"What's wrong?" he asked.

I turned my back to him before I said something I might regret, and found myself staring out at the empty harbor. My heart began to pound as worries about Kat disappeared.

Whistler and Dylan were gone. I searched the horizon, but the boat was nowhere in sight. What if he ran into trouble? What if a giant storm came up? What if he never came back?

I inhaled the sea air. It was too late to panic. Dylan would be back. I'd stayed for Takumi. It was the right thing to do. And so what if Takumi laughed with a beautiful girl? He wasn't the type of guy who would say he loved me one minute and then go off with someone else the next. I'd only known him for a few weeks, but a girl can tell, can't she?

The important thing was the danger to us was over. My brother knew what he was doing. I was being silly. Takumi had the right to laugh with Kat. I wanted him to laugh.

I just wanted him to laugh with me.

I finally swiveled back around. "I can't believe Dylan and *Whistler* are gone."

Takumi laid his pack down. "Are you sorry you stayed behind?"

I peeked at the bay, then back at Takumi. "No. I wanted to."

His sparkle was back. "Let's go for a hike, then."

I took his hand in mine. "Okay! But before we leave, will you help me pitch the tents and get this gear stowed. It's going to rain."

Takumi's shoulders slumped. He glanced up at the sky and grimaced. When had I become the *not fun* girl? I didn't want to be that girl, but someone had to put our stuff away.

We set up camp under the clump of trees I'd spied earlier. The scruffy pines had withstood the tsunami and would provide a little shelter. Also, the ground had a type of leafy plant growing on it that would be a little cushion. The island campers had set up on ground that was rocky and hard, but they had air mattresses. We didn't.

The first tent was already put together when Nick and the girls arrived from the beach. Makala and Angelina dropped their loads and headed to the doctor's hut to dry off and change. Takumi raced after them and handed Angelina her gun. Nick stayed to help us finish setting up.

The moment the tents were up and everything was finally stowed, Takumi took my hand again. "Let's get away from here before something else needs to be done."

I grabbed a raincoat. "Okay. Nick, Takumi and I are going for a hike. We'll be back by dark."

Nick was busily arranging two sleeping bags in one of the tents. If he answered me, I didn't hear it.

Takumi led us on a trail that headed inland.

I looked back at the empty bay. "I thought we were searching for a good place to anchor *Whistler* and set up a more permanent camp? Why are we headed away from the coast?"

Takumi kept walking. "I need a break from the sea. The pamphlet we took off the yacht said there was a campground close by. I thought it might be a cool place to check out. There might even be some supplies there. And if there's a damaged building, maybe we could use the scraps to build a shelter for ourselves."

Lost in thoughts of fire pits and a possible chemical toilet, I didn't watch where I was going, and stumbled over a rock.

"You okay?" Takumi steadied me.

I nodded and tried not to limp, but my ankle hurt.

In some places we walked on a clear path, in others, the tsunami had completely scraped the plants and soil away, leaving deep ruts. What plants we did see were mostly tall grasses, although in the distance, like little mirages, stood clumps of evergreen type trees.

"Before the tsunami, the path was probably pretty easy. But it can't be too far. We just have to go inland, keeping the water to our backs, and Devil's Peak to our right."

"Devil's Peak?" In the distance I could see what appeared to be the pointy top of a mountain. I hadn't noticed it before. "Scary name!"

A little further up the trail, I found a patch of low-growing yellow shrubs with small white flowers.

"Flowers!" I hadn't seen a flower since we'd left home. "They are so delicate. How did they manage to survive? I'd think the salt water from the tsunami would have killed them." I picked a small bloom and stuck it behind my ear.

"Island plants are used to salt spray." Takumi smiled. "You look good with flowers in your hair." He pulled me into his arms. "My island girl," he whispered in my ear and kissed me.

I couldn't stop grinning. We held hands as we hiked and kept sneaking glances at one another.

At a bend in the path we discovered an even larger bush with purple flowers.

"On the way back I'm going to pick some for Zoë. She'll be so excited, to have real flowers for her wedding." I smelled the purple blooms. "She might even forgive me for laughing at her."

For about a quarter of a mile we saw nothing but the tall grasses we'd seen before, but up ahead stood an oasis of trees. I hoped the campground was there. My ankle was starting to throb.

Then the rain I'd worried about came down. I scrambled to put my raincoat on and pulled up my hood. Takumi took out a rain hat and zipped up his jacket. The bare spots of rocky ground became slippery, and I stepped carefully, not wanting to damage my ankle more.

The rain fell hard. There was no shelter, and after a few minutes, my pants and shoes were soaked.

I checked my cell. It was after six. "Maybe we should head back."

Takumi pointed down the trail. "The trees will keep us dry. Let's get there and wait out the storm."

My ankle ached, but I moved as quickly as I could.

The rain finally slowed to a drizzle. We came around a huge boulder and Takumi placed his finger to his lips. We watched the field of wet grass on our left side. A ripple was flowing through it. Something alive was headed toward us.

We took a couple of steps back and searched for some kind of weapon. We had nothing. Takumi took his pack off, and raised it over his head.

"Do you have a rock or something in there?" I whispered.

"No!" Takumi answered.

"Great!" I hid behind him. We were so screwed.

Whatever was in the grass was charging right at us. All of a sudden, a bird's head popped up. And it gobbled.

"A turkey?" Takumi lowered his pack.

"A killer turkey!" I chuckled.

The turkey waddled out of the grass and gobbled again.

"Don't move," Takumi whispered, as he slowly took off his coat, and crouched down.

"What are you doing?" I asked softly.

"Catching it."

Takumi and the turkey stared at one another for a long moment. With his jacket open wide, Takumi pounced. The turkey flapped its wings. Feathers slapped Takumi in the face. Feathers floated in the air. The turkey squawked. Takumi yelled. The turkey broke free and launched itself into the air. It flew low but fast, and was soon only a tiny speck in the distance.

Takumi lay in the grass face down. His coat was spread out beneath his face. Feathers covered his back.

I giggled so hard I had to sit. Takumi rolled over in the grass, looked up at me, and began laughing too. That relaxed, deep laugh I'd heard earlier.

"Missed," he said with a gasp.

"Sure did." Another wave of hysteria hit me.

Takumi brushed the feathers off as best he could. I helped pick off the ones stuck to his wet shirt and stuffed them into my pocket.

Takumi got to his feet and stared out at the direction the turkey flew. "I didn't think turkeys could fly."

"Well, it appears they can." I wiped my eyes.

"Yeah!" Takumi put his coat back on and adjusted his hat. "But how cool is it that turkeys are on the island! The brochure talked about foxes, but not wild turkeys. Next time I'll be prepared. We can set traps."

"Nah! You should give your coat at least one more try." I snorted.

"Very funny." Takumi wrapped his arm around my shoulders, and kissed me.

I reached up, pulled a feather out of his hair, and tickled his nose.

Our eyes met, and he laughed. And laughed. And laughed some more.

With me.

Chapter Nine

The rain finally stopped, but everything was so wet, it almost didn't matter. We continued on toward the oasis of trees. I couldn't remember the last time I'd felt so happy. If my ankle hadn't hurt as much as it did, I'd say it was a perfect afternoon.

I smiled as I replayed Takumi's adventure with the turkey in my mind. But the more I thought about it, the more I was sorry we hadn't captured it. We'd been eating fish and seaweed for days. The thought of roasted turkey made my mouth water.

"You know, where there are turkeys, there are eggs. Maybe we could capture and raise a few hens, just for the eggs."

Takumi glanced over at me. "You think we'll be staying on the island that long?"

I stopped to think. I liked the feel of land under my feet. Now that the cons were gone, I felt safe. From what the President had said, the mainland didn't sound all that great. Maybe we should find my parents and come back here to stay.

Takumi guided me along. "There is so much we don't know about this island. What other animals are here? I bet some of the campers could fill us in. They had hours to research Santa Cruz before the tsunami hit. All we have is a little tourist pamphlet."

I reached out to brush the top of a clump of tall grass that grew along our path. "How did Kat and her dad end up here? He doesn't seem like the wilderness type."

Takumi smiled when I mentioned her name. I had a sudden urge to pinch him.

"No," he said. "Her dad isn't Mr. Outdoors. He didn't even know how to paddle the kayaks they came in."

I recalled my first attempt at kayaking in Grays Harbor. I kept going in circles. Had Takumi shared that with Kat? I scowled. My perfect afternoon was fading. I walked faster.

Takumi didn't notice. "Kat's parents divorced and her mom remarried. Her stepdad is big into camping and kayaking. He told Kat about the island." Takumi started laughing again. "She showed us how her dad tried and tried to put up a tent, but couldn't. Kat is so funny."

I walked even faster. Takumi kept chuckling. I told myself to ignore him. It was hard, however. My ankle was killing me.

"Wait up," he cried. "You're limping."

I pretended I didn't hear him and kept hobbling ahead.

Takumi ran to catch up with me. "Stop. Are you hurt, Toni?"

"Yeah," I finally admitted.

We were almost to the camp. Debris lay scattered about. Mostly broken fence posts, signs, and parts of buildings. A small shed was lying under a large fir tree and appeared to be dry. Takumi helped me over to the metal surface and we climbed on top of it.

"Let me look at your foot." He rested my leg across his lap.

I grimaced as he took off my shoe.

"I don't think anything's broken." He felt around my ankle and the bones of my foot. "But it's really swollen. Did you twist it?"

"When we first started out."

"Why didn't you say something?"

"I thought I could just walk it off." I pulled my foot back and massaged it.

Takumi's brows knitted together. "I'm going to take a look around. Just rest, okay?" He handed me a bottle of water. "That's all we have, so don't drink it all."

Takumi climbed over to a pile of bricks. Except for the roof, nothing was recognizable as a building or even a part of one.

"Find anything?" I called out after he'd been exploring for a while.

"Just bricks and some wooden beams. If we had the whole crew, we could move the bricks. There might be good stuff underneath, but it would take too long to clear it by myself."

I closed my eyes and pushed my jealous thoughts away.

"Toni!" Takumi's urgent whisper startled me.

My eyes popped open. He bent over and picked up a broken two-by-four from the wreckage.

"Don't move!" he hissed as he stared at a spot near me.

I grinned. "What? Another turkey?"

I turned my head and swallowed a scream. Slithering up from under the roof was the biggest snake I'd ever seen.

"Stay still!" Takumi carefully stepped toward me with his board. "Focus on me."

I was too afraid to move. From the corner of my eye I could see that the snake's head, and its enormous body, were now all the way up on the roof. Right beside me. The snake's tail was still coming up from under the metal building. The snake just kept growing. Longer and longer. Its tongue darted in and out. I knew that was how snakes smelled.

I was smelly. It was coming for me.

Takumi was still a few yards away. The snake started to coil its long body. What did that mean? Did it coil before it struck?

I gulped.

Takumi was two feet away. "Okay, when I say roll, stay low, and roll away from the snake and off the roof. Got it?" he whispered.

I nodded.

The snake kept coiling.

"Roll!" Takumi yelled.

I rolled. Takumi swung the board like a baseball bat.

I crashed to the ground, whimpered, and grabbed my ankle.

Takumi knelt down beside me. "Are you okay?"

I looked up. "Did you get it?"

"Yep. It's over there. In the grass." Takumi stood tall and proud.

"My hero." I shivered. "What kinda snake was it? It was as big as a cobra."

"I don't know, but we're taking it back to camp. I'm sick of fish, and snake is supposed to taste like chicken."

I made a face. "I'll have to take your word for it."

Takumi examined the dead snake. "Not as good as a turkey, but it will do."

"I'm not eating anything that tried to eat me." My nose wrinkled.

Takumi helped me up off the ground and tried to get me to sit back on the roof.

My hip was bruised. My ankle was worse. But all I wanted was to be far away from that roof. "There might be more snakes under there." I hobbled to the pile of bricks.

He supported me, but kept looking back at the roof. There was a weird gleam in his eye.

"Seriously? You are not going to hunt for more snakes. We don't even know if they're poisonous or not." I moved the bricks around to make a place to sit.

"Okay, okay," he said. "But I need to go back and get the water bottle."

Takumi stepped carefully to the roof. He got down on his knees and peered under it.

"Takumi!" I imagined a giant snake jumping out and devouring him.

"All right!" He snatched the water bottle up off the ground and turned it upside down. It was empty.

"Sorry! It fell." I painfully put my shoe back on. "I'm ready to go."

Takumi took his coat off and kneeled next to the dead snake. "Thing's too heavy for my backpack." He laid his jacket on the ground and tried to bundle the snake up on it, but it was too long. Finally, he wrapped the snake around his neck and shoulders and wore it. It almost hung down to his feet.

I offered to carry his backpack but he insisted he could carry both.

It took us twice as long to hike back to camp. I tried not to complain, but I moaned a lot. Toward the end, I forced myself to ignore the snake and leaned on Takumi. That slowed us even more. When we got to where we could see the ocean, he left me at the base of a tree and ran to get help.

I limped over to where I could look down on the bay. *Whistler* hadn't returned. It had been gone six hours, but now it was growing dark. I began to worry.

The doctor confirmed nothing was broken, and told me to stay off my ankle for at least two days. The sprain would take some time to heal.

While I was being helped from the doctor's hut and back to our campsite, Takumi and Nick told me how they skinned the snake, sliced it into hamburger-patty sized pieces, and were grilling snake burgers over our campfire.

As soon as I was situated near the fire, Makala ran up to me and claimed snake was the best thing she'd ever eaten. "It's so good. I could eat snake every day. I could eat snake for breakfast. I could eat snake for lunch. I could eat snake for dinner. Even Boots likes snake, don't you, boy?"

Boots was too busy staring at the pieces still grilling to respond.

"You should try it," Angelina said. "It really does taste like…"

"Chicken," Nick and Makala said together and giggled.

I made a face. Nick and Makala laughed.

Takumi winked at Makala and handed me a bowl of rice. "Sure you don't want to try it?"

"Come on," Nick said. "You need protein to heal properly."

"Fine," I sighed. Takumi beamed and dropped a small portion of snake onto my rice. I picked at it with my fork. It fell apart in chunks. At least it was well done. I held a bite up to my nose. It actually smelled good, kinda like roasted pork.

All eyes were on me. I put a tiny piece into my mouth and chewed. It really did taste like chicken. I raised my head and smiled. "You're right."

Everyone cheered. Takumi was the loudest.

The fire crackled and lit up the darkness as I finished my meal. I even had seconds of snake and studied our new home.

While we'd been snake hunting, Nick and Angelina had created a nice little campsite. The two tents were sheltered by the trees and the fire pit was close by, but in the open. When I stood, I could see the bay below. Even though it hurt, I kept checking.

But *Whistler* didn't appear.

Chapter Ten

I hobbled to a stump near the fire and sat down. I zipped up my jacket to stay warm. It was so dark that just a few feet away from the fire everything looked pitch-black.

"So, what did you do this afternoon?" I asked Makala.

Angelina pulled her sister up onto her lap. "She learned how to skip rocks. I got my shoulder re-bandaged and Makala and Sophia swam for a while, didn't you?"

Makala grinned. "Then it rained and Sophia and me played in her tent. We made clothes for her doll. I tried to dress Boots, but he ran away."

Boots heard his name and barked.

Takumi and I laughed. Makala looked up at Angelina and grinned.

Nick said he'd worked on getting the campsite ready. "I spent most of my day searching for wood. But I also gathered pine needles and piled them under the sleeping bags. Hope they help. The ground's pretty hard."

I smiled at my friends. On the boat, we were together night and day. There weren't these kinds of stories to tell. Hearing about everyone's day was nice. Normal.

When it was my turn, I told the group about Takumi's and my adventure. Takumi acted out his attempt at capturing the turkey. Everyone chuckled, but then began plotting ways to really trap or shoot a turkey.

Angelina said we shouldn't waste bullets. Takumi suggested he hunt with the spear gun. Nick described a box-type trap he'd seen. It was fun to bounce ideas around.

I leaned over the fire and soaked in the heat. I sat back on my stump, then hobbled over to check out the bay. When my ankle wasn't shooting stabbing pains up my leg, it throbbed. I finally gave in and announced that I needed to go to bed. Nick pointed to the tent on the right and said it was the girls' tent.

Angelina was apologetic. "I'm sorry, but Makala wanted to sleep in a tent like Sophia instead of the doctors' hut, and I don't feel right…"

I glanced at Takumi. He shrugged. I kissed his cheek got ready for bed.

The ground was hard under the sleeping bag, even with the pine needles Nick stuffed under them. I lay there and decided that when *Whistler* got back, we should bring some of the cushions from the boat ashore to sleep on.

Dylan and *Whistler*! Where were they? I checked my cell. Still no service. I put my phone in my pack and threw the bag to the end of my bed. I'd just propped my foot up on the backpack when the tent flap opened and Kat came in.

"Angelina said you were still awake. Dad thought you might need these." She shook a baggie with four pills in it. "They're pain pills. They'll help you get some rest."

"That's okay," I said with the wave of my hand. "I don't like the way pain pills make me feel."

"Well, I'll leave them here in case you change your mind." Kat left the pills and a mug of water down in the corner by the head of my bed. "You're supposed to take two, but you're small. One might be enough." She smiled her perfect white teeth smile.

"Thank you," I muttered and readjusted my foot.

Kat's eyes narrowed and she left.

I laid back and listened to the conversations around the fire. Kat joined right in. She told a story about when she was a little girl and collected snakes. She hid one in her shirt and it bit her in the stomach. She described running down the street, holding the snake out by the tail and screaming. The crew roared with laughter.

I gritted my teeth. The story wasn't that funny. And where was Kat sitting? I couldn't stop myself. I had to know. I spun around painfully and crawled to the tent flap. Kat was perched on a stump right beside Takumi. Their legs were almost touching. He was grinning from ear to ear.

My ankle caught on the edge of the sleeping bag as I hurried back into bed. I yelped quietly with the pain. It was killing me. There was no way I was going to get any sleep hurting as much as I was, but no way would I touch the pills she gave me either.

With a sigh, I laid back and tried to rest. I didn't know what hurt worse, Takumi being with Kat, or my ankle.

****

I woke the next morning still tired, but not as angry with Takumi. Maybe it was because my ankle felt better, but probably because I hadn't heard that *Whistler* was back. I was beyond worried about Dylan.

A thick fog had come in during the night and covered the bay and the camp. It was cold and damp. I hated leaving my warm sleeping bag, but I had to check to see if *Whistler* was anchored. Takumi was already up and building a fire.

"How's the ankle?" He crumpled a page from a *National Geographic* magazine and then tossed some twigs on top.

"Better." I hobbled over to the edge of the cliff. I couldn't see anything but white. It was like being in the middle of a cloud. "Can you see if *Whistler*'s there?" I squinted.

Takumi lit the paper and the fire blazed to life. "Couldn't see a thing. I'll go down to the water and check as soon as I get the fire going." He blew on the sparks. "It's freezing this morning."

"It is." I picked up some pine needles and threw them on top of the small flames. The fire sparked and crackled. Takumi crisscrossed two large boards across the fire. When they caught hold, he stood.

"Be right back." He took off down the trail to the beach.

Nick crawled out of his tent and joined me. "Did the Ice Age find us again?' he hugged himself.

"It's the fog. The moisture in it makes it so cold. It should burn off." I held my hands over the flames and fed the fire as I impatiently waited for Takumi to come back.

Nick went back to his tent with a sleeping bag wrapped around him. "I should have grabbed a heavier coat before *Whistler* left." He sat bundled in the sleeping bag and poked at the fire. "Didn't it come back during the night?"

"I don't know." I adjusted the boards on the fire. "Takumi went to check. We couldn't see the bay through the fog."

His sleeping bag looked cozy. I quietly snuck mine out of my tent without waking Makala or Angelina. Boots woke and sneezed in annoyance. I covered him back up and he didn't move. My sleeping bag dragged along the ground as I walked to the fire, but I felt much warmer.

Takumi returned and shook his head. “Fog’s even thicker down there. But I’m sure *Whistler* isn’t in the bay.”

“Where can they be?” I stared wide-eyed at Takumi.

“They’re fine.” Nick’s eyes narrowed with concern. “I bet their plans changed and they had no way of letting us know.”

Takumi stirred the fire and added another board. “Nick’s right. They could be floating just outside the bay, waiting for the fog to clear.”

I started limping back and forth from the cliff to the fire. Makala and Angelina woke and joined us. Someone had thought to bring metal coat hangers. Takumi crisscrossed them over the fire, then sat a pot of water in the center of them. Soon the water began to boil. He handed out cups of hot water, and joined us.

He blew on his cup, and took a sip. “M-m-m! This is the best mocha I’ve ever had.”

Makala stared down at her cup of water and tipped her head. All of a sudden she caught on and continued with the game of pretend we’d played on the boat. “I have the best hot chocolate!” Then her lower lip trembled. ‘Ervis always puts marshmallows in my cocoa.”

Angelina gave Makala a hug. “When Jervis gets back, he’ll give you double marshmallows. I’m drinking hot apple cider. Ummm!”

Makala shook her head. “I want ‘ervis.”

I knew how she felt. “So, what is everyone planning to do today?”

“I’m making breakfast. How does snake sound?” Takumi said.

“Snake?” Makala’s eyes lit up.

Takumi sighed with relief. "That's right. We still have lots of snake to cook and no refrigeration. I've been thinking. Maybe we could find a way to smoke the fish and meat we find. If we catch a turkey, we won't be able to eat the whole thing right away. It's a shame to let it spoil. Smoked meat can last a long time."

We spent most of the morning discussing different ways we could smoke the snake and any other meat we might find. Nick and Takumi talked about bringing some of the bricks we'd found back to camp and building a smoker. The fog slowly lifted. I made endless trips to the edge of the cliff to check the bay, but *Whistler* didn't appear.

When we were finishing our breakfast of cold rice and warm snake, a small group of islanders came to visit, including Jeremy, Sophia's father. There were also four men I didn't know and an older woman with long gray hair.

Jeremy handed me a tree limb in the shape of a 'Y'. "My wife hurt her leg when we got here and I made this for her. Thought you might need it."

I smiled. The makeshift crutch was a little long for me, but if I angled it away from my leg, it took some of the pressure off my ankle.

A woman gave Angelina a covered woven basket. "I made the basket," she said.

Angelina opened it and gasped. Inside were tiny purple grapes.

Makala jumped up and down. "Grapes!"

The woman grinned. "A wine maker planted grape vines on the island years ago. Some of the vines survived."

Takumi offered them hot water and grilled snake. They didn't seem surprised at all by the snake and accepted the cups of water. They moved to the fire and opened up the camp-stools they'd brought with them. I envied them their camp-stools and air mattresses.

When they were settled around the fire Jeremy cleared his throat. "We had a meeting last night."

"Who's *we*?" I asked.

"Everyone from the island." He glanced around at the group he'd brought with him.

"Everyone but us," Nick responded.

Jeremy nodded. "You're right. We didn't include you. You're just kids."

"Just kids? Really?" I glared at him. "We 'just kids' saved you from the cons."

"You acted irresponsibly. Makala could have been hurt." Jeremy stood. "You proved that you are not old enough to make adult decisions. I get that you don't want to be told what to do. But here's the deal. We voted that there are to be no guns on the island. We are here to confiscate your guns. It's not safe with all the children around. And Makala needs an adult to make decisions on her behalf."

Angelina's face turned red. "You think you know what's best for my sister?"

"Honey," the old lady addressed Angelina. "I know you think you are all grown up, but when you get to be my age, you'll look back and realize how young and foolish you really were. We can't stand by and watch you make a mistake that might harm your little sister. How old are you anyway? Fourteen, fifteen?"

Angelina pursed her lips and glared at the woman.

I gritted my teeth. "Did you survive a tsunami, sail the Pacific coast, fight off navy sailors, a motorcycle gang, and convicts, when you were young?"

The old lady stood and turned to the islanders. "I told you. Teenagers never listen. They think they know it all."

Jeremy motioned for her to sit back down. "We understand what you've gone through. It has been a difficult time for all of us. You are a remarkable group of kids. But you are not adults, and we are not leaving here without the guns."

"You will not touch my pistol," Angelina said in an angry voice. "Our daddy was a police officer. He taught Makala and me to respect guns. The gun I brought was his and I'm almost as good a shot as he was."

"Is that so!" the old lady said. "Where is your daddy now?"

Angelina clinched her fists. Her father had been killed in the line of duty. She threw the basket of grapes on the ground and stepped toward the woman. I'd never seen her so angry.

I blocked her path, and crossed my fingers that Makala wouldn't give my lie away. "All the guns are on *Whistler* … and *Whistler* isn't back yet. When it does return, I promise we will keep the guns onboard the boat."

Angelina squeezed Makala's shoulder. Makala seemed puzzled, but for once kept quiet.

"That's not good enough," one of the men said.

Jeremy shook his head. "If you won't give us the guns, Makala will no longer be welcome in our camp and none of the children will be allowed to visit her here."

Makala's eyes got big and filled with tears.

"How can you be so mean to a four-year-old?" Nick stood. "Leave!"

"Not before we search your tents for the guns," Jeremy said.

Takumi walked over to his tent and came back with his spear gun. "Is this the way you thank us for getting rid of the convicts?" Takumi aimed the tip in the air. "The world has changed. We're changed. Adapt or suffer."

"Is that a threat?" a man I didn't know asked.

Takumi shook his head. "We've never been a threat to anyone. We only protect ourselves. But we will do whatever we need to defend our own."

"I knew it!" The old lady snatched the basket up off the ground. "They had no intention of working with us. They planned all along to keep their boat full of food and supplies for themselves."

Angelina handed Makala to Nick. "We came here looking for friends. All we've found are convicts and arrogant, arrogant…"

I placed my hand on Angelina's shoulder. "When *Whistler* returns, we'll leave. We'll find another bay, far from here, to make our camp in. You can stay and tell yourselves how superior you are, at least until someone shows up with a weapon and wipes you out."

"I want to play with Sophia," Makala cried.

"I hope you're proud of yourselves." I pointed toward their camp. "Go!"

They finally left. I kept the crutch.

Chapter Eleven

Makala cried and clung to Angelina.

"Look, Makala!" Nick found the grapes the Islander woman had dropped in the dirt and showed them to her.

"Can I eat them?" Makala wiped her eyes.

Angelina carried her over to an upside-down cooking pot and sat her down. "Not yet. The grapes need to be rinsed off. They were in the dirt." Angelina filled a bowl with fresh water, picked out one tiny grape, dropped it in the water, brought it out, and inspected it.

Makala sniffed. "Can I eat it now?"

"It's not clean enough yet." Angelina dropped the grape back into the bowl.

Makala kept watching. After the second rinse she was allowed to eat the grape.

Her face lit up. "It's sweet."

"Good. You can wash the rest of the grapes and pass them out to everyone."

Makala become totally focused on dunking the grapes, one at a time. Angelina examined them before Makala could eat or pass one out to us. She often made Makala go back and rinse it again. They *were* sweet.

I used my new crutch to walk to the edge of the cliff. Once there, I leaned on it while I studied the horizon. The fog was lifting in wispy waves, but there was no sign of the boat.

"Jerks!" I picked up a rock and threw it as hard as I could over the cliff. Without missing a beat, I hurled another. We'd tried to help those people. I gripped a third rock tight, and with all my might, threw it as far as I could.

"I can't believe they'd hurt Makala like that." Takumi joined me at the bluff's edge.

"They are so full of themselves." I aimed the fourth rock at a single tree barely hanging on to the side of the cliff. The rock thumped off the tree's trunk and I felt even worse. The tree had survived the tsunami. Just like us. It didn't deserve to have rocks thrown at it.

"Feel better?" Takumi asked.

"No," I sighed.

He rolled a stump over for me to sit on. "The doctor said to rest."

I dropped the crutch on the ground. "The crutch doesn't help much either."

"It's really pretty cool. I wonder how many trees Jeremy tested before he found a branch that formed the exact 'y' he needed."

"It hurts my under arm, though. I have to choose between arm pain and my ankle aching."

Takumi grinned. "I have an idea." He hurried to his tent and came back with a thick grey sock.

"Your dirty sock?" I wrinkled my nose. "Thanks."

"It's your father's dirty sock. It's wool and will make great padding."

I reached into my pockets and pulled out the turkey feathers I'd picked up the day before. "I knew I'd find a use for these."

Takumi stuffed the sock with feathers and wrapped it around the V of the crutch.

"Much better," I said as I hobbled back and forth, leaning heavily on the crutch. "Thanks, Takumi."

With the fog gone, the air grew warmer. I used the now-padded crutch for support while I stared out at the horizon, hoping any minute *Whistler* would appear. Takumi paced back and forth between the fire and me. Nick and the girls decided to hike to the ruined camp and bring back some bricks. Mostly, they wanted to do something to take Makala's mind off her friend.

Makala raced over to me and showed me a handful of leftover cooked rice.

"Rice? Are you taking food for a picnic?" I asked.

Makala tried to roll her eyes, but only managed to look up and then down. "No, silly. This is turkey food. When we find a turkey, I'll feed it, and it will follow me back here."

"Of course." I felt around in my pockets and found a couple of tiny feathers. "Here! You can also give him back his feathers too."

Makala hurried to her sister gripping the feathers in one hand and the rice in the other.

Nick called out to Takumi, "Coming with us?"

Takumi wrapped his arm around me and shook his head.

"You should go and show them the way," I suggested.

Takumi looked across at Nick. "The trail is easy. You won't have any problem finding the camp."

As soon as they left we let the campfire die. The day grew warmer and we took off our coats. Takumi found the deck of cards and we played crazy eights. I stared at the bay and had trouble keeping my mind on the game.

I was in the middle of dealing out the cards when Kat showed up.

"What happened?" she cried. "You pulled a weapon on Jeremy?" She stared at Takumi.

I bolted upright. "They were threatening us! He only showed them the spear gun. And he didn't aim it at anyone."

Takumi looked more shocked at my outburst than Kat did.

"What?" I put my hands on my hips. "She just accused you of threatening her people."

"I don't need you to defend me, Toni," Takumi said.

Kat stepped closer to him. "I was worried. I know you. You would never have brought out the spear gun unless you felt threatened."

I turned my back on them and moved closer to the ridgeline. *She knows him? What does that mean?*

Takumi filled Kat in on what the islanders had said. I heard her gasp when he told her about how upset Makala had been. They moved to the fire, rebuilt it, and spoke softly. I couldn't make out their words.

After a long time, Takumi wandered over to me. "What was that all about?"

"She accused you of threatening her people," I said again.

"Her father is the only *people* she has on the island. She was concerned for us."

"Really?" I said. "Then why didn't she warn us about the convicts?"

"Toni, this isn't like you. What's wrong?"

I studied my shoes. "I don't trust her."

"Why? Kat fought the cons and took great care of Angelina. Before we came, she was the only teen on the island. She just wants to be friends with us."

My face burned. *Not us. You.*

"I thought I'd take the kayaks and search the coastline for a place to anchor *Whistler* and build a new camp. Kat offered to go with me."

"Of course she did," I blurted out before I could stop myself.

Takumi frowned. "You have to rest your ankle. Would you prefer I go by myself?"

"No, you need to have someone with you." My shoulders slumped.

"Okay, then. Kat and I are going to go kayaking. I'll bring you back a lobster." He brought my lips to his, kissed me, then left with Kat.

From my perch at the cliff's edge I watched Takumi and Kat kayak out of the bay. She paddled almost as well as Takumi. Their laughter floated up off the water and chipped away at my heart.

I'd waited all morning for the fog to lift and *Whistler* to appear. The fog had been gone for a long while, but the boat, and my brother, didn't show up. Takumi and Kat soon disappeared from view too. On the boat, I had missed being alone, but not anymore. Now, I wanted everyone I cared about close by. There was too much danger in the world.

Boots yipped. I quickly wiped my eyes, grabbed my new crutch, and moved to the head of the trail.

The little dog ran and jumped all around, and on me. I was always amazed at how high he could leap on his short little legs. Nick, Angelina, and Makala were close behind. Nick pulled a chunk of canvas loaded with bricks behind him. It had to be heavy.

Makala showed me a handful of flowers she'd picked. They were beautiful in a small, delicate way. "We didn't find any turkeys," she said sadly. "I think they're scared of Boots."

I picked Boots up. His doggy kisses made me smile. "You're probably right. Dogs weren't allowed on the island before… before…"

"Before the giant wave tried to kill everyone?" Makala said.

I put Boots down. "How'd you get so smart?"

Makala grinned and hurried over to help Nick with the bricks.

Angelina and Nick discussed ways to make a smoker. Angelina complained her shoulder hurt and leaned back on a log. Nick moved bricks around to demonstrate his ideas. Makala had fun building with them.

I elevated my foot on a rock and tried to rest, but my mind wouldn't quiet down. What had happened to Dylan? How long would Takumi and Kat be gone? I hated just sitting and waiting.

I finally hopped up. "I'm going for a short hike," I told Angelina.

She stared at my foot, started to argue, but saw something in my face that made her stop. I adjusted the padded crutch and headed for a trail. Before I had gone more than a few steps, I heard a woman's voice behind me.

"Where's my husband?" the voice said. "He left on your boat. He promised me he'd be back yesterday. It's a new day, and he still isn't back."

I turned and faced a young woman with stringy hair that fell past her waist. She held her hands up in the air. "I don't have any weapons."

I glanced at Angelina, who was trying not to laugh.

"That's good, because I don't either," I replied.

The woman lowered her arms and crossed them tight across her chest. "Where is he?"

I shook my head. "I don't know. I'm worried, too."

"What do you mean, you don't know?" she snarled at me.

"I have no way of contacting the boat. Is your cell working?" I asked.

The woman huffed. "If he doesn't come back by this time tomorrow, you and your group are going to be arrested."

"Arrested for what?" I crossed my arms too.

"For kidnapping our men." The woman turned to leave. "You have one more day."

"That's ridiculous. Dylan asked for volunteers. Everyone heard him. If my brother isn't back with the boat, it means something is wrong. We should be working together to find them. I love my brother as much as you love your husband."

"This time tomorrow!" the woman screeched, then left.

Angelina and Nick moved to stand beside me.

"This is insane," I whispered. "Can they do that? Arrest us?"

Nick scowled. "They can do whatever they want. Somehow we've been painted as the bad guys."

"More like disrespectful teens," I shook my head. "But that isn't something they can punish us for."

Angelina stared at Makala. "We should pack up and leave. They're looking for a reason to take Makala away from me."

My jaw dropped. Was this all about the guns, and Makala being here without an adult? "But if we leave, how will Dylan and Jervis find us?" I asked.

Nick turned on his cell. "It's two o'clock. If the boat isn't back by morning, Angelina, Makala, and I will pack up and head across to the other side of the island. You and Takumi can hide somewhere and wait. If *Whistler* still doesn't come back, you can follow after us."

Angelina put her hand on my arm. "But the boat will be back before then. I know it."

"I'm going to see if I can find Takumi." I took off walking along the edge of the island and away from the bay.

** * *

There was a trail of sorts that I followed, although it was washed out in most places. I had to crawl over a number of large boulders. Some were barely hanging on and I crossed my fingers they wouldn't tumble down with me on top of them.

Most of the trees and shrubs were gone. The mud had dried to a flaky, dry sort of dirt that started blowing around me. But I didn't mind. Wind meant that *Whistler* could sail.

My ankle throbbed and I had to rest often. I perched on a rock that had split, leaving an almost flat surface, and tried to figure out how far I'd gone. Below me, at least a hundred feet down, giant rocks made up the shoreline. Huge ocean waves crashed on them. A knot formed in my throat. The waves were too rough for the plastic kayaks to handle.

There was no sign of Takumi or Kat. I turned on my cell again and checked the time. It was after four. A short way ahead, the edge of the cliff jutted out into the ocean. I stood up and decided I would walk as far as the bluff. If I didn't find them, I'd head back.

It took me longer than I'd expected, and twice I almost turned back. Finally, I'd made it. The bluff was wider than it had seemed from a distance, and it took me fifteen minutes to cross it and get to the edge. I found a large tree and leaned on it as I inspected the calm bay that was over forty feet below me.

Suddenly I gasped. The kayaks! They were there. But no one was in them. I kneeled down and squinted. Kat and Takumi were in the water. Were they just swimming around? I kept watching. Something was wrong. Kat was holding onto Takumi with one arm and a kayak with the other. Takumi wasn't moving.

I cupped my hands around my mouth and yelled, "Takumi!"

Kat stared up at me. "Help!" she called out. "He's hurt."

Chapter Twelve

Takumi needed me. I dropped my crutch and pulled off my shoes, pants, and jacket. I found a rocky ledge that jutted far out over the sea. I scooted to the edge on my bottom and stared down into the bay.

I was at least forty feet above the water. The number one rule of diving was to never dive into water you were unfamiliar with. But, I didn't give myself time to think about that. Takumi was in trouble.

I searched for the darkest part of the sea and dove. My body was long and straight. The minute my fingers sliced through the surface, I tucked and rolled, trying to stop my momentum.

My underwater summersaults slowed me and I searched for the light above. My legs shot out and touched bottom. I pushed off and followed the bright beams. The surface was a long ways away, through water that stung my eyes.

Something grabbed my leg. Precious air escaped my lungs. I kicked and pulled. My right leg was caught. I fought the panic and clasped my lips together.

I had to confront whatever had hold of me and forced myself to look down. It was just seaweed, wrapped around my ankle. I swam hard for the surface. The seaweed held me back. I pulled and pulled. My leg didn't budge.

My lungs screamed for air.

I reached down and tried to unwrap the strand. I couldn't find a way to unwind it. I couldn't feel the edge. It was all slimy. Panic filled me. I was going to drown.

Anger washed over me. I'd failed. And Takumi! He would die too. With her. All because of a stupid strand of seaweed.

Then I heard Takumi's calm voice in my head. "The harder you pull, the tighter it becomes!"

When had he'd said this? Stars swam before my eyes. I needed air.

All of a sudden, I remembered. Takumi and Makala had been playing with a woven finger puzzle. "The harder you pull, the tighter it becomes."

Was seaweed like the finger game? Every instinct screamed at me to swim to the surface. Instead, I used my arms to push myself down.

My lungs ached.

I was dizzy.

The seaweed loosened its grip. I pulled my foot free and shot up.

I had a long ways to swim. My lungs demanded oxygen. Stars flashed before my eyes. Just when I thought I couldn't hold my breath for another second, I broke the surface.

I gulped mouthfuls of air and floated on my back.

But only for a short moment.

Takumi! Where was he? I turned from side to side trying to get my bearings. He and Kat were a short way off to the right. I took one more deep breath and swam to them.

"What happened?" I grabbed Takumi's arm.

Kat sank under the sea. I worried I'd have to rescue her, but she popped back up with the kayak line. "Takumi dove to catch a lobster. When he came up, he was in terrible pain. He said he stepped on a stingray, and then passed out."

I grabbed the lifejacket from the bottom of the kayak and managed to get it on him. The jacket held his head up and out of the water. I held onto the loop on the back of it.

Kat rested her head against the hull. "I tried to get him into the kayak, but couldn't. I don't know how much longer I could have held on."

I rolled Takumi onto his back and let him float. "Takumi," I patted his face. "Takumi!"

His eyes fluttered open. He groaned. "Toni!" He began to thrash around and moan. "God. It hurts so…!" He winced and grabbed his foot. "Stingray. Stinger's still in."

"What should we do?" I stroked his face.

"Pain's spreading. Need to get it out." Takumi gasped. He was having trouble breathing.

I searched the bay for a place to go ashore. The edges of the steep cliffs seemed to shoot straight up from the bay. There was not a beach or land area to drag him to.

Kat was shivering. They'd both been in the cool water too long.

"Kat?"

"What?" She raised her head.

"If we float him on his back, maybe I can take out the stinger."

Takumi cried out with pain.

She held him while I examined his foot. A sharp barb with a hook on the side was sticking out of his foot.

"Do you have a knife?" I asked.

Kat shook her head.

"It needs to be cut out. Okay then. We leave it alone until we get help. Let's get him out of the water." I held Takumi facing the kayak. He passed out again. I was glad he wasn't feeling any pain, but he also couldn't help us.

I motioned for Kat to go to the other side of the kayak. "I'll dive and push him up from below. You pull. Just get him up and across the top."

Kat was shaking so hard I worried she wouldn't be able to lift Takumi at all, but I couldn't do it alone. She leaned across Takumi's kayak and grabbed the straps of his lifejacket.

"Ready?" I inhaled two deep breaths. When she nodded I dove, wrapped my arms around Takumi's legs, and kicked as hard as I could, propelling him up. When my head broke the surface, Takumi's feet dangled in my face from the kayak. He'd made it.

We rolled him over and pushed him as far down into the bow of the kayak as we could. He was still unconscious.

I searched the bay. "Where's the other kayak?" I had to find it. There was no way all three of us would fit into one.

Kat helped me look.

"There it is." I pointed. "Stay with Takumi."

Her teeth chattered. "Hurry!"

I sprinted toward the loose kayak, found the line that was tied to the bow, and towed it back. I wrapped the long line through the handles on the sides of both kayaks and tied them together, side by side.

"Okay! Now get in this one," I told Kat.

Kat shook her head. "I can't."

"Yes, you can." I clenched my teeth. "You have to. I can't do this by myself."

Kat took a deep breath and pulled herself up on the side of the kayak. She kicked to propel herself higher. The kayak tipped over far on the side she was trying to enter from. Both kayaks rocked. I dove down and pushed her up from below. On the third try, Kat made it up onto the flat kayak deck. She managed to wiggle around and stretch her legs out.

The cold was getting to me. I started to pull myself up onto the back of Takumi's kayak.

"Wait!" Kat cried. "We need the other paddle."

"What!" The cold was seeping into my bones. I looked around. "Where is it?"

Kat searched the calm bay. "I don't know. Takumi bungeed his to his kayak, but mine floated away."

I couldn't see the other paddle anywhere. One would have to do. More than anything I wished it were a real, two-bladed kayak paddle, and not the single dinghy paddle we'd found in Grays Harbor. But one was better than none.

I tied Takumi's kayak to our stern. I was shivering hard. My strength was almost gone. When I got up on the side of Kat's kayak, she yanked on my sweatshirt and pulled me across the stern. Now all I had to do was figure out how to straddle the thing.

"Squeeze in behind me." Kat moved as far forward as she could, leaving a small gap behind her.

It was tricky, but I managed to squeeze in and wedge my legs down alongside her.

"Ready?" She pulled out the paddle.

"Ready!" I checked on Takumi. He seemed secure in the kayak behind us, but his head was down. Was he still breathing? I couldn't tell. Fear engulfed me.

My trembling intensified.

Kat paused paddling and took off the lifejacket she'd been wearing. "Here! Maybe this will warm your back."

I stared at her full, pink bra as I took the lifejacket. She'd been swimming with Takumi in her underwear.

My imagination took flight. Takumi and Kat. All alone. In their underwear. I tried to shake the images out of my head, but they wouldn't go away. I argued with myself. What they'd been doing before didn't matter—Takumi was dying. And the entire crew had been swimming around in our underwear when we first got to the island.

But my face burned. Jealousy was doing more than the lifejacket had to warm me.

We paddled in silence out of the bay. The gentle ocean waves rocked the kayaks. I spent my time focusing on Takumi: Furious with him one moment, then concerned about him the next.

Kat was slowing down. I was about to tell her I'd take over paddling, when I saw a couple of fins. "Look!" I smiled.

"Oh my God. Sharks!" She squealed.

"I don't think so. Yesterday we saw some…"

Before I could finish, dolphins leapt in the air and swam up and around us. One stood on its tail and squeaked.

"Maybe they'll tow us," Kat whispered.

"They aren't trained animals. We can't *make* them tow us," I sneered.

I glanced back at Takumi. He was awake and gulped in air like a fish out of water. All of a sudden I didn't care that he'd been almost naked with Kat. I loved him and he was hurting. I took the paddle from her and started stroking hard.

"But I've heard stories of how dolphins have saved swimmers," Kat insisted.

The dolphins came alongside us. Then, almost as if there was a signal, they took off.

"Wait!" Kat yelled. "Come back."

The dolphins swam incredibly fast, just under the surface. They reminded me of torpedoes. I searched the horizon for their target. It was a game I'd seen them play during our summer sailing trips.

"Is that *Whistler*?" I squinted and searched the horizon.

Kat shaded her eyes even though there was no sun. "I can't tell. But it's a sailboat. "Help!" she screamed and waved her arms.

I joined her in yelling, even though I knew we were too far for them to hear us. I lifted the paddle high above my head and waved it back and forth. The sailboat continued on its path. It was entering Prisoners' Harbor, the bay we'd made our home in.

I told Takumi to hold on. He was moaning and writhing with pain.

Exhausted, I pushed myself to keep paddling. The dolphins returned. They both scooted on their tails, squawked, and shot back out toward the boat.

I kept paddling.

"Don't go!" Kat yelled. "Toni, make them help us."

"Right. How do you suggest I do that?" I passed the paddle across to the other side. Kat ducked.

"I don't know, but we're too far out. They don't see us." Kat started to cry.

"Keep waving your arms." I pulled the paddle through the waves.

The large boat kept heading toward the shore. It was going into the bay. Either Kat was right and they didn't see us, or they didn't care.

This time when the dolphins returned, Kat wiggled a line in the water and pleaded with them to take it and tow us. They seemed to laugh, got into formation, and took off for the sailboat again.

The large boat slowly disappeared behind the cliff that protected the bay. They weren't coming to help us. We had about a quarter of a mile to go. Both Kat and I were beyond tired. Takumi was thrashing around, his pain growing. I'd never felt so helpless.

Tears streamed down my cheeks. Kat sobbed as she took the paddle from me.

"Toni!" Kat cried.

I didn't respond.

"Toni, look. The boat. It's back. Maybe it did see us."

I sniffed and stared at the horizon.

Takumi screamed in pain. He thrashed around from one side of the kayak to the other. His kayak almost tipped over.

I pulled my legs up and out of Kat's and my kayak and slid into the water. I swam to Takumi and grabbed his hand. "You have to stop moving around so much. Squeeze my hand instead," I begged him.

I checked the sailboat's progress. Its sails were full and it was headed straight for us.

The dolphins appeared behind me. I reached out to them. One almost let me touch it, changed its mind, and rolled onto its side. It stared at me with one eye.

"Thank you!" I sniffed. "You showed that boat where we were. They wouldn't have spotted us if you hadn't."

The dolphin jabbered at me, joined its friend, and swam out to sea.

The sailboat kept coming.

I ignored the cold and stayed at Takumi's side. He yelled and squeezed my hand so hard I thought my fingers might break.

"Hold on, Takumi! Help's on the way. Just hold on," I said, over and over again.

Chapter Thirteen

The boat heading toward us was *Whistler*. It had a dark blue hull, the sails had duct tape hanging off them, but the biggest clue was Zoë's high-pitched voice. It carried out over the sea.

For the first time ever, I was excited to hear it.

Dylan dropped the main sail.

Zoë stood at the wheel and shouted, "Where's the brake on this thing?"

The boat glided past us.

I would've laughed if I hadn't been shivering so hard.

"What's going on?" Zoë yelled as they zoomed by.

"Takumi kicked a stingray," I shouted. "The stinger's still in. He's having an allergic reaction. Can't breathe."

Banks and Brad, the two guys from the island, arrived on deck as Zoë disappeared below. Dylan hurried down to the swim step and threw us a line. Kat rowed both of the kayaks to the line. I swam to it, tied it to Kat's kayak, and Dylan towed us to the stern. I told the guys to lift Takumi on board first.

In seconds, Takumi was out of his kayak and in the cabin below.

I prayed Zoë could help him as one of the island guys tied the kayaks to the back cleats.

Dylan reached down for me. "Are you okay?" He yanked me out of the water and onto the swim-step.

I threw myself into his arms and dripped all over him. "What took you so long? I was so worried." My voice cracked.

"We made an extra stop and had no way to tell you." Dylan kissed my forehead. "Sorry!"

"I want to hear all about it, but first, I need to check on Takumi." I started down the steps.

"Where's Jervis?"

"Um! Well. That's part of the story." Dylan's head lowered.

My hand flew to my mouth. "Jervis?"

"No, nothing like that. He's fine. At least he was. Go! Check on Takumi. We can talk later." Dylan turned to help Kat out of the kayak.

The island guys nodded to me as I made my way down the stairs. Takumi was lying on Jervis' mattress in the middle of the main cabin. Zoë held his head in her lap and spooned a red liquid into his mouth.

She glared at me. "About time you showed up. Hold his head. I'm trying to get some Benadryl into him. I don't want him to choke." She timed the doses carefully so he wouldn't inhale the liquid into his already troubled lungs.

He struggled with every dose and his breathing sounded terrible.

"I hope that's enough." She tightened the lid on the medicine bottle. "I want to check his foot before he wakes up."

Whistler heeled hard to port. We were sailing. I steadied Takumi. Dylan needed to know about the island people and their threats before we sailed back into the harbor. But I couldn't leave Takumi.

"Is he going to be okay?" Kat appeared behind me. I hadn't even noticed that she'd come down.

Zoë stared at Kat's bra, raised her eyebrows, and lifted Takumi's foot. We almost bumped heads as we studied the stinger close up. It was buried deep into Takumi's foot.

"Does your father still have lots of antibiotics?" Zoë asked Kat.

"I wouldn't say lots. He has some." Kat crossed her arms around her chest.

"We need to get this thing out." Zoë gestured at the stinger. "But first, you two need to put some clothes on. You're getting the bandages wet."

"I left my things up on shore when Takumi and I went kayaking," Kat said.

"Really?" Zoë glanced at me.

"I'll find something." I searched through the clothes I'd left on the boat, changed, and handed an old, torn, Seahawks sweatshirt to Kat.

She pulled it on over her wet bra and picked up a razor blade from the first aid kit. "A neighbor brought his dog to Dad with porcupine quills in his back. Dad said the secret was to make a small incision alongside the barb, and lift out the quill. Not pull it out."

Zoë peered down at Takumi's foot. "Makes sense."

Takumi took a breath. His chest made a rattling sound. We heeled way over to the starboard side and I grabbed the over-head handrail to keep from falling. We were sailing fast and would enter the harbor soon. I was out of time.

"I'll be right back." I ran for the stairs, stood at the top of the cockpit opening, and called to Dylan. "We need to talk."

"Okay. Talk!" Dylan adjusted the wheel.

"Alone. Come down."

Dylan turned to the island guys. "Take the wheel for a minute."

I shook my head. "You have to drop the sails. We can't go into the harbor."

"What do you mean?" Banks, or maybe it was Brad, shouted. "I need to get back. My wife must be worried sick."

Dylan stared at me. "Just spit it out."

I sighed. "The people on the island threatened us. I'm worried they might do something to Angelina, Nick, or Makala if we don't give our guns and maybe even the boat to them."

"That's bull." One of the 'B' guys stood. "No one from the island would harm you."

"I'm dropping the sails and you're going to explain," Dylan told me.

"You promised to bring us back," the other B argued.

"I'll do what I promised as soon as I know what's going on," Dylan vowed.

I checked our location. We were just behind the cliffs that sheltered the bay. Hopefully, the islanders hadn't spotted *Whistler* yet.

Zoë called out. "Toni, we need you!"

I hurried back to Takumi's side. He was gasping for air. His skin appeared almost blue.

"Shouldn't we let the doctor do this?" I stared at the razor in Kat's hand.

"The poison in the barb is still going into him. We need to get it out and soak his foot in hot water," Kat said.

"Hot water? To clean it?" Zoë asked.

"No, hot water neutralizes the poison. I grew up around here. Remember?" Kat poured alcohol over the razor blade.

"Okay." I pumped water into the tea kettle and handed it up to the guy still sitting in the cockpit. "Get a fire going and heat this up."

"Now?" Dylan asked.

"Kat needs to soak Takumi's foot in hot water." I raced back down to the cabin.

The island guys continued to argue with Dylan. I tried to tune them out and concentrate on Takumi.

I kneeled at the head of the mattress and pressed down on Takumi's shoulders. Zoë placed Takumi's foot in her lap. Kat held the razor and a navy blue pot-holder.

"Ready? Hold tight!" Zoë made a slit in his swollen foot and wrapped the pot-holder around the stinger.

Takumi yelled. I did my best to hold him down.

"Keep him still!" Zoë yelled.

"Got it!" She held up the pot-holder with the bloody stinger sticking out on both ends.

I loosened my hold on Takumi. His eyes popped open.

"Wanna see the stinger?" Zoë asked.

Takumi rolled to his side and threw up on the teak floor.

"Gross!" Zoë held her nose and ran up top.

"Sorry, dude." Kat made a similar face and followed Zoë.

Takumi moaned while I cleaned up the mess and opened the hatches. I gave him a sip of water and wiped his mouth. He laid back and closed his eyes again. I wrapped his foot in some bandages from the kit. It was swollen, but not bleeding too hard.

I moved to the top stair where I could watch Dylan but still check on Takumi. Zoë and Kat were perched in the bow.

Dylan noticed me. “Explain!” he demanded.

“Not until you tell me where Jervis is.” I put my hands on my hips.

Dylan stood on top of the cabin and neatly folded the main sail over the boom. “We listened to the shortwave radio while sailing the cons to Santa Rosa. An Emergency Broadcast announcer mentioned a number of military camps along the coast. When Jervis learned there was a camp in Santa Barbara, he insisted on being dropped off there. His dad is in the Army, remember? He figured that even if his dad wasn’t in Santa Barbara, they would know where he was.”

“Jervis is in Santa Barbara?” I handed him a green tie for the sail.

“Yeah!” We anchored a ways from shore and Brad and Banks rowed him in.”

“But, what if the base doesn’t know where his dad is? What if his dad is dead? How will he get back to us?”

Dylan grimaced. “I tried to get him to wait until cell service was up, but he was determined to go.”

Tears filled my eyes. Jervis was gone. We might never hear from him again. I didn’t even get a chance to say good-bye. And Makala! She was going to be so upset.

“Your turn. What happened back at camp?” Dylan knotted the last of the green ties around the lowered sail.

Brad and Banks leaned forward in their seats and glared at me.

I sniffed. “Sophia’s father and a couple of others from the island showed up at our site. They said we had one day to turn in our guns to them, or else. They claimed to be worried that a kid would find the guns and get hurt.

We're not welcome in their camp. They also said we weren't qualified to care for Makala."

"What?" Dylan's eyes got big.

"And they told us we're selfish for not sharing the boat and all we have with them."

"Do you really think they'd try something?" Dylan glanced at the B's.

Banks and Brad exchanged looks but said nothing.

"I do!" A wave hit us from the side. I grabbed hold of the dodger pole. "They're angry and they think we're just a group of stupid kids. Nick, Angelina, and I talked about hiking to the other side of the island if *Whistler* didn't return soon."

I crouched to check on Takumi in the cabin below. He was very still. I waited for him to take a breath. He didn't. I kept staring. His chest didn't move. I moved down two steps, and continued to watch. I counted to ten. He wasn't breathing.

"Zoë!" I screamed and leapt down to the cabin below.

I knelt next to Takumi and started mouth-to-mouth resuscitation. Zoë and Kat stood helplessly by. I breathed into his mouth and pushed on his chest.

"His pulse is weak." Zoë held his wrist.

"The Benadryl isn't working." Kat took his other hand.

"Takumi, come on!" I'd already lost Cole. I couldn't bear to lose him too.

His eyes finally flew open and he struggled to inhale.

I sat back and prayed he'd breathe again.

He did. Takumi took in a second and then a third breath. Each one was less of a struggle.

"Pulse is stronger." Zoë smiled at me.

Takumi's chest rose and fell in a regular pattern.

One of the B's came down and shoved the blackened teapot at me. "Water's hot," he growled, then hurried back on top.

I poured the steaming water into a large stockpot, stuck my finger in, and pulled it out fast.

"Bring it over here," Kat said.

I added two cups of cold water to the pot and tested it again. It was bearable. I bent Takumi's knee and raised his foot up while Zoë slid the pot under it. When his foot entered, he yelped and tried to pull it out.

I used both hands and all my strength to keep his foot in the water. "Takumi. Relax. The heat will stop the poison from spreading." My hands were burning, too. "Just a few more seconds," I whispered over and over.

Kat studied her watch. "Okay! That's long enough."

I yanked his foot out. My hands and his foot were bright red, from the heat as well as his blood. He passed out again. Zoë dried him off and wrapped his foot in a gauze bandage.

We stared down at him for a long while. When he woke up, he stared back at me with clear eyes. "What happened?" He took in a solid breath.

I held his hand. "*Whistler* showed up. You're going to be fine."

Kat moved to the other side of the mattress and threw herself on top of Takumi. "I was so scared. You almost died."

I dropped Takumi's hand.

Zoë yelled, "Get off of him, you idiot. He can barely breathe as it is."

Takumi patted Kat’s shoulder and took in another steady breath.

I bit my lip and climbed on deck.

Chapter Fourteen

My head hurt. My hands burned. Dylan and the guys from the island could be overheard, yelling at one another.

"Knock it off," I screamed as I stepped into the cockpit. "Everyone sit down."

The island guys appeared shocked at my outburst, and plopped down in the corners of the stern. Dylan gripped the wheel tightly. A big wave rocked the boat. The anchor chain clanged. Dylan and I watched to see if the anchor was holding.

"You can't keep us here." A 'B' guy slapped the seat beside him.

"Stop!" I held up my hand. "We get it. You two want to go home. And you will. We just need to get our people off the island first." I turned my back on the guys. "Dylan, do you have a plan?"

"I haven't had a second to think with these two yelling at me." Dylan rubbed his eyes.

I grabbed Dylan's arm and pulled him to the bow. "Someone has to tell Nick and Angelina what's going on. Takumi and Kat left this morning in two kayaks. The campers will be suspicious if only one returns. So, we need two people to paddle the kayaks back, find Angelina and Nick, help them pack up, and when it gets dark, carry everything down to the beach."

"And then?" Dylan asked.

"At sundown, you sail *Whistler* into the bay. The B's row the dinghy to shore. We climb aboard the dinghy and kayaks and paddle back to *Whistler*. We'll sail away before the B's make it back to camp."

"Sounds good," Dylan said and we headed back to the stern.

One of the B's leaned on the rail. "You expect us just to wait here all day? Let me take one of the kayaks. I promise not to say anything to anyone. I just want to tell my wife I'm okay."

Dylan shook his head. "I appreciate all you guys did to help with the convicts, but we can't take a chance. You'll have to stay onboard for just a few more hours. Sorry."

"You're keeping us against our will!" The guy without a wife got to his feet. "No wonder our friends don't trust you."

Zoë arrived on deck. "What's going on up here? Why's everyone angry?" She sat down on the cockpit bench. "Takumi's fine, by the way."

Dylan filled her in on what I'd told him about the camper's threats.

She swiveled to face me. "What are you doing? First you alienate Takumi. Then you make enemies with our island friends. What's your problem?"

"I didn't alienate…" I stammered, and then squared my shoulders. "The islanders convinced themselves that we're just a bunch of ignorant kids. They think we need adult guidance. But what they really want is what we have."

"I can't believe it. You're ruining everything." Zoë began to sob. "Sophia's father was going to officiate at our wedding. The campers were going to be our guests. Makala and Sophia would have been the flower girls. And…"

Dylan held his head in his hands.

The guy with a wife motioned to Zoë. "Let Brad and me go back and talk to them. I'm sure they'll let you all leave, if that's what you want. And if you agree to keep the guns on the boat, I bet they'll let you stay at the camp and have your wedding."

Zoë sniffed. "Do it, Dylan. Don't you want a big wedding? Don't you want lots of guests and presents and everything? Please, Dylan. Please. Do it for me. Do it for our baby."

I grabbed Zoë's arm. "Stop it! Listen to yourself. You'd risk the boat and Makala? Just for a fancy wedding?"

Zoë shook her head. "It's not fair."

The guy without a wife said, "You're wrong about our friends. Your perfect wedding should be here."

Zoë looked pleadingly at Dylan. Tears and snot streamed down her face.

I stared at the island guys. "You've been on this boat for what, two days now? Look me in the eye and tell me that you never once thought about how sweet it would be to live on the boat. Or that you didn't notice how nice it was to sleep on a mattress instead of the hard ground. Assure me that you never considered how cool it would be to sail back to the mainland instead of paddling."

The B's studied their feet in silence. At least they weren't liars.

"All right, then. Kat and I should be the ones to kayak back. Dylan, you need to stay with the boat. You can pull up the anchor. Zoë needs to monitor Takumi. Unless… Zoë, does Takumi need to see the doctor?"

Zoë was ignoring me.

"Zoë?"

Before I could shake her, Kat appeared on deck and tapped me on the shoulder. "Why did you take off like that? Takumi's been asking for you."

I glared at her.

Kat scowled back. "What's your problem? Takumi tells me how great you are, but all I see is a bossy, mean girl. I can't believe he's crazy about you."

If he's crazy about me, then why was she throwing herself at him? I bumped her as I headed down to the cabin.

Takumi was sitting up and looking more handsome than ever. I couldn't believe he could recover so fast.

"Why'd you leave?" He seemed totally clueless.

"Really?" I asked. "Maybe it was because Kat was draped all over you."

"Kat? That's ridiculous. She..." Takumi reached out to me.

I took a step back. "Nice pink *bra*, by the way." I shook my head. "We don't have time for this. I'm glad you're feeling better. We're making plans to sneak back to shore and pick up Nick and the rest of our crew."

"I want to help." Takumi struggled to get up off the mattress.

I stopped him before he could fall. He wrapped his arms around me and pulled me down with him.

"Takumi. Let me go. I have to go ashore."

"Not until you explain everything."

"Fine," I sighed. "Five minutes." I rolled away and told him my plan. When I was almost done, I sat up. "I'm concerned about Dylan and Zoë keeping the island guys under control. They really want to go home." I glanced at the chart table. "I wonder if they know where the gun is hidden. I think we should find another hiding place."

Takumi thought for a moment. "What about under my pillow? They wouldn't think to check there."

"That's a great idea. I don't want anyone to get hurt. But if they try to warn the campers or take control of the boat, it would be nice to know they wouldn't find the gun."

Takumi turned onto his side and pulled me back to him. He traced the outline of my cheek with his fingers. "Be careful, okay?"

"I will," I promised and kissed his forehead.

I found the gun buried deep under papers in the chart table. I checked to see if it was loaded. It wasn't. I put two bullets in the chamber, and left the rest in the back of the silverware drawer.

He shoved the gun beneath the two pillows he was propped up on. "We should offer Kat and her father a spot on the boat."

My heart skipped a beat. "You want Kat to come with us?"

"There are no teens on the island but us. She was lonely until we showed up."

"I bet." My voice was icy. "I'll talk to Dylan."

"Toni, wait. You know that there is nothing…" Takumi tried to get up again.

I turned my back, ignored the thump and moan I heard behind me, and climbed up on deck.

****

Kat was head down in the cockpit locker. Dylan stood behind the wheel even though we weren't moving. Zoë wiped her eyes and stared out at the water. The B's were huddled together on the bow.

"Are they going to be a problem?" I gestured at the islanders.

Dylan seemed uncertain. "They're great guys, but they really want to go home."

I moved beside him and whispered in his ear, "Takumi has the gun under his pillows."

"Good!" Dylan whispered back. "I don't think they'd try to find it, but I'm glad he'll be my backup."

"Oh! Takumi thinks Kat and her father should sail away with us." I shoved my hands in my pockets.

"Really? What do *you* think?" Dylan's eyes narrowed.

Zoë, who had been ignoring us the whole time, piped up. "I'm going to have a baby. We need a doctor."

"Okay. That settles it. Assuming they want to come," I said loudly.

Kat pulled herself up from the locker. "Look! Two dry lifejackets." She handed one to me. "Did I hear you say you wanted my dad to take off with you guys?"

"Takumi suggested it," I mumbled as I put on the lifejacket. "You too, I suppose."

"That's good, because if we help you escape, we might not be popular at the camp."

Kat was acting as if she hadn't insulted me earlier. I shrugged. Maybe it was for the best, at least for now. I could play that game, too. "So, Dylan told you the plan?"

"Yeah." Kat studied me. "If you and I are kayaking back, I think you need more of a disguise. Is there a dark beanie you could hide your hair in?"

Zoë stood and wiped her eyes. "Dylan has one. I'll go get it."

Dylan moved to the bow to talk to the B's.

Zoë returned and handed me one of Dylan's dark blue knit hats. "Takumi wants to talk to you."

"Tell him we can talk when I get back." I stuffed my long hair into the hat. The hat puffed up high on my head.

Zoë snickered. "You look like Marge Simpson."

Dylan spun around, stared at Zoë, and sighed with relief. The idea of having a doctor onboard had settled her. He held onto the lifelines and returned to the stern. The wind was picking up.

"The guys aren't happy about it, but they agreed to wait to go ashore later," he whispered to Zoë, Kat, and me. "We've gotten to know one another. I think I can trust them." He noticed my lifejacket. "You and Kat should leave. The sun is starting to set."

Chapter Fifteen

Kat and I paddled in silence. We made good time, but my ankle started to throb. I worried I'd slow Kat down when we got to shore.

The sunset turned the clouds a greyish pink. It almost made me sad to leave this side of the island. We finally glided into the calm waters of the bay. The tide was low, and had left behind a whole new collection of debris.

At the surf's edge, a plastic tabletop splashed ashore. A short ways up on the beach, a small pine tree and a wooden flagpole, complete with a tattered American flag, lay covered in mud. The usual wrecked parts of buildings were scattered all around. Most would be scavenged for firewood, although some of the larger pieces would be stacked in a pile high up on the beach. The islanders were saving this wood to build more permanent structures.

We dragged the kayaks near the pile of saved lumber. I was surprised that none of the islanders were around to check out the wreckage, especially the table-top.

The camps we passed on the way were empty too. We heard loud voices yelling, and Boots barking, as we grew closer. I moaned. We were too late. Whatever the "or else" threat was, the islanders were in the process of acting on it.

Kat and I crouched behind a couple of trees, listened, and watched. I'd been limping badly and rubbed my ankle.

There were almost twenty villagers at our camp. I recognized Sophia, her parents, and the woman who'd come to scold us before. Angelina held Boots in her arms. Makala clung to her leg. A large fire burned in the center of the gathered group, its flames creating shadows. They danced along the edges of the dark forest and veiled the tents.

"I don't know where your daughter is." Nick paced back and forth. "She and Takumi went kayaking and haven't come back." He faced the doctor. "I'm sure they're okay, though."

"First you take two of our men, now the doctor's daughter?" A woman with a whiny voice poked Nick in the chest with her long fingernail.

Kat hissed, "I'm going to diffuse this. Stay here."

I swallowed my clever comeback, and moved behind a boulder.

Kat stepped into the center of the group gathered around the fire. "What's going on?"

"Kat? Where ha… have you been?" Kat's dad raced to hug her in his too thin arms.

"I told you we were going kayaking," she replied in an annoyed tone. "We just got back."

"Where's that Asian boy?" an older man with a huge pot-belly said behind her.

"He's Japanese-American." Kat glared at the man. "Takumi stayed on the beach to gather firewood. There's lots of new debris down there." Kat nodded at Nick and Angelina. Makala smiled shyly. Boots wagged his tail and struggled to greet her.

"See! I told you they were stealing all the firewood. I haven't found a piece to burn since they arrived," a gray-haired woman cried.

"I still don't know why everyone's here." Kat stood with her hands on her hips.

Jeremy, who was Sophia's father, stepped forward. "Hand over your gun before someone gets hurt."

"We told you. We left our pistol on the boat." Angelina's eyes narrowed.

Makala hung her head. "Sissy! Mommy said we shouldn't *never* lie!"

Jeremy went down on one knee in front of Makala. "Sweetie, do you know where the gun is?"

Angelina squeezed Makala's shoulder. "Don't say another word."

"Makala, look at me," Jeremy demanded.

Makala looked at her sister. Angelina shook her head.

Jeremy cleared his throat and said in a friendlier voice, "We're starting a little school. Do you want to go to pre-school with Sophia?"

Makala grinned. "Can I, Sissy? Can I go to school?"

Angelina handed Boots to Nick, hefted her sister up into her arms, and headed to her tent. "Stop trying to bribe my sister, you jerk."

Boots growled at Jeremy.

Jeremy kept his eyes on Makala. "Sweetheart, tell me where the gun is, and you and Sophia can go play."

Makala slowly turned her head, and stared at a hollow stump she and Angelina were passing by.

Jeremy jumped to his feet and sprinted for the stump. Nick shoved the dog at Kat and ran for it too. Both arrived at the same time, body-slammed one another, and fell to the ground. A couple of big guys from the island ran towards them.

My pulse raced. I had to help. I ran through the dark bushes, tripped on a root, and moaned with pain as I went down.

Makala began screaming. Jeremy and one of the big guys held Nick. The second guy dug in the hollow of the stump and pulled out a plastic bag that contained the gun.

Makala cried hysterically.

"You got what you came for, now leave!" Angelina cuddled Makala close.

Kat zipped Boots into a tent, turned, and walked up to the guys holding Nick. "What are you doing? What's wrong with you?"

Nick struggled to get free.

Jeremy pointed the gun at Nick, then spun around and aimed at the tree I hid behind. "Dude in the trees, come out or I'll shoot your friend."

"Dad, do something!" Kat cried.

Kat's dad held out his hand. "I think you sh-should give the gun to me, son."

Jeremy ignored the doctor and stared at my hiding place. "I'm going to count to ten. One…"

I limped into the clearing. Jeremy jerked the hat off my head, and turned the gun on me.

"You're not the Asian dude. Tell me where he is. Now!"

Jeremy and I glared at one another.

A guy I didn't know stared out at the bay. "White sails. The sailboat's back."

"Just in time," Jeremy smirked.

The islanders hurried to the cliff's edge and stared down at the sailboat rapidly approaching the beach.

Jeremy swooped in and snatched Makala from Angelina's arms. He aimed the gun at Makala's head.

Angelina screamed, "Makala!"

The group on the beach gasped.

"Dude! Not cool!" a young man cried.

A woman yelled, "Put that gun down, Jeremy. Now!"

"Jeremy! Don't do this!" Jeremy's wife grabbed his arm and tugged on it.

Jeremy turned to his wife, still holding Makala fast. "Go to our campsite and pack our things. We're trading these kids for the boat."

"You're threatening Makala with a gun." His wife slugged his shoulder.

"We're leaving on that sailboat. Go pack our things," Jeremy said.

"I don't want to have any part of this!" Sophia's mother cried.

"I'm not letting my daughter grow up sleeping in the dirt. I asked these guys if we could leave with them. They told me, no. They had their chance. With that boat we can sail to South America. We can make a new life for ourselves."

"We can't make a new life by destroying the lives of others," Sophia's mother argued.

"Go pack. Come or don't. I'm taking Sophia."

Sophia's mother glared at Jeremy. She reached down to pick up her daughter.

"Sophia stays with me," Jeremy spat.

"You'd risk her too?" Sophia's mother's shoulders slumped. "Jeremy, what's wrong with you!"

Jeremy gestured for her to go.

She slowly walked away, pausing to look back at her daughter and Makala every few feet.

"Mommy!" Sophia screamed.

Makala struggled in Jeremy's arms and whimpered.

A young couple standing at the edge of camp stepped forward. "We came here to make sure the gun didn't fall into the wrong hands." The young woman stared at Jeremy. "You're the wrong hands. Put the gun down before someone gets hurt."

"Enough!" Jeremy turned in a slow circle, the pistol still pointed at Makala. "Listen up! I'm going down to the beach and tell the kids on that boat that if they want their friends back, they'll have to give us the sailboat. Anyone who helps me can come with us. If you try and stop me, the girl gets hurt."

The young couple shook their heads and backed away.

"Help us!" I pleaded.

A man with a beer belly shook his finger at me. "This is your fault. You brought the gun to our island."

My mouth dropped open. "The convicts brought a gun here. If we hadn't shown up, they would have made your lives miserable."

A young man with a beard stepped toward Jeremy. "Come on, bro. Hand over the gun."

Jeremy aimed at the sand in front of the young man and pulled the trigger.

I held my hands over my ears.

Makala and Sophia screamed.

Jeremy turned the gun on the young man. "If you aren't with me, you should leave."

The young man raised his hands in the air. Most of the group gathered on the beach followed his example. After a few minutes, one by one they left.

Kat, her father, and six of the younger guys stayed. The young guys shifted from one foot to another.

I wanted to scream. We'd saved these people from the convicts. We'd risked our lives for them.

Jeremy signaled for us to start moving. "Head to the beach. I'll follow with Makala… Anyone makes a wrong move, the girl gets a bullet." Kat and her father started down the path. Four island guys followed after them. Two held tightly onto Nick's arms. Angelina stayed close to Jeremy and Makala.

Sophia clung to her father's leg.

"You!" Jeremy pointed the gun at me. "Take my daughter's hand and make sure she doesn't fall."

I reached for Sophia. She screamed, "Mommy!" and darted off into the woods before I could grab her.

"Stop her!" Jeremy yelled at me.

"No!" Sophia's mother arrived back in the clearing. "I heard the gunshot. I'll find her. We'll meet you on the beach."

Jeremy stared at his wife. "If you don't show up, I'll come looking for you. Don't let that happen."

She took off after her daughter. "Sophia, it's Mommy. Where are you?" Her cries grew faint as she moved farther and farther away.

While we hiked down the steep path, we peeked through openings in the trees and brush, and watched *Whistler*'s progress. I kept shaking my head. How had my plan failed so badly?

When we got to the beach, I couldn't take my eyes off *Whistler*. It was sailing too fast. It should have lowered its sails and needed to drop anchor.

I limped faster. "Kat, they aren't slowing down. Something's wrong." Kat and I began to run. The others followed close behind.

"Slow down!" Jeremy yelled. I didn't know if he was talking to me or to the boat. I ignored him and moved as fast as my ankle would allow. When we got to the shore, I stared in horror. The sails were still up. The boat was headed straight for the beach.

Without thinking, I limped into the water and headed to the spot where *Whistler* would crash. Kat and her dad pulled me back. "You can't stop the boat!"

"It's going to hit the beach! We have to do something." I screamed. "Dylan! Takumi! Drop the sails!"

No one answered. I could see people on deck, but it was so dark, I couldn't tell who.

Whistler was only a few yards off the beach.

A shot rang out from the boat.

Loud voices began arguing.

Dylan yelled, "Grab the day anchor!"

Whistler kept coming.

The sails were still up.

The hull of the boat hit the rocky shore.

There was a terrible crunching sound. The bow was held fast.

Whistler was beached.

Chapter Sixteen

The shoreline was in chaos. Jeremy held Makala under his arm and aimed the gun at me, at the boat, then back at me. Nick yelled and struggled to break free from the guys holding him. Makala kicked and flailed her arms.

"Let her go." Angelina edged closer to Makala.

Jeremy turned the gun on her. "Back off," he growled.

Two guys held onto Nick. The four remaining island guys, Kat, her dad, and I sloshed around in ankle-deep water and stared in horror. The boat was stuck, bow first, up on the shore. The keel was dug in, and *Whistler* was heeled over almost thirty degrees, although water still surrounded the mid-ship and stern.

How had this happened? "Dylan! Takumi!" I screamed.

"We're all okay. Give us a minute," Dylan yelled back.

Jeremy ran down to the shoreline with Makala under his arm. "It's beached," he bellowed, then turned to me. "You and your brother! You did this on purpose."

I shook my head, speechless.

"You've ruined everything." He marched back and forth, huffing and puffing.

"Get a grip." I found my voice. "I don't know what happened, but I know Dylan would never do this to our family's boat."

Whistler was so close, I could now make out the people onboard. Takumi leaned on the mast and held a gun on two guys huddled on the bow. Their backs were to us, but they had to be the 'B's'.

Dylan lowered the main and wrapped lines around the sail to keep it folded onto the mast. The jib fluttered back and forth and made a terrible noise. I didn't see Zoë anywhere.

"Toni?" Dylan began rolling in the jib. "What's going on?"

Jeremy grabbed my arm. "I've got a gun aimed at Makala and your sister. Get that boat off the beach. Now!"

"Toni! Are you okay?" Takumi stepped to the rail.

"I'm fine." I shook Jeremy's hand loose.

Dylan tied the jib in place and moved beside Takumi. I could see them whispering.

Dylan gestured at the guys on the bow. "Brad and Banks beached the boat. They jumped me and took over sailing. Jeremy, if you want to blame someone, blame them. There's nothing I can do now. We'll have to wait until the tide comes in. Then hope it'll float off."

"We have a gun too, and it's pointing at Banks and Brad." Takumi went back to leaning on the mast. "Give us our friends, and we'll give you, yours."

"You said they're responsible for crashing the boat. They get what they deserve," Jeremy cried.

"So, we can just shoot your friends?" Dylan sounded incredulous.

Banks and Brad hunched over even farther.

Jeremy looked back at the path to camp and then the boat. "I don't want anyone injured, but I'll do whatever it takes to get off this island."

Dylan took the gun from Takumi. "The boat isn't going anywhere until high-tide. Are you just going to stand around for eight hours?" When there was no answer he continued. "It's getting cold. At least let Makala come onboard and get warm."

"Let all the girls go. I'll stay. I'll be your hostage," Nick offered.

"We wait for the tide." Jeremy shifted Makala to his other arm and faced the four young men still hanging around. "Guys! Make a fire." He leveled the pistol at *Whistler*. "Dylan, if you try anything, I'll start shooting."

"Dude, this is going too far," a young man in a cowboy hat said, and stepped away. "The boat's beached. Give it up."

"The tide will free it," Jeremy insisted.

"I'm outta here." The cowboy put his hands in the air and walked away.

Another guy mouthed, "Sorry," and followed him.

Two of Jeremy's friends tied Nick's hands together with a plastic bag, pushed Nick onto an upside-down bin, and perched on a log behind him.

The islanders who were not guarding Nick collected wood and dried seaweed. In no time, a large smoky fire was ablaze. I was chilled and held my hands out to the flames. But the warmth didn't make me feel any better. *Whistler* was stuck. There might be cracks or a big hole in the hull. And Jeremy was starting to lose it. Waiting would only make him worse.

Jeremy cradled Makala and sat on the edge of a partially destroyed wooden rowboat near the fire. Makala cried herself to sleep. Kat and her father huddled together on a beached tree.

We settled in to wait for the tide. Time seemed to stand still.

I rested my head in my hands and closed my eyes. I tried to think of a way to end the standoff, but couldn't.

We seemed to be in gun-related conflicts a lot. Were the pacifists right? Were our guns the reason we were threatened everywhere we went?

I opened my eyes and checked on Dylan. He was waving the gun around as he talked with his hands. He'd never even held a gun before this journey.

I thought back on our trip. Back on all we'd gone through. Without Angelina's gun, our voyage would have failed. We'd have lost the boat to the sailors—and if not to them, then the motorcycle gang. It made me sad to think how much control the gun seemed to have over our lives.

Zoë appeared on the boat deck with an arm full of blankets. She even handed a couple to the 'B' guys and spoke in a quiet voice to Dylan. I realized I hadn't seen Takumi on *Whistler's* deck for a while.

"Is Takumi feeling okay?" I tried to keep the worry out of my voice.

Zoë glanced at Dylan, then called back, "He's making dinner."

Dinner! I couldn't remember when I'd eaten last. I plopped back down. My stomach rumbled. My mouth was dry. I needed to go to the bathroom.

The tide had only just started to change.

We had at least six hours to go.

Makala whimpered and sucked her thumb in her sleep. I'd almost woken her. Kat and her father threw some wood on the fire.

"Doc! Kat! I'm surprised you stayed to help me," Jeremy whispered.

Kat squeezed her father's hand before he could respond. "We want to get off this island too."

Jeremy snarled. "Let's hope those idiots haven't ruptured the hull. We'll find out soon enough."

I bit my lip. Nick kicked the sand and pebbles at his feet.

"Knock it off!" One of his guards gripped his shoulder.

We watched and waited. I tried to doze. Makala slept.

The sea came farther and farther up the beach. The stern of the boat bounced with the gentle waves, but the hull and bow were still held fast.

A gust of wind blew sparks from the fire toward Kat and the doctor. They hopped up and brushed the embers off their clothes.

I checked on the boat. If the wind or tide pushed it broadside onto the beach, it would roll onto its side, and we'd never get it off. But so far, the anchor Dylan had thrown off the back was holding the stern in place. The boat remained perpendicular to the shore.

Jeremy kept checking the trail for his wife and daughter. Finally, he sent two of the island guys to find them. Our numbers were improving. Now there was only Jeremy and the guys guarding Nick. I could tell Nick and Angelina were thinking the same thing, but with Nick tied up, I didn't have a clue what we could do. Besides, we couldn't risk Makala.

Time dragged on.

I checked my watch. We'd been sitting, doing nothing for almost four hours. I popped up and told Jeremy he could shoot me if he needed to, but I couldn't hold it any longer: I was headed to the bushes. Jeremy scowled, then ordered Kat to guard me.

Kat leaned on a tree with her back to me while I did my business.

"What kind of game are you playing?" I asked.

"Game?" Kat replied.

"You told Jeremy you'd help him." I zipped up my jeans.

"That's what he heard. What I said was that I wanted to leave the island. I do. Dad and I are here to help you. Believe it, or not."

"Kat! Toni!" a voice whispered from behind a nearby tree.

I jumped. "Who's there?"

"Shusssh!" Takumi stepped out from behind a tree.

I wanted to throw myself into his arms, but held back. He was dripping wet. I stared at his skin-tight rubber outfit and ace-bandaged foot. The wet suit! He was wearing the wet suit I'd loaded in Seattle. I'd forgotten we even had one.

"Good thinking, on the wet suit! What are you doing here?" I watched to see what Kat would do.

She grinned at him.

"I'm rescuing you. Are you okay?" Takumi studied my face.

"I'm worried." I relaxed and caressed his cheek. "The boat's beached … and Jeremy's dangerous."

Takumi held my hand to his face for a moment, then turned to Kat. "And you? Your dad?"

"We're okay." Kat stepped towards him. "How's the foot?"

"Almost good as new." Takumi walked in a circle and only limped a little.

"How did you manage to get off the boat?" Kat asked.

"I slid off the stern and swam down the beach. I hoped no one would hear or see me." Takumi hurried over to the tree and returned, seconds later, with a spear gun.

Kat raised her eyebrows. “Umm. Hate to tell you, but pistol beats spear gun.”

Takumi grinned. “Dylan is going to distract Jeremy. When he does, I’ll sneak up behind him, press a spear into his back, and tell him to drop the gun.”

“And if he doesn’t?” I narrowed my eyes.

Takumi locked a spear into the gun. “He will.”

Jeremy bellowed from the beach, “Kat. Is everything okay?”

Takumi moved away from Kat. “What? You’re guarding Toni?”

“Jeremy thinks Dad and I stayed on the beach to help him. I’m kinda letting him think that.” Kat cupped her hand around her mouth and yelled that everything was fine.

We started back to the beach. Takumi reached for my hand. I shoved it in my pocket.

“What happened after we left the boat?” Kat led the way.

“When Dylan was bringing up the anchor, Banks and Brad attacked him. They sailed the boat here. I was below, sleeping. Zoë woke me when she learned what was going on. I pulled the cons’ gun on the ‘B’s and we got the boat back. But it was too late,” Takumi sighed.

“Is Dylan okay?” Cole’s head injury flashed before me.

“He has a headache.” Takumi grimaced. “And he feels stupid for trusting those guys.

At least he had time to throw out a small stern anchor before we hit. We hope it will keep *Whistler* from floating broadside onto the beach.”

Kat held a branch up for us to walk under. “But how are you going to get the boat off the shore?”

Takumi and I exchanged glances. I didn't trust her enough to tell her we could still motor. I waited to see if Takumi would. When he didn't, I was even more confused.

"Just hope Whistler doesn't have a crack or big hole in the bottom." I pushed past her.

Kat didn't ask any more questions.

We crouched down at the edge of the bushes and studied the scene below. On the far side of the fire, Jeremy held Makala in his arms. She was awake—and screaming for her sister.

Angelina, Nick, and the guys guarding Nick were close by. The guys who'd left to find Sophia and her mother never returned. Kat's dad sat across the fire from Jeremy and Makala.

"Wait for the distraction. When Jeremy gets up, see if you can grab Makala from him. We need to get her out of the line of fire."

"Got it," Kat said softly.

At the last second, I squeezed his hand. "Be careful, okay?"

"I will." He turned to Kat. "You and Toni take cover when the action starts."

Kat and I hiked back to the fire. I could hear Takumi rustling in the bushes behind us.

Makala was still calling for her sister.

"You were gone long enough." Jeremy glared at Kat.

"Princess here needed the perfect spot to pee. Took a while." Kat made a face.

Jeremy chuckled.

Angelina got up and kneeled in front of Jeremy. "Please. Makala's scared. Give her to me. I'm begging you."

Jeremy turned the gun on Angelina. He switched Makala to his other arm and shook his head. His arms had to be aching from holding onto her so long.

Makala whimpered, “Sissy!”

“You’re fine…” Angelina reassured her.

“Come on. Hand Makala over to her sister. Point the stupid gun at me. I’m a bigger target,” I said.

Jeremy repositioned Makala to his knee. “Makala’s your little darling. You might risk one another, but not her. Now, make her stop whining.”

Nick popped up and growled. His arms were tied tight behind his back. Jeremy’s friends shoved him down.

“Enough!” Dylan yelled from the bow of *Whistler*. “This has gone far enough. Banks. Brad. Go. Just leave.”

The guys huddled on the boat deck scrambled to their feet and stared at Dylan.

“You heard me. Get off my boat!” Dylan yelled.

‘The B’s’ climbed over the rail, dropped to the water that came up to their chests, and began to wade to shore.

Kat, Nick, Angelina, and I leapt to our feet. My heart raced. I forced myself not to turn and check on Takumi.

The guys guarding Nick stood and gazed at the scene on *Whistler*.

Jeremy jumped up, while holding Makala as his shield.

It was time. Jeremy had his back to Takumi’s hiding place.

Dylan continued speaking and gesturing with his gun. “Jeremy! I’ve let my hostages go. Now, it’s your turn. Put the gun away. Give Makala to her sister. If you want off this island, work with me.”

I glimpsed Takumi darting behind a large boulder from the corner of my eye. I held my breath. The plan was working. Everyone was focused on Dylan.

Jeremy shook his head. "You had your chance to let us on. The boat's mine now."

Dylan raised his hands in the air with frustration. "If we don't get the boat off the beach, it won't be useful for anyone."

Jeremy's face grew purple. "The boat *will* float off the beach. It *will* float, or you'll be sorry." He spun and turned the gun on me.

I froze.

Takumi roared, "Drop the gun!" He jammed a spear into Jeremy's back.

I'd been expecting it, but still jumped.

"I said, drop it!" Takumi sounded fierce.

In one quick motion, Jeremy dropped Makala, twisted, and elbowed Takumi in the face. Takumi lost the spear gun. Nick, hands behind his back, body slammed into Jeremy. I snatched Makala and dove behind a bin. Angelina raced over and covered Makala and me with her body. Kat sprinted to her dad. Jeremy's friends stayed by the fire and held their hands in the air.

Nick, Jeremy, and Takumi rolled around on the ground. Nick head-butted Jeremy. Jeremy threw a punch that knocked Nick away. Takumi grabbed Jeremy's arms. Jeremy flipped Takumi onto his back, straddled him, and held the gun tight to his forehead.

"*No*!" I screamed.

Takumi worked an arm free and tried to push the gun away. Kat's dad came out of nowhere and leapt on Jeremy's back. Jeremy, Takumi, and the doctor fought for control of the pistol.

Then the gun went off.

Chapter Seventeen

I raced toward the fight. Kat ran to her dad. The Doctor lay on the beach, groaning, holding his left side. A pool of blood was already starting to form beside him. He gripped the pistol tight in his fingers.

Takumi was pounding on Jeremy. Jeremy held his arms up to protect his face, then dropped them. Takumi punched him again and again. Blood went flying everywhere.

"Takumi! Stop!" I cried. "You're killing him."

Takumi stared at his bloody fists, then at me. He pushed himself away and stood, trying to catch his breath.

Jeremy didn't move. I knelt beside him to take his pulse. He moaned and opened his one good eye.

Takumi stumbled over to Nick. He untied the plastic bag from Nick's wrists and handed the bag back. Without saying a word, Takumi wandered to the water's edge. Nick began securing Jeremy's hands behind his back with the shredded plastic bag.

I watched for a second before hurrying over to Kat.

She crouched beside her father. "He's been shot!" Shock bleached all color from her face. She flew into action, ripped off her sweatshirt, and pressed the cloth over the bloody open wound on the side of his stomach.

"Zoë!" I yelled at the boat. "The doctor's been shot. We need help."

I pried the gun from the doctor's fingers. I was surprised Nick's guards hadn't already snatched it. But they sat on a nearby on a tree trunk and stared at their feet.

"We didn't really help Jeremy!" one of the guys who'd been guarding Nick mumbled, when he saw me glance at them.

"We could have gotten the pistol," the other added.

"But you did nothing for hours while Jeremy held us hostage." I aimed the pistol at them while Nick finished securing Jeremy, then lowered it. "Just, just… go away." I motioned with the gun. "Leave!"

Kat glanced up. "Wait! I need bandages, disinfectant, and sutures." She checked her dad's wound and stared at the guys. "Get the supplies and hurry back."

Jeremy's friends seemed uncertain and didn't move.

"You heard her," I cried. "Here's a chance for you to make good."

They turned and ran. I hoped at least one would return with the supplies. I passed the pistol to Nick and found the spear gun in the sand. He rubbed his swollen chin. Angelina wiped the blood off Nick's face. Makala hid behind Angelina.

"How bad is Kat's dad?" Nick turned the gun on Jeremy.

"Not good. Zoë's on her way." I pushed the gun so it aimed down. "Maybe it's time we put the pistol away."

Jeremy tried to get up, groaned, and fell face first into the sand. Nick stuck the pistol in the back of his waistband.

Takumi limped into the shallows and leaned over to wash the blood off his hands.

I ran to the water and handed him his spear gun. "Are you all right?"

"I lost it. When he aimed the gun at you, I wanted to…" Takumi dried his hands on his pants.

"But you didn't." I hugged him, then jumped at the sound of an oar splash. It was Zoë. She was having a hard time rowing the dinghy. I left Takumi and waded into the cold water past my knees.

"Throw me a line," I yelled.

"How can I do that? I'm rowing!" Zoë snapped.

"Stop. Lay the paddles in the boat." I reached my arms out for the line. On the third throw, I caught it, and towed her to shore.

Takumi remained at the water's edge and stared at his scraped knuckles. He didn't react when Zoë and I passed by.

"Takumi, are you okay?" I paused at his side. He didn't answer. "I'm going to take Zoë over to the doctor. I'll be right back."

Takumi bent over and began washing his hands again. He was scrubbing so hard that the blood on them was now his.

Zoë and I hurried to the doctor. He was propped up on coats a little ways from the fire.

Kat stood as we approached. "He needs a hospital. There's no way to tell if he's nicked a vital organ without an imaging machine. You have to help him."

I held my hands up. "There aren't any hospitals left. Everything's been wiped out."

She shook her head. "Zoë told me that your friend went to a military base on the mainland. When the military sets up a base, they bring in doctors and equipment."

Zoë took over pressing Kat's already bloodstained sweatshirt on the still oozing wound. "She's right. He might need a surgeon. The bullet went clear through, but we can't tell what damage it did. The gun went off at close range. And stomach wounds are among the worst."

"But, but," I stammered.

Kat shook her finger at me. "He risked his life for you guys."

The doctor moaned.

I sighed and stared back at *Whistler*.

"Is everything under control?" Dylan called out from the boat.

I searched for an answer. Angelina, Nick, and Makala were huddled by the fire. Boots was wandering around, sniffing. Takumi waded around in the bay, scrubbing his hands raw. The doctor lay bleeding.

"We have to take Kat and her dad to the army base. He's hurt. It's bad," I yelled to Dylan.

Dylan stared out at the bay, then back at me. "Can't Zoë sew him up like she did Angelina?"

"The girls think this it is a lot more serious. He needs surgery."

Dylan shrugged. "That's too bad."

"Dylan. We have to help him. He risked his life for us."

"Damn!" Dylan turned away, then faced back. "Do we have time to grab our camping gear?"

I thought a moment. "We'll make time. Can you come ashore?"

Dylan walked to the bow and lowered his voice. "I have to stay here. If the stern anchor slips, I'll only have seconds to keep the boat aimed at the shore. Actually, I could use some help."

I hurried closer to the boat. "I'll ask Nick and Takumi to pack up our gear. Kat and Zoë can get the doctor ready. I'll row Makala and Angelina to the boat right now. Makala needs to go to bed. When everything is ready, I'll row back to get the doctor and the others."

"Okay, but make it fast. When the keel lifts, we're backing out. *Whistler* can't survive another tide change."

I was beyond exhausted and cold. I pulled Takumi up the beach to the fire. He avoided looking at Jeremy.

When I told the crew that we needed to pack up and take the doctor to the army hospital, I could tell they were just as wiped out as I was. Nick groaned, but said he'd help. Angelina was happy with my offer to row Makala and her to the boat.

Takumi followed slowly behind Nick as they headed up the trail to our camp.

Kat nodded when I told them we would be leaving for the hospital as soon as the boat floated free. We were helpless until then.

She and Zoë discussed whether or not to try to stitch up the mess that was the side of her father's stomach. I'd sewn Angelina's wound, but had no interest in doing that again. I told them my plan, and headed for the dinghy.

A small group of islanders ran down the beach towards us and stopped me.

"We heard a gunshot. Is everything…?" Sophia's mother started to speak, then spied Jeremy. Tears filled her eyes. When she learned the doctor had been shot, she quietly took off her wedding ring and stuck it in Jeremy's shirt pocket. "We're done, Jeremy. Sophia and I never want to see you again."

Jeremy closed his eyes and fell back onto the sand. His wife left sobbing.

Jeremy's followers became helpful. Some broke away and carried the supplies Kat had asked for over to her. A man and woman I didn't know said how sorry they were for what had happened.

My face burned. "You're sorry? You're sorry? You left us. You saw how Jeremy was threatening Makala, and all of us. But you took off anyway!"

Another man in the group stepped forward. "You brought the guns to the island. What happened is on you."

"Really!" I took a step toward him. "Twenty days ago, that might have been true. There were police and firemen around to protect you. But the world has changed."

"That's why we came here. Away from all the violence." The man watched his companions. A couple of people nodded their agreement, but most looked away.

I took another step. "The violence followed you."

He moved back. I moved forward. "The convicts were here before we even got here."

He bumped into a woman standing behind him. I was right up in his face. "Violence will find you again. You can protect yourself, or be victims."

"Get away from me!" the man turned and walked away.

A woman with long gray hair took his place. "You're going to leave, then?"

"We're going to take the doctor to the mainland." I glared. "We won't return."

"I'm glad the guns will be gone." She frowned. "But we never wanted you children or the doctor harmed."

"Whatever!" I glanced around at the group gathered around me.

"We should have done more to stop Jeremy. What can we do to make amends?" A woman I'd not seen before had asked the question.

"Nothing." I rubbed my arms. "No, wait. You can take care of him." I gestured at Jeremy.

One of the guys leaned over to help Jeremy up. "What do you want us to do with him?"

"I don't care," I said. "But just so you know, he held a gun to a little girl's head for almost six hours."

The man's face turned red. "We were wrong to leave you kids with him." He shoved Jeremy toward the trail.

A young guy grabbed my arm and smiled charmingly at me. "Can my friends and I hitch a ride to Santa Barbara?"

He'd been one of the first to walk off and leave us with Jeremy. I glared at him. He dropped his hand from my arm and slunk away.

I hurried to the dinghy. Angelina and Makala were already onboard and I quickly paddled to the stern of *Whistler*. Makala complained as the cold worked its way through her layers of clothing.

The boat had been heeled over earlier, but was now almost sitting straight up in the water. Angelina carried Makala below. I stayed on deck with Dylan. He asked me to throw our makeshift depth finder out, and see how much water we had.

The rope with the broken brick was dripping on the bench. "How shallow did it get?"

"At the lowest, we were in five feet of water. The hull must be dug in pretty deep." Dylan peered over the side.

I lowered the brick and counted the marks on the rope that entered the water until the brick hit bottom.

"We have over six and a half feet, mid-ship." I checked the stern. "Over nine feet back here."

"The keel goes down six feet eight inches. Let me know when there is exactly seven feet at the mid-ship."

As I measured, I worried about Takumi. We'd been through a lot. I'd never seen him acting the way he was.

"I think Takumi's in shock." I laid the depth finder down on the bench. "And I told Kat I'd be right back. I'm going ashore and tell them what we're doing."

"No. They can wait. The tide won't. We're close to floating free. I need you here." He handed me back the depth finder rope. "Keep measuring. When we have seven feet, yell."

I wanted to argue, but knew he was right. The water under the hull was growing deeper.

I went back to my job. All of a sudden I felt the boat break free. We were afloat. I dropped the depth finder, and called out, "Six feet four inches. Six feet eight inches... Dylan, we got it. Seven feet."

"Okay. I'm going to start the engine. Cross your fingers." Dylan put the key in the ignition. "Keep an eye on the stern anchor. Hold the line off to the side as we back out. Don't let me drive over it."

I ran to the starboard cleat where the stern anchor was tied. The anchor line went straight down.

Dylan turned the key. Nothing happened. He tried again. There was a little sputter, then the engine died.

"Use the choke," I yelled.

Dylan adjusted the choke and tried again. The engine roared, fizzled, and finally started.

"Hold on," Dylan yelled down to Angelina and Makala and threw the gear into reverse.

The prop churned the sea floor. There was a terrible grinding sound. Sand and pebbles whipped around in the water. The prop stirred the bottom, but we were not moving. The boat shuddered. The engine roared.

The boat shook. All of a sudden we lurched and broke free. Whistler was backing away from the beach. We made slow progress at first. The boat would start to move, stall, and move a short distance more.

I fought to keep the stern anchor line away from the propeller below. It was tight and I ran from cleat to cleat, wrapping it so it wouldn't slip through my fingers. All of a sudden, something felt wrong. We'd backed out past where the anchor was buried. It was pulling the hull of the boat toward the beach.

"Haul in the anchor. It's pulling us sideways," Dylan screamed.

I yanked on the line. The stern anchor was stuck. I pulled and pulled. It didn't budge. "I can't move it." I shoved Dylan out of the way and took over the wheel. "You try."

Dylan heaved up on the anchor line. I spun the wheel away from the shore. Nothing I did helped. Whistler was now parallel to the beach.

"Let it go!" I screamed. "Let the anchor go."

A wave hit us broadside. The keel hit bottom. The boat listed over onto its side.

It was high tide. If we beached sideways at high tide, we'd never get off.

Dylan tossed the line that was attached to the stern anchor overboard. I turned the wheel the opposite way and revved the engine. The stern swung back around. The keel scraped bottom. I throttled down. We zoomed off and away from the beach.

"Slow down!" Dylan yelled.

I adjusted the throttle and took a breath.

We were over a couple of hundred feet from the beach. I spun *Whistler* around and motored, bow first, to the middle of the bay and put the engine in neutral. The engine roar died down. Dylan threw out the depth checker.

I closed my eyes and gulped in air. We'd made it. We'd saved *Whistler*.

When my pulse slowed, I searched the shore for Takumi. He wasn't there. I gripped the wheel and kept the rudder straight. Dylan used our depth finder and reported that *Whistler* had twenty feet of water under her, perfect for anchoring. I ran below and checked for leaks. So far, there were none.

While he readied the bow anchor, a shrill voice carried across the water. Dylan and I stopped to listen.

Zoë stood on the beach and waved frantically. "Dylan! Come back! Don't you *dare* leave me!"

Chapter Eighteen

Dylan's mouth hung open. I elbowed him and grinned and he closed his mouth and smiled back. All of a sudden we began to laugh. We laughed so hard our sides hurt, and tears ran down our cheeks. We had to hold each other up.

I don't know why we thought the situation was funny. The doctor was badly hurt. Takumi and Makala were in shock. But we'd saved the boat, and at that moment in time, Zoë seemed hilarious.

"You didn't tell her what we were doing?" Dylan chuckled.

"I told you I needed to go back." I snorted. My snort set us off again.

After a lot of yelling back and forth, Dylan managed to convince Zoë that we weren't leaving her and we anchored the boat. I stayed on the lookout for debris while he dropped the anchor.

The floating pieces from buildings were now all broken up. It made it easier to find firewood, but the wood had been in the water for a couple of weeks. Trees that had been knocked down were still intact and a threat, however. I still saw the occasional plastic flower or rubber toy, and the always-present plastic bins.

Takumi and Nick finally appeared on the beach. Their arms were full of camping gear. A couple of villagers held loads too. Boots sensed something was going on and ran in circles, yipping.

"I'll go ashore this time," Dylan offered. "It'll take a few trips."

Even though I was anxious to talk to Takumi, I was glad to let Dylan row back to the beach this time.

Dylan returned with our gear along with Nick, and Zoë. Takumi stayed to help Kat with her father.

Disappointed, I paced back and forth the length of the boat and tried to see what Takumi and Kat were doing. I knew I was being stupid—her dad was badly injured.

Dylan and Nick unloaded the dinghy while Zoë complained about our leaving the shore without telling her.

"What was so funny, Dylan?" Zoë placed her hands on her hips.

"Nothing," Dylan replied. "Toni got the hiccups. We were tired. Silly."

"Really? You weren't laughing at me?"

"Never, babe. I'd never laugh at you. Only with you. Forever. Remember?"

I turned my back to them, grabbed the rails, and grinned. My brother was good. I picked up a rolled up tent and carried it below. There was work to do.

"How's Kat's dad?" I asked Zoë as Dylan unloaded the last of the camping equipment from the dinghy.

"He's okay. We stitched him and wrapped the wound. A couple of guys offered to help us load the doctor into the dinghy. I don't know how we are going to get him from the dinghy onto the sailboat, however."

"He doesn't look like he weighs a lot. We'll manage." Dylan headed back to shore.

I couldn't wait to leave the bay. We'd had nothing but problems since we got here. But I had faith that we'd come back after we got the doctor to the military compound and find my parents on the island. Just at a better spot.

I was sorry the doctor had been shot, but I couldn't wrap my head around the idea of Kat coming with us.

Nick and Takumi carried the doctor down to Jervis' mattress on the floor of the main cabin. Kat followed after them. Her eyes were red and swollen. She hovered beside her father, checking and rechecking his wound.

I dug out the last jar of peanut butter and handed it to Kat with a spoon. "Sorry, it's all we have left onboard."

She took a spoonful and closed her eyes. "I forgot how amazing peanut butter is."

"How about your dad? I could make some hot water with peanut butter in it."

"No, just plain water." She scooted beside me on the couch and whispered, "His stomach is swollen. I'm worried he's bleeding internally."

"I…I… can hear you." Her dad tried to sit up, moaned, then fell back. His fingers gently felt his stomach. "I'll be fine. Glad we a… are going to a hospital, though. Thank you."

Kat helped her father take sips of water. Takumi came down and we shared a spoonful of peanut butter. I screwed the lid back on.

Dylan appeared and took a seat. I handed my spoon and the jar to him. "How's your father?" he asked Kat as he opened the jar.

Kat looked at her dad and waited for him to answer. "I hurt. Thanks for s… sailing to Santa Barbara."

"Just hang on. We'll get you there as soon as we can." Dylan started digging out a huge helping of peanut butter. "We're all sleep-deprived. What do you think about taking two-hour shifts? Zoë and I will do the first one. Toni, you and Takumi take the second. Angelina and Nick, you have the third. Santa Barbara is only thirty miles away, and with good wind, we should be there by late this afternoon." Dylan shoved the heaping spoonful into his mouth.

"Fine with me," I said. "Two hours of sleep sounds like heaven." I pulled my dead cell phone out of my pocket. "Is there any battery power left? We should all charge our phones. We might get service when we get close to the mainland."

Dylan turned on the battery meter on the electrical panel. "It's low," he said and pulled out his cell. "But cells don't use much. Jervis mentioned we should unhook the batteries to make them last longer."

"I remember." I checked my phone for messages. None. "We should figure out how to do that before the batteries all die."

Dylan said something with his mouth full of peanut butter, and went up on deck with the plate of peanut butter for Zoë and Nick. I heard the anchor fall into the anchor locker and the sails go up. We were on our way.

After a short while, Nick came down, checked on Angelina and Makala, and joined Takumi at the chart table. They opened up the large maps and began to study the California coastal charts. I found blankets and handed them to Kat. She covered her father and lay down on the couch above him.

The guys marked a few places they wanted to avoid and noted the shallow areas of Santa Barbara Bay. Nick found his cell, plugged it in too, yawned, and joined Angelina and Makala in their cabin. Takumi and I looked around for a place to sleep, then headed to Dylan's bed. Kat watched us leave, but I couldn't read her face. I snuggled into Takumi's arms and instantly fell asleep.

It seemed like it had been only a few seconds, when my eyes popped open and I stared into Zoë's face.

"What are you doing in my bed?" she growled.

"What time is it?" I felt even more tired than I had before sleeping.

"You've been here for over two hours. Dylan and I haven't slept forever. Now *get out* of my bed."

Takumi and I washed our faces in cold salt water. We'd finally run out of soap. I grabbed our coats, and headed up top. I was pleased to find a small fire burning in the barbecue pit and warmed myself while I tried to wake up. Takumi took directions and the wheel from Dylan, then Dylan headed down to bed.

Dylan had filled the water tanks with water from the stream but it had to be boiled. I filled the teapot with stream water and placed it over the fire. *Whistler* was flying down-wind. The boat was only slightly heeled.

"I'll leave my phone charging for a few more minutes, and then you can charge up yours," I told Takumi.

He shrugged. "Okay. But I don't see why I should bother."

I placed my hand on his arm. "Are you okay?"

"Are any of us are okay…" He stared at my hand. "The islanders had a good point. We do use the guns to get our way. We're becoming bullies. I've never lost control like I did with Jeremy. If you hadn't stopped me, I might have beaten him to death."

"But you did stop. And now you regret what you did. Next time you'll stop yourself. We're all doing the best we can."

"Well, we have to do better."

"I think we're doing pretty well. We only bring out the guns when we're threatened. Maybe, because we know we have the guns, we don't feel the need to discuss or compromise as much as we would if we didn't have guns. I don't know. But I'm not going to feel guilty that Angelina brought a pistol. It saved us more than once."

Takumi pursed his lips and stared up at the sail. I dug a small log out of the wood storage bin and tossed it on the fire. It was damp and smoked a lot.

The wind changed, and we tacked. Takumi brought in the sail and let it out while I turned the wheel.

When we'd first arrived in California, the sky was cloudy, but seemed lighter. Now the clouds were thick and the wind had a chill to it. Was the Ice Age still following us?

I zipped up my coat. "Do you think there really will be cell service?" Butterflies swirled around my stomach. What would it mean if we didn't hear from our families? But then, if I heard from mine, I'd have to tell them that Cole was dead.

"The closer we get to that base, the better our chance."

The tea kettle whistled. I tiptoed below and hunted for tea. There was none left, but I found some old Crystal Light mix, along with two mugs, and carried them up top.

"How does hot lemonade sound?" I asked.

For the first time in two days, Takumi smiled, and it was almost as if the sun came out. We sailed along in comfortable silence. I stared out at the gentle sea. Snow-white seagulls followed behind the boat and called to us. We had to adjust the sail to maneuver around a huge floating tree. I spied a red storage bin, but let it pass.

It felt good to be back on the sea again, although I hadn't missed the cold. Fog floated off the water and added to the overall chill. I checked my watch. *Whistler* had been sailing for more than four hours. We had to be getting close to the California shoreline.

It was time to ask the question that had been bothering me for days. I took a deep breath. "Takumi, what's the deal with you and Kat?"

Takumi squinted and stared straight ahead. We entered a bank of fog, and he stood on top of the captain's seat to get a better view. "What?"

"You heard me. Are you and Kat…?"

Takumi held up his hand for silence. "Look!"

"Really? You're not going to answer?" I swiveled to see what he was so focused on.

In our path, a huge cruise ship floated, upside-down. My hand flew to my mouth. What had happened to all the people on board? Was the boat full of bodies?

I studied each and every window and porthole for survivors. No one appeared. I couldn't tell if the life rafts had been used or not. The top half of the boat was under water.

The breeze we needed to fill our sails was non-existent, blocked by the massive ship. We almost came to a stop. When we finally made it past the ship, we were struck by a massive blast of wind. *Whistler* heeled far over. I struggled to let out more sail. We picked up speed. The California shoreline appeared on the horizon.

We were surrounded by hundreds of large vessels. They all floated, either on their sides or fully capsized, in the waters off the coast. I wondered how many had already sunk. Maneuvering through them took all our concentration.

"We need to get close enough to the beach to see landmarks. Something we can use to navigate," Takumi told me.

I shivered as much in fear as with the cold. We could easily run into a submerged ship. And he was right. We needed to figure out where we were.

As we drew close to the shore, the famous California beaches appeared rocky and dotted with clusters of tents and huts made from debris. There were no permanent structures. No high-rises. No hotels. Nothing. Even the famous highways had disappeared. And most of the palm trees were gone.

An endless mass of people swarmed the beach in both directions. They seemed to roam, back and forth.

There had to be thousands of them.

How were they surviving?

And which cluster of tents was a military base?

Chapter Nineteen

Takumi and I scanned the coastline for military uniforms or some other sign the army was close by, but nothing appeared.

A toddler wading in the water got knocked down by a wave. I waited for a concerned parent to rescue the child, but none came. I waved my arms. No one noticed. The child's head disappeared under the water. Another wave washed ashore over the top of where the toddler had gone down. A second child, not much older than the toddler, ran into the water and dragged the drowning child to shore by his or her arm.

I couldn't breathe. I lowered my head and gasped for air.

"What was that all about?" Takumi asked. Before I could answer, he spun the wheel. The sail got back winded and the boom jived across the stern. I tried to bring in the boom before it crashed, but I was too slow. The jib spun around itself and became useless. The main sail flopped in the wind.

Dylan raced up the steps. "What the hell?"

Takumi shook all over. "The top of an antenna was sticking up in the water directly ahead of us. I turned to avoid going over the top of whatever was under it."

"Without controlling the sails?" Dylan jumped around the deck, inspecting the boom and main. "We're lucky the mainsail didn't rip off the boom. What were you thinking?"

Takumi shook his head. I put my hand on his shoulder. He shrugged it off.

I took a step back and leaned against the wheel.

Nick came up on deck. "Holy cr…" He nodded toward the shore. Dylan finally stopped ranting and looked too.

"That's what we were trying to tell you." I gestured at the sea. "Look at all of the damaged ships. And just as many have probably sunk. Takumi swerved to miss a sunken ship."

"Don't make excuses for me," Takumi snapped. "I panicked. It's my fault."

Nick moved to the jib, untangled the lines, and pulled out the sail. "All good," he cried.

Dylan watched the waters around us as he pulled in the sheet and tightened down the boom.

Takumi brushed past me and went below.

This wasn't the Takumi I knew. Had the fight with Jeremy affected him more than I'd realized? Or was it something else—something to do with Kat?

I stayed on deck to give him some space, even though our shift was finished. I took the wheel and headed into the wind while Dylan checked out the sail. "How are we going to find the base?" I asked Dylan. "You were here before, right?"

"No. Not here." Dylan turned his back on the view of the beach. "We were further north." Dylan gripped the wheel. "That's where the base is. There were people camping, here and there, but not like this. And the tents were a ways away from the military compound. You'll know when you see the army base. It's easy to find. Barbed wire and lots of soldiers with guns."

I checked the little wind arrow at the top of the mast. "How did Jervis get in? Did you see him actually go inside the base?"

Dylan nodded. "Before he left *Whistler*, he told me he planned to tell the military guys that his dad is in the military and he's looking for him. Brad and Banks dropped him off about a quarter-mile north of the base and rowed back. Jervis hiked to the base, held his hands in the air, and started yelling. All of a sudden, he was surrounded by soldiers with guns. When they escorted him inside, we sailed away. Fast."

"So, we don't have any idea what happened to him?"

"None. But the US Army, they take care of their own … at least that's what Jervis told me. I bet he's okay."

"I hope so," I mumbled.

Nick brought up the chart for Santa Barbara and he and Dylan studied it. They tried to compare it to what we were seeing of the coast.

"There should be cities here, but they're gone. I'm sure the base is farther north."

I checked the wind and turned the boat as far north as I could without losing the sail again. "So, do we have a plan? How are we going to get the doctor inside that base? I bet a lot of those people on the beach have tried."

"Yeah, I've been thinking about that. Jervis said he was an Army brat. Maybe the doctor should say he is a military guy too."

I thought for a moment. "They'll take one look at him and know he's not military, but I bet if they discover he's a doctor, they'll want to help him. Kat can bring some of their medicine and offer it too."

"They might just take the medicine, and leave Kat and her dad to fend for themselves." Dylan scowled.

Nick raised his head. "I'll row them ashore and watch what happens. If they don't get in, I'll bring them back to *Whistler*."

"Once they're onshore, you should row out a ways to keep the boat safe. Are you taking one of the guns?" I checked the sails.

"No." Nick went back to the chart. "I'll take one of the spear guns instead. Angelina is worried we're getting short on bullets. And one gun isn't going to do any good against the soldiers, anyway. But it might deter a swimmer from trying to swim out and steal the dinghy." He motioned for me to leave. "You can go back to bed for a while. It's Angelina's and my turn."

"I'm awake now. Let Angelina sleep." Dylan took the wheel from me.

Nick grinned. "I hoped you'd say that."

"Fine then," I said and headed below.

Kat's dad was very still on the mattress. Takumi and Kat sat together on the couch above where the doctor lay. Takumi had his arm around her and she wept on his shoulder. Takumi jumped when he saw me.

I kept my eyes on the doctor. "Is he… did he?"

Kat wiped her eyes on her sleeve. "He's asleep or in a coma. I'm not sure. His stomach's getting bigger. I'm sure he's bleeding internally."

"We're almost there. The doctors on the base will be able to fix him." I kept my head down, entered Zoë and Dylan's cabin, and closed the door behind me. Zoë was sound asleep. I climbed in the bed next to her and stared at the ceiling.

There was a soft knock on the door. I ignored it. Takumi stepped inside.

"Go away!" I whispered.

Takumi hung his head. "Please, Toni, talk to me."

"What's there to say?" I growled.

Zoë rolled over and mumbled in her sleep.

"Not here." Takumi reached out to me. "Please."

I was so full of dread my body felt heavy. Every step was an effort. But I followed him out of the bedroom and into the head, our private office.

Takumi sat me on the toilet lid and stepped into the shower stall. “Toni, I love you. Nothing about that will ever change.”

“Really? Then why are you…?” I paused. “No, I’m not doing the drama thing. Are you with Kat now?”

“No, I’m with you. But right now, Kat needs me. She has no one else.” Takumi stepped out of the shower. “Kat and I are just friends. I swear.” He kneeled down in front of me. “I messed up with the rescue, and now Kat’s dad is hurt. I have to go ashore with her and carry her father from the dinghy to the base. I *owe* her that. Kat can’t do it by herself and Nick can’t help. He has to stay with the dinghy or it will be stolen.”

He took my hand. “As soon as the soldiers start to help Kat and her dad, I’ll race back to Nick.”

“What if something goes wrong?” Tears welled in my eyes and I bit my cheek to stop them. “I need you as much as she does. It’s Jeremy’s fault that Kat’s dad got shot, not yours.”

Takumi turned my hand over and kissed my palm. “I should have shot him in the leg when I had a chance. I didn’t, and now Kat’s dad might die.”

“If Jeremy hadn’t taken our gun and held us hostage, Kat’s dad wouldn’t have been injured either. You rescued us. You don’t owe Kat anything.”

“I know it’s hard for you to understand. You are so strong. You took control of *Whistler*. You kept Jeremy calm. And now, you’ll hear from your family, and have them on your side, too.” He dropped his eyes. “Kat’s not as tough as you. All she has is her dad, and if he dies… I love you, but I have to help her.”

Suddenly, it all made sense. Kat needed someone to lean on, and Takumi liked being needed. But that wasn't love. A tear escaped and rolled down my cheek. "Takumi, you are not alone. Everyone on this boat cares about you. We are your family now. We count on you." I sniffed. "Besides, if you're gone, who will cook for us?"

Takumi chuckled.

"I love you. And I believe you love me. But I'm worried Kat…" I took a deep breath. "I'm scared you'll leave and won't make it back to me."

"I'll be back. I promise." Takumi held my face and kissed my tears away.

A cold dread spread from my feet up to my heart. I grabbed Takumi and squeezed him tight. "If you don't come back to me, I'll find you. And I won't play nice."

Takumi laughed and helped me up.

"Give me your cell." I held out my hand. "I'm going to make sure it's at least partially charged before you go."

Takumi pulled up cushions and opened cupboards. "I'll make a big pot of rice and beans." He hauled out large bags of each. "There's about a month's supply here. Let me show you how to soak the beans. You know you have to do that before you cook them, right?"

I grimaced. Despite what he'd said, he was worried that he wouldn't make it back too. "No! I know nothing about cooking. The crew and I need *you*." I turned and left to go on deck and feed the fire.

"Is everything okay?" Dylan asked.

I shook my head. "Can Zoë teach me how to be the damsel in distress?"

Dylan frowned. "What are you talking about?"

"Never mind. Keep the fire going if you want to eat today." I swiveled and went back below. I was starting to feel like a yo-yo. Up and down.

Kat changed her dad's bandage. The wound was still oozing. She opened up one of her packs. "Can I wake Zoë? I need to give her this medicine. I'm pretty sure I know what each one is good for."

"What about your dad? Won't he need the medicine?" I tried not to sound as icy as I felt.

"I'll take what I think he might need, and a little extra to bribe the guards. Dad has some insulin, some heart disease medicine, and other medicine that might be in short supply. It won't do you guys any good."

Dylan called out that the base was in sight.

My heart raced. I didn't care that Kat was standing only a few feet away. I grabbed Takumi's arm. "Take me with you. Let me help."

Takumi kissed my cheek. "It's too risky."

"Please!" I begged. "I need to go with you."

Takumi pulled me into his arms and held me.

I breathed in his scent and closed my eyes. Had I really just begged him? My cheeks burned and I stepped away.

He grabbed for me. I moved out of his reach.

Kat acted as if she hadn't seen and heard us, but her hand shook as she filled a bottle of water in the galley.

Zoë came out of her cabin and rubbed her eyes. "Can't you guys keep it down?"

Kat turned to Zoë. "I'm leaving some of Dad's meds with you." She held up the bottles and boxes and told her what each was for.

"Slow down," Zoë complained. "Let me write the info down." She took a page from Dad's logbook and began scribbling the names of the drugs and what they were for. Kat gave her a lot of medicine. I hoped some of the containers held antibiotics.

I dug out a large plastic garbage bag and handed it to Kat. She shoved her camper's backpack and sleeping bag into it. Her dad's pack she put on her back. We didn't speak.

Dylan dropped the sails and Whistler slowed to a stop. I climbed on deck and scanned the beach. We were in a huge open bay. Damaged boats and the tops of sunken ships dotted the waters here, too. There were lots of tents and lean-to's, but not nearly as many as we'd seen further south.

What had once been a long pier was now a row of pilings that stretched out to the sea. Huge ships and smaller vessels were tied to the pilings. People in uniforms were removing equipment, furniture, and supplies from the ships, and barging the stuff to shore.

Dylan had been right. The military base was distinct. Two large portable buildings had been brought in as well as a number of long, barracks-type tents. Rolls of barbed wire circled the base and people in uniforms with rifles paced back and forth. I wondered if Jervis was somewhere behind all that security.

Angelina came out of her cabin. "Why are we stopped?"

Makala rubbed her eyes and carried Boots up on deck.

Takumi and Nick helped the doctor up top and sat him on the bench. His head rolled forward. He was unconscious. Kat kept him from falling off the bench.

Takumi and Nick loaded the dinghy. Nick tossed in a spear gun. Both guys wore shorts. "Where are your packs?" I asked.

"We won't need much." Nick held up a plastic bag. "Just a change of clothes. We'll have to jump into the water to land, and tow the dinghy out and over the breakers when we leave."

Dylan showed Nick the spot where the B's had rowed Jervis ashore. There was considerable surf, and they would have to time the landing just right. "Since Kat's dad is hurt, maybe you should beach a little closer to the base."

Angelina hugged Kat. "I'll never forget how you and your dad helped me."

"Bye, Kat." Makala held Boots in her arms. When Kat leaned down to kiss Makala's forehead, Boots' tongue got Kat first. The girls giggled.

It was my turn. I searched for something I could say that wouldn't sound bitter. "I hope your father's better soon." I tipped my head toward the bag of meds. "And thank you for all that medicine."

"You're welcome." Kat turned and climbed aboard the dinghy.

Nick and Takumi lowered the doctor down to Kat and followed after him. Nick untied the line.

"Wait! Why's Takumi still in the dinghy?" Dylan's brows cinched together.

Kat rested her hand on Takumi's shoulder. Takumi kept his eyes on me. "Kat can't carry her dad to the base. Nick will have to stay with the dinghy. I'm going to help her."

"What? When was that decided?" Dylan held his hands up in frustration.

"We'll return in an hour." Nick attached the oars to the boat.

"Be safe," Angelina cried.

Makala waved and yelled good-bye. Boots barked.

"The rice and beans will be ready." I stared at Takumi.

His shoulders relaxed and he smiled back as Nick began rowing toward the beach.

Chapter Twenty

Zoë went back to bed. Angelina, Boots, and Makala left the deck to find food. Makala carried a piece of cooked snake and a bowl of grapes back to her bed. In minutes, she was asleep.

I dug out the binoculars and stood on the bow watching the dinghy. They were headed toward the shoreline, which was about five hundred feet from the barbed wire. I held my breath while the little boat rode a wave to shore. It could have easily flipped over, but it didn't.

Takumi's legs dangled over the bow and he jumped off when the dinghy hit the sand. As he dragged the boat up onto the shore, a number of people camping along the beach came out of their tents or structures, and headed toward them.

I couldn't tell if Takumi and the rest could see them or not. I checked my cell to see if I could call Takumi and warn him, but there was still no service.

The beach people seemed to move slowly. Many of them appeared weak or sick. I couldn't begin to imagine the horrors they had encountered. Some were being helped to walk.

Why were they following Takumi and Kat? What did they want from them? "Hurry!" I whispered to myself as they unloaded the dinghy. It seemed to take forever. The beach people started to gather into a huge group.

Takumi and Nick had a heated discussion. They gestured at the approaching crowd, then at the dinghy. Finally, Takumi hoisted Kat's dad onto his back. Kat threw one pack on her back and picked up the bag with the rest of the gear.

While they were busy, Nick leapt from the boat, and handed the spear gun and extra spears to Takumi. Before Takumi could react, Nick dove into the bay. He disappeared under the surf for a moment, but then his head appeared out past the breakers.

The dinghy followed after him. He had to be towing it.

Takumi and Kat took off for the military compound. The crowd on the beach stood for a moment and watched the dinghy head out into the bay. A number of people just sat down, their heads bowed. Part of the group followed after Takumi and Kat. Three young men waded into the surf and swam toward Nick and the dinghy. Without the dinghy to slow them down, they were rapidly gaining on Nick.

"Nick!" I screamed.

Angelina raced up from below.

"What! What's happening to Nick?"

I pointed to the shore and handed her the binoculars. "Over there, see? That's Takumi with Kat and her dad." I moved my finger. "Those people are chasing them. And in the water, a short ways in front of the dinghy is Nick. I can't see the guys swimming after him, but there are some."

Angelina raised the binoculars and gasped. "They're going to catch Nick. But he has the spear gun, right? He can stop swimming and warn them off."

I shook my head. "He gave it to Takumi."

Angelina shoved the binoculars at me. "I'm getting the pistol. Meet me at the stern in two minutes with the kayaks. We're going to help them."

"Right." I began untying the straps holding the kayaks onto the side of the boat. It felt good to be doing something. Anything.

When I pulled the kayaks around to the stern, Dylan argued with me. "Takumi and Nick can take care of themselves. The crowd might take away their packs, but they won't hurt them."

"How do you know that? Nick is going to have to fight off three guys. They want the dinghy and won't care if they drown Nick to get it. Takumi at least has a weapon."

"Why didn't they both take a spear-gun?" Dylan sounded exasperated. "We have two."

Angelina came on deck with the police pistol and checked the bullets. "It doesn't matter why they didn't. It's done. Toni and I will paddle to Nick and help him." She shoved the gun into her daypack. "Then we'll wait for Takumi." She looked at me. "Let's go."

Dylan offered to go in my place, but I'd had enough of being left behind.

"Zoë would have a fit if you left, and you know it. We won't be gone long." I grabbed a couple of lifejackets and shoved off. We made good time even with Angelina's sore shoulder. Two weeks of practice had increased my paddling skill. Soon we were closing in on the dinghy. Unfortunately, the guys swimming after Nick were too.

All of a sudden, Angelina stopped paddling and pulled out the gun.

"What are you doing?" I couldn't believe she'd start shooting the guys in the water. At least, not before we talked to them.

But she aimed and fired. Between our location and the dinghy a huge fin popped up out of the water. A barbed tail thrashed about. This time it really *was* a shark. The water around the shark turned red.

"You shot a shark? Oh my God! You shot a shark!" The kayak felt really small. I fought the panic welling up in my chest. "Won't its blood bring others?"

"It's better than letting it eat Nick. There are probably lots of other sharks around anyway. The coast has been a feeding ground." She gestured at all the damaged boats. "Sharks will go after their own if they smell blood. I made it bleed to distract them."

Nick and the three guys had stopped swimming when they heard the shot.

"Sharks!" Both Angelina and I yelled.

Nick pulled the dinghy close to him and heaved himself over the side. He fell into the bottom of the boat just as a shark passed by.

The three guys stared at the dinghy, the shore, then back at the dinghy. One of the guys began swimming for the beach. The other two swam toward the dinghy. The two guys heading for the dinghy soon came to a stop and treaded water. Three sharks circled around them.

"Help us!" The guys screamed.

"Really?" Nick called out. "Is that what you were planning to do? Help me?"

"Dude. *You can't let us die this way*!" one of the guys screamed as a shark disappeared beneath him.

Before Nick could answer, the sharks circling the guys in the water abruptly turned, and headed for the shark Angelina had shot. A feeding frenzy began. A half a dozen sharks appeared and attacked the dead or dying shark. Tails and teeth gnashed and ripped chunks of flesh off. The bay turned red.

Nick used the distraction to paddle to the guys in the water. "Angelina and Toni, stay back," he cried.

Angelina and I stopped paddling. A shark came alongside me, circled Angelina's kayak, then raised its head and sharp teeth out of the water. Angelina shot it in the eye. It immediately sank.

"Paddle to the dinghy before more come!" Angelina screamed.

But it was too late. Sharks converged on the shark Angelina shot in the eye. A tailfin slapped my kayak and I almost tipped over. I focused on paddling to the dinghy and getting as far away as I could from the shark action. I hoped Angelina was behind me, but I was too busy to check.

Nick was hauling the swimmers onto the dinghy when I arrived. I grabbed the side of the dinghy and held on, hoping the sharks would think I was a part of the larger boat.

I took a deep breath and checked on Angelina. A shark was attacking her kayak. She shot at it twice, but it kept coming. She made it to the dinghy just as the shark bashed the bottom of her kayak. Nick and one of the swimmers pulled her aboard moments before the kayak flipped over. The shark bit into the end of the kayak and shook it, shattering the little plastic kayak.

Both Nick and Angelina were shaking.

"Are you okay?" Nick searched for signs of injury on Angelina.

Angelina kissed his cheek, then turned the gun on the swimmers. "I watched you two going after Nick. Try anything, and you're back in the water."

The gun in her hand shook. I yelled and pointed. Two more of the frenzied sharks were headed our way.

"Use your paddle. Hit the sharks in the nose." Angelina moved to the side I was holding on to and steadied my kayak so my arms were free.

I swung at a shark. It grabbed onto my paddle with its sharp teeth and swam away with it. Angelina shook her head at me.

While the shark was busy eating my oar, I started to climb into the dinghy. “A little help here!” I begged as I almost tipped the kayak over. Angelina helped me aboard. Nick pulled my kayak out of the water and laid it across the stern of the dinghy.

Sharks circled all around us. We rocked back and forth so hard, I was sure we’d go over. Twice my kayak fell off the stern. We got it back onboard moments before it was eaten, too. There were only three paddles left. With the blunt ends, we took turns bashing shark noses.

“We’re just making them mad.” I whacked a small one. It sank beneath the boat.

“Their noses are sensitive,” Angelina cried. “Haven’t you watched *Shark Week*? We’re doing the right thing.”

“I liked it better when we just shot them.” I passed my paddle to one of the swimmers. He smashed a big one, hard. It shook its head, as if stunned.

Angelina shot another shark in the head. It was soon devoured too.

Finally, one by one, the remaining sharks began to lose interest in us. No idea if it was because we hit them, or because their stomachs were full.

We fell back in the boat and gasped for air. Angelina crossed herself. Her lips moved in a silent prayer. I closed my eyes, and said my own prayer. Tears streaked my cheeks.

I wiped my eyes and searched the shoreline. Takumi and Kat had made it down the beach to the barbed wire. The group had followed them all the way. For some reason, Kat’s dad was lying on the beach.

Takumi stood with the spear gun aimed at the crowd behind him. Guardsmen remained in a row in front of the barbed wire, and aimed their guns at Takumi and the crowd.

"Takumi!" I yelled.

Everyone in the boat turned to watch.

Takumi rotated back and forth, talking to the military guys, then warning off the crowd with his spear gun.

A young woman jetted out of the crowd, ran at Kat, and grabbed Kat's backpack. Kat held on tight and a tug of war ensued.

Two shots rang out. The line of guardsmen parted, and an older man with gray hair stepped out.

The woman fighting with Kat let go of the pack, backed away, and disappeared into the mass of people. More soldiers appeared. Two guys carried a stretcher. Takumi lowered his spear gun. Kat supervised while her dad was loaded onto the stretcher.

The older man spoke to Kat and Takumi. A soldier inspected Kat's bags, nodded to the older man, and threw both packs over his shoulder. Takumi and Kat were soon surrounded by men and women in uniforms.

A few individuals from the crowd came forward and seemed to be pleading with the soldiers. Another shot rang out and the group backed away.

Takumi became agitated and appeared to be arguing with Kat and the soldiers. He pointed at *Whistler*. He shaded his eyes and stared for a long moment at the dinghy. Could he see me? I stood and waved my arms. The boat rocked.

"Sit down!" Nick yanked on my jacket.

"We have to help him!" I slapped the seat.

"We can't. We're outgunned." Angelina frowned. "I'm sorry."

My heart pounded. I watched Kat grab Takumi's hand and pull him toward the gate. Takumi shook free and folded his arms. One of the soldiers motioned with his rifle for him to move. When Takumi didn't, he shoved his rifle into Takumi's back.

Takumi's head dropped. In a matter of seconds, he and Kat were escorted to the gate. He turned for one last look in my direction, then disappeared inside the U.S. Army compound.

I held my breath. And waited. And watched. Fear gripped my stomach. Takumi didn't return. "He'll explain everything to them. He'll be back," I muttered.

"Yes!" Angelina scooted beside me. "And the doctor is getting the help he needs. I wonder what they said to get inside. Most of the people in that crowd looked like they needed medical help, too."

Nick checked for sharks and then tossed the kayak back into the water to make more room on the dinghy. "I'm sure the bags of meds and medical equipment helped. And the fact that Kat's dad is a doctor." He tied the kayak line to the stern and faced me. "Toni, Takumi made me promise that if he wasn't back in an hour, I'd head back to *Whistler* without him."

I gritted my teeth. "We are *not* leaving here without him."

Angelina and Nick glanced at one another.

"I mean it." I narrowed my eyes.

Angelina gave my hand a squeeze. "We know you do. We want him back too."

"Is that the sailboat you've been talking about?" One of the guys gestured towards *Whistler*.

I'd almost forgotten about our two extra passengers. I nodded at what was left of Santa Barbara. "Time for you guys to go."

"No way," the second guy grimaced. "You can shoot me, but I'm not getting back into that water. Not with sharks around."

"Look! We saved you. I don't even want to know what you were planning when you swam after Nick. But I know it wasn't good. You don't get to call the shots." I moved to the bow where there was more room now the kayak was gone.

Nick locked the oars into place on the dinghy. "We'll row closer to shore and watch for Takumi. You two can body surf in."

"Let me go with you on the sailboat. I know a lot about sailing. I'd be a big help," the first guy pleaded.

"Boat's full." I turned to study the beach once again. "Did you see if your friend made it to shore okay?"

The first guy shrugged. "I was too busy trying to stay alive. He's not my friend anyway."

"Not my friend either." The second guy stared back at *Whistler*. "You people got to let us go with you. You don't know what it's like on shore. The soldiers come out once a day and distribute bottles of water and some food, but it's not enough. We're starving. People are sick. Dying."

"Then why do you stay?" I asked.

"Because something is better than nothing. The rivers up north are frozen over, and the streams around here are drying up. The military is taking water-makers off of the big ship and turning salt water into fresh, but it's not enough," the first swimmer said.

The second swimmer shook his head. "If you have a water bottle, they will fill it for you.

Sometimes, even two bottles. But more and more people are coming and…"

"We just left the island of Santa Cruz." I pointed to the East. "There's water, live game, and lots of seafood. Find a boat. Go there. It might take a few days to locate a stream, so bring back up water. But there are creeks and marshlands. The island's only thirty miles away."

"Thirty miles? Right!" The second guy stared at the dinghy, then his friend.

Angelina raised her gun. "Don't even think about it."

"Okay. Toni's right. Time for you guys to leave. Takumi's not back yet, but I don't mind making two trips." Nick picked up the oars and began rowing towards shore.

"Angelina will shoot you if you try anything. You're going back into the water, with or without our help," I said.

The first swimmer grinned at Angelina. He had a nice smile and knew it. "You won't kill me."

Angelina thought for a moment. "No. You're right. But I would shoot you where it would hurt. Your foot would be a good target. You could swim with only one foot. The blood in the water might be a problem, however."

The guy's eyes got big. "You wouldn't!"

"Try me." She released the safety on the gun.

Chapter Twenty-One

The swimmers made it to shore safely. Sharks stayed away from the dinghy for the time being. We floated outside the breakers while Nick changed into dry clothes. I shivered and rubbed my arms. Nick and Angelina snuggled to stay warm. I missed Takumi and studied the shore for signs of his return.

"You're getting pretty badass with that gun," Nick told Angelina. "Would you really have shot them?"

"For sure." Angelina grinned. "If there'd been any bullets left."

Nick laughed. "You were bluffing that whole time? God, I love you."

Angelina's face turned red and she rested her head on his shoulder.

I smiled at Angelina and scooted down in the bow to get out of the wind. I peeked over the side and waited for Takumi. To stay awake, I busied myself by counting the damaged and partially sunken boats in the bay. Thirty-seven. Then I counted the number of tents close to the base. Sixty-two. Still, we floated, and watched. I began naming the military men and women who were scavenging parts off the damaged ships. Somewhere between the man I named Fat Willy and the woman I called Betty, I dozed off.

"Toni." Nick gently poked my shoulder.

I bolted awake and refocused on the shore. "Is he there?"

"No." Nick checked his watch. "It's been an hour. We need to get back to *Whistler*."

"We are not going—"

Angelina slid down beside me. "I left Makala sleeping. I'm sure she's awake now. I have to get back. We can watch the shore from *Whistler*."

"When he sees us leave, he'll think we gave up. I won't do that. Ever."

Angelina sighed. "Toni, we can't sit here all day. We are out of water and it's cold.

Makala is probably scared. We'll take turns watching the beach with the binoculars from

Whistler."

I shook my head.

Angelina sighed. "Fine. We'll give it another half-hour, and then we absolutely have to go back. Agreed?"

I bit my lip. "He'll come."

I stared for thirty minutes at the barbed-wire gate, but he never showed.

****

Makala jumped up and down and waved her arms at Angelina as we approached *Whistler*.

Boots yipped and chased his tail with excitement. At least *they* were cheerful.

Dylan stood on the stern and held up something in his hand.

Nick squinted. "I think he's holding up his cell."

"His cell phone?" I was so lost in worrying about Takumi that I didn't get what he was trying to say.

"Service!" Angelina cried. "I think he's trying to say he has cell service."

I yanked out my phone and waited for what seemed forever for it to boot up. All of a sudden there were a series of dings. A sound I hadn't heard for weeks. Text messages. Lots of text messages were coming through.

I started to hyperventilate. I'd been checking for messages every day. Now that I had some, I was afraid. What if they contained bad news? I slapped my phone face down on my leg.

Angelina nudged me. "Toni. Maybe one of the messages is from Takumi."

Takumi! She was right. I took a deep breath and checked.

None of the texts were from Takumi. Six messages were from my best friend. I skipped over them. My hand began to shake. The rest were texts from Mom and Dad. I closed my eyes for a moment, took a deep breath, and started reading. Their first messages were from before the tsunami.

Dad texted:

Hi Guys. Was I wrong to send you out on the boat? Your Mom is upset with me. I know you will handle the boat well. You will take care of it and each other. We left Grandma's and are driving South with Aunt Susan, your cousins, and Grandma. We have two cars and enough bikes for all of us. The tsunami will hit in twelve hours and we want to get as far from the coast as we can. Text us back and let us know you are okay.

Mom wrote:

Cole, Dylan, and Toni. I can't believe Dad left you guys with instructions to take the boat out by yourselves. We should all be together. I don't know what he was thinking. We are driving east, to avoid any problems with the tsunami, then we will head south. Grandma isn't doing well. She begged us to leave her, but of course we couldn't. I don't know what we will do when we run out of gas. Dad says

phone service is difficult to find out at sea, even when it is working well. I hate to think of you out in the ocean. Text us. Please. We love you.

I skimmed the rest of their messages. They'd made it almost to the California border before they ran out of gas. Traffic was backed up. They'd unloaded and camped for the night along the highway.

Mom said that Aunt Susan had gotten a message from Uncle Mike. They made plans to meet outside San Francisco and ride their bikes to his parents' place in Arizona. At the end of every message Mom talked about how angry she was that Dad had sent us out on the boat alone.

My hand flew to my mouth. "No!" I gasped.

Angelina touched my arm. "What happened?"

I lowered the phone. "My grandma…" I sniffed.

"I'm so sorry, Toni." Angelina hugged me.

"This is what I was afraid of. Bad news. And now I have to text them back and tell them about Cole."

Angelina patted my back. "Maybe you should wait until you can tell them in person."

"I'll talk to Dylan before I do anything." I sniffed. "Why aren't you guys checking your phones?"

Nick was rowing furiously. "We left them on *Whistler*."

I sat up and forced myself to read on. Mom had simply written that Grandma had died.

Dad texted the details.

Grandma had a sudden heart attack and died yesterday. We called 911. There was no response. We buried Grandma under a beautiful oak tree. Your Mom and Susan are having a hard time dealing with the way she died. I feel so helpless.

After that, Dad's texts became more and more about how concerned for us he was. He begged us to text or call. Service seemed to come and go for them. They kept their phones off to save power and hoped every time they had service there would be a message from us. They'd begun to fear the worst.

They met up with Uncle Mike ten days into the trip. Uncle Mike, Aunt Susan, and my cousins were heading inland to Arizona. Uncle Mike didn't have a bike, so he was going to ride my ten-year-old cousin Bella's bike and Bella would ride in a little wagon Dad had been towing. Mom hated to say good-bye to her sister and family.

In the last text, they both wrote that their cell batteries were dying. They were going to continue on to Santa Barbara, trade the bikes for some kind of boat, and go to the north end of Santa Cruz Island. They would wait for us there.

I read and re-read their messages.

Dylan stood on the swim step and helped me onto *Whistler*. "Did you get the texts?"

I fell into his arms. "Grandma died."

He hugged me and then held me at arm's length. "I know. I loved her too." He gazed across the water toward the island. "Just think. Mom and Dad might be right over there."

I followed his gaze. "I know."

"Let's go find them." Dylan smiled.

We helped Angelina and Nick aboard. Makala and Boots acted as if Angelina had been gone for days instead of only a few hours. Nick hurried below to find his and Angelina's cell phones.

Zoë appeared on deck dressed in a floor-length silver gown and twirled in a slow circle so I could view her dress from all angles.

My jaw dropped. "What are you wearing?"

Makala pushed between us and held up her hands. "Zoë painted my nails, and we made flowers, and I get to be a flower girl, an—"

"Slow down," I told Makala and stared at Zoë.

Zoë held her hands on her hips. "I am not going to meet your parents until Dylan and I are married. I read somewhere that a ship's captain can perform a wedding at sea. And since you and Dylan are co-captains, I want you to marry us. Will you?"

I picked up the binoculars and searched the beach for Takumi.

"Toni?" Zoë swung me around to face her.

"Really!" I dropped the binoculars on the couch. "We just fought off sharks. Who knows what danger Takumi is in? My grandma died and you want me—"

Dylan held up his hand. "What? What are you talking about? What sharks?"

Zoë glared at me as she smoothed the wrinkles on her dress.

I bit my lip. "We were attacked by sharks! Giant, hungry sharks. They tried to tip my kayak, they went after Nick, and they surrounded the guys swimming after him. If Angelina hadn't had her gun, we wouldn't have survived."

Dylan slid his cell into his pocket. "Sorry. We started getting texts, and…"

Zoë held her hand in the air. "Are you going to marry us or not?"

I literally bit my tongue.

Dylan stepped in front of Zoë and whispered. "It will only take a few minutes and it will make Zoë happy."

"And you? Will it make you happy? How about Boots? Will it make Boots happy? Will it make—"

Dylan grabbed my arm and pulled me to the bow. "What's the matter with you?"

"Our grandma is dead, Dylan. Dead. I don't know what's happening to Takumi. Oh! And by the way. Are you going to text Mom and Dad and tell them Cole is gone, or do you want me to?"

Dylan glared.

I'd hit a wall. It didn't matter to me that I'd hurt Zoë or was angering my brother. "Look at the people barely surviving on that beach." I gestured at the shore. "They don't have enough water or food. And Takumi might be hurt or…" I took a deep breath. "I haven't slept for two days. And now you want me to throw a wedding and party like everything is fine?"

Dylan closed his eyes. "Toni, I'm sad too. And I know this is tough. All of it. I didn't know about the sharks, I swear. Zoë's been barely hanging on since we started getting texts. I'm worried about her. She doesn't act like she gets it. She keeps talking about the huge wedding we're going to have in Seattle. Sometimes I don't think she understands what's happened."

I glanced back at the stern where she stood watching us. "So we're supposed to go along? Humor her?"

"Not everyone is as strong as you are. And she's having a baby. Doesn't that make women a little …I don't know. Emotional?"

"Yes. If she's really pregnant."

"Toni!"

"Fine. I'll perform the service. But not until I get a few hours of sleep. And I'm doing it for you and the baby. Not for Zoë. Are we clear?"

Dylan's eyes narrowed. "Fine."

"Good," I snarled and started for the girls' cabin.

Dylan cleared his throat. "As soon as the wedding's over, we'll head back to Santa Cruz and find Mom and Dad."

I stopped. "Not until Takumi shows up. Give him the rest of the day and night to talk his way off the base."

"Mom and Dad are right over there." Dylan stared at the island in the distance.

"I know. But we are all exhausted. If Mom and Dad made it to the island, they should be okay for one more night. If we don't get some rest, we won't be. I mean it. You and Zoë can do your wedding thing, but not until I take a nap. I'll take the first watch afterward. I'll want to check the shore for Takumi, anyway. We can leave in the morning if he doesn't show up."

"I'll tell Zoë." Dylan started to walk away, then paused. "Maybe you should brace yourself. There's a chance we may never see Takumi and Kat again."

"Takumi said he would be back." I elbowed Dylan in the ribs and headed below.

Chapter Twenty-Two

I was halfway down the steps to the main cabin when Angelina jumped up and squealed. "Mom's alive." She grabbed Makala and swung her around. "Mommy's alive!"

Makala clung to Angelina and squealed. Boots barked and jumped on the girls.

"What did she say?" I asked.

Angelina held up her phone. "A few doctors and nurses bused everyone in the hospital up to higher ground, in the mountains. After the wave, they returned to Seattle, but the hospital had been destroyed. Mom stayed on the bus and helped with some of the patients for a little while, then began looking for us. She couldn't get to the waterfront where I'd told her we were camping. There was too much debris."

Angelina put Makala down. "Shush," she told Boots. He chased his tail.

"After a couple of days of searching, mom found a motorcycle, and headed to Mexico." She glowed with pride. "I can't believe she rode a motorcycle with her arm in a cast."

Boots yipped and Angelina took out the bag of dog food and began smashing the giant pieces of kibble.

"Mom says she knows in her heart we're still alive. She wants us to go to our grandparents' house. Her last text was ten days ago. Her cell was dying and she had no way to charge it. She'd made it as far as Bakersfield."

Nick came down to the galley. His brows were cinched. "I could hear your news up top. That's so cool, Angelina. Where do your grandparents live?"

"Mexico. On a ranch, part way down on the Baja Peninsula. Grandpa's the mayor of a small town. What about you? Did you hear from your family?"

Nick smiled. "I did. My brother, my sisters, and my parents are helping my uncle and my cousins bring a huge herd of cattle south. Of course the tsunami didn't hit Idaho, but it got dark and started getting real cold, real fast. The military bases began to disband and head south. My family hopes to find a place in Texas or New Mexico where the cattle can graze. They couldn't just take off and leave the poor animals to freeze to death. And they have horses and dogs too. At the very least, they'll give the cows to the military. The resettlement camps need food. But they hope to keep some and find a place for them to graze."

Nick moved to stare out the port window. "It's a huge job driving that many cows. I wish I were there to help them."

"You can meet them when they get settled in the south, though. That will be great. And they are alive!" Angelina grinned.

Nick turned and hugged her. "You're right! My family is still alive." They laughed and danced around the tight space. Makala joined in and the three spun in circles.

Zoë came out of her cabin and smiled at them. Was it because of what Dylan had said, or were her eyes almost a little too bright?

"Did you hear from your family?" Angelina asked her.

Zoë grinned. "Mom wrote that the tsunami was coming and they were trying to get a flight out of Hawaii. That's all she texted. But, my parents are terrible about keeping their cell phones charged." She giggled and fidgeted with her rhinestone bracelet. "I bet they are sitting in a beautiful resort just waiting for the power to come back on. When it does, they'll call or text me. I'm not worried."

"I'm sure you're right." Angelina gave me a concerned look.

I checked the beach for Takumi one last time and then I headed to bed. Angelina promised she'd wake me if Takumi showed up on shore.

I snuggled down in the covers as the boat rocked gently and read the messages my best friend sent. Her first were full of excitement and adventure:

"You wouldn't believe the traffic. We almost ran out of gas just getting to the cabin. But we made it and the cabin is so cute. You'd love it. Uncle Paul has been busy chopping wood. We all brought food and we have enough to last us forever. Dad keeps talking about wanting to leave after the tsunami, but Paul thinks we are better off just staying here. I still can't believe you are on a boat. Text me.

After the tsunami she wrote:

We lost power and had our first snow fall today. Snow in August? Mom and Dad are fighting all the time about whether or not we should leave. We don't have much gas left in the car, so I don't know what good it would do to leave. Paul has a radio and we heard that Seattle was completely destroyed. Guess there's no going back.

She wrote four more messages. The last one gave me chills.

The snow is now so deep that we have trouble opening the door. And it is freezing. We can't be out

for more than a few minutes. The guys hunt for food, but there aren't any animals around and no grocery stores. We are going through the food we brought too fast. If the snow doesn't stop soon, I don't know how long we'll last. I can't charge my phone anymore. I guess this is good-bye. It's not fair. We should be the high school diving champs. We should be going to the Homecoming dance. I miss you.

I laid the phone on the shelf above my head, closed my eyes, and let the tears flow. When I finally fell asleep, I dreamt I was covered in ice, and about to dive into a pool of sharks.

It was a relief when Angelina shook my shoulder and said, "Wedding time!"

Chapter Twenty-Three

The crew had been busy preparing for the big event while I slept. Paper flowers had been made from pages torn out of our *National Geographic* magazines. Pictures of butterflies from the butterfly article had been cut out. The decorations, hung off the rails and dodger with fishing line, swung back and forth with the rocking of the boat. Small votive candles were scattered around in votive holders, bowls, and even coffee mugs.

"Oh, good. You're up." Zoë grabbed my arm. "I have the perfect dress for you." She pulled me into her cabin.

I mouthed 'help' to Angelina. She was wearing a lovely light blue cocktail dress. I forced a smile. If Angelina could go along, I would try. Zoë held up a red silk dress. It was a simple wrap-around style with a v-neckline.

I plopped on the bed and lowered my head. It was the dress Takumi had asked me to wear to the Homecoming Dance we were never going to attend.

My eyes misted over and I fought for control. I told Zoë to give me a few minutes to clean up and washed up as best I could with a bucket of room temperature salt water. My hair was greasy and I didn't have time or soap, so I piled it up on my head, pulled a few tendrils down around my face, and called it good.

Zoë gave me instructions while I dressed.

"I have it all written out. Even the marriage certificate. You'll need to sign it. Nick and Angelina will be our witnesses and sing. Makala will be the flower girl and ring bearer. Angelina can be maid-of-honor since you're doing the ceremony." She bit her lip. "I wish Takumi were here. I planned on him being the best man, but oh, well. Nick will have to do that too. This is just a formality anyway. Just until my parents can throw us a huge wedding at our country club." I narrowed my eyes and studied her while she went on and on about what her real wedding would be like.

I tied the belt around my waist and turned around. Zoë stopped talking and tipped her head. "You're actually kinda pretty." She sounded surprised. I kept smiling like I'd promised Dylan I would.

When we opened the cabin door and stepped out, Nick whistled at me. "Wow. You clean up good."

Zoë shooed everyone but me up top. She handed me a sheet of lined paper from dad's logbook. It was written like a script for a play. I read the words next to my name. It seemed simple enough.

"This is the last thing." She pulled out a sheer lace shawl. Dad's black comb stuck through the lace near the edge of the shawl. She showed me where she wanted it placed in her hair. I did my best and she adjusted it in the cabin mirror.

With the veil, Zoë actually looked like a bride. The lace draped around her shoulders and down her back. The silver dress glimmered pale in the twilight. "Just a minute." I grabbed my phone and took her picture.

"We're going to be sisters, can you believe it?" She hugged me. Tears welled in her eyes and she threw her head back. "Now stop it before I ruin my make-up. Go up top and stand behind the wheel. When you're ready, send Makala down, and tell Angelina and Nick to start singing."

The candles were all lit and glowed in the increasingly darkening light. Nick stood on one side of the companionway, Angelina on the other. Boots lay on the deck behind Angelina, quiet for once. Dylan was in front of the wheel I was to stand behind. I nodded and Angelina and Nick hummed *Here Comes the Bride*.

Makala came up first wearing a glittery gold dress that had once been a woman's dressy sleeveless top. Angelina and Zoë had taken in the sides with duct tape so it fit Makala. It ended up looking like a roaring '20s flapper dress and Makala loved it. She was carrying a small garbage pail.

She slowly climbed the steps from the cabin to the deck, rested the garbage pail at the top of the steps, brushed off her dress, and began tossing tiny pieces of colored paper on the ground. The tiny bits blew around the boat, into the barbeque grill, and onto the water. When she ran out of room to walk, she turned the pail upside down, shook out any remaining paper, and ran to Angelina.

We all smiled.

Then it was time for Zoë. She was a vision. But then the shawl blew up and off her head, caught the wind, and landed in the water. The little butterflies and flowers rapidly swung back and forth, almost frantic. One by one, the candles blew out.

I tried hard not to laugh. Zoë tapped her stiletto heel and glared at me.

I checked my script and read the, "We are gathered…" part.

Angelina said a prayer.

As the sun set, we began to shiver. I couldn't see a thing, so Dylan ran down below and found the flashlights. Nick and Angelina kept singing some song they both knew from church. Over and over again.

Next on the list was Zoë and Dylan's message or poem to one another. Zoë cleared her throat and recited a poem about love and flowers, and love growing like flowers, or maybe it was growing like a tree, or into a tree. I shivered, rubbed my bare arms, and thought about my friend who was trapped in the cold.

Then it was Dylan's turn. "I…I didn't know I was supposed to say anything," he whispered.

"Just say what's in your heart, darling. You must know a poem that captures the love we feel for one another."

I wondered how well Zoë really knew my brother.

Dylan raised his eyebrows. "Roses are red, violets are blue, sugar is sweet, but not as sweet as… I love you."

I held my breath and waited for Zoë to explode at the childish poem Dylan had corrupted.

Instead, Zoë giggled hysterically, and threw herself into his arms. "You are so funny. I love you so much."

The group sighed with relief. The gleam in her eyes seemed almost maniacal in the dimming light.

They said their vows. Dylan put the ring on her finger.

"And, by the power vested in me by the history of maritime weddings," I said, and declared them husband and wife.

Nick and Angelina took pictures of the wedding couple, and then we all set up our phones to take group photos. A sudden gust of wind blew across the boat and we were done. Zoë, Angelina, and Makala hurried below. I went around and gathered up the darkened candles.

Dylan began raising the sails.

"What are you doing? I thought we were going to wait until the morning."

"We are, but the boat has been floating towards shore. I'll take her out a long ways, and we should be okay floating until morning. Of course, we'll have to take turns watching, just in case."

"Okay. But don't take too long. We're all cold and hungry." I headed for the warmth of the cabin below.

On top of the mattress that covered most of the floor of the main cabin, the girls were spreading a tablecloth. "Close the flap, close the flap," they yelled as I started down.

Angelina handed the plates and silverware to me and I set the table. We placed the candles I'd gathered from the ceremony on top of a cutting board on the center of the 'mattress table' and lit them. They brightened the room and actually seemed to give off a little heat.

Zoë found another shawl and wrapped it around her shoulders.

"I'm going to change into some warmer—" I turned toward my cabin.

"But it's our wedding reception!" Zoë's lower lip stuck out in a pout.

"Really?" I huffed. "I'm freezing." She continued to pout. "Fine. Do you have any other shawls in there, then?" I motioned towards her cabin.

Zoë found each of us a perfectly coordinated pashmina. They helped with the cold, a lot. Makala's shawl dragged on the floor but Angelina wrapped her up in it when she finally sat down and Boots burrowed under it.

Zoë went on and on about how lovely the wedding had turned out. Angelina and I kept looking at one another. Was she serious? I'd never seen a wedding as strange as the one we'd just had. I didn't trust myself to respond to her raves and moved to help Angelina in the galley.

I expected just a big bowl of rice and beans for dinner. And there was a bowl of it on the counter, but then Angelina opened up the oven we hadn't used for weeks, and pulled out three big lobsters.

"Wow!" I exclaimed. "When did you catch these?"

Zoë smoothed out her dress. "Dylan put out the crab pots and caught these instead of crabs. They have sharp spines, so be careful. Dylan got pricked. We boiled them this afternoon while you guys were out screwing around."

"Screwing around?" My hands formed a fist.

"Zoë and Dylan's wedding!" Angelina reminded me as she shoved a cookie sheet of lobsters my way.

"I found some tools for cracking crab, but I'm not sure how to crack lobsters." Angelina held up a silver tool.

I was more familiar with crab, too, but on a few special occasions, Mom served lobster. "Mom uses scissors to cut open the tail."

"Scissors?"

"Yeah." I washed the scissors we stored in a kitchen drawer and cut along the back of the lobster tail. Using pot-holders to protect my hands, I grabbed hold of both sides of the cut, and opened up the back. With a fork, I pulled out the big chunk of sweet white meat.

"Cool," Angelina said and went to work cracking open the claws while I cut the meat up into bite-sized pieces.

Soon, Dylan and Nick joined us in the cabin.

"I can't see us floating into anything out here for a while." Dylan plopped down next to his wife. Wife? That felt so strange.

Nick helped Angelina and me dish out the food. We all found places around the mattress and feasted. Angelina said she'd added some chili powder to the salt water she cooked the rice and beans in. It gave it a spicy flair. The lobster pieces melted in my mouth.

While we ate, we pulled out our cells and took turns talking about the messages we'd just gotten. Angelina was excited to see her grandparents again. She felt certain her mom would be waiting.

"I don't understand why we can text, but when we try to make calls, they don't go through." I quickly texted my parents, my friend, and checked again for a message from Takumi. Still nothing.

Dylan said he'd tried to search the web and check the GPS, but that didn't work either.

Nick seemed to know the most about how it all worked. "During an emergency, the government can flip a switch so only emergency personnel can use their phones," he said. "Add to that the problem of the thousands of cell towers that were knocked down when the tsunami hit. I'm surprised we have service at all. Especially on the coast. We're probably only getting texts because we are close to a military base."

"So why do you only have one text message? Your family was inland," I asked Nick.

"They're horseback riding. Your families could keep charging their phones in their cars. Mine couldn't."

"Horseback?" Makala's eyes lit up. "Your family rides horses?"

"Yeah. They're camping and herding cattle from Idaho to Texas."

"Do you know how to ride a horse?" Makala's smile beamed.

"I do." Nick showed Makala pictures of his family that he'd taken the summer before. "The official on the radio said the government was restoring cell towers and nationalizing the cell companies. We probably need to hook up to the government cell program, but we don't know how. Text messages are the easiest and least costly form of communication, so the government probably just lets them go through for now."

Zoë slammed down her fork. "Why are you guys all talking about cell phones? This is our wedding reception. Doesn't anyone have a speech? And you're supposed to give us presents, you know."

Presents? Was she serious? Even Dylan's mouth hung open.

"Good idea," Angelina smiled. "Nick and I wanted you to have a wedding cake. We didn't have much to work with, so this is our present to you. We hope you like it." She went to the freezer that had been turned off since the start of the trip and pulled out what appeared to be a pile of snowballs.

Zoë grinned and sat up tall.

Angelina held up her creation for us all to see. "We added sugar and vanilla to some of the cooked rice, squeezed the rice into balls, and stacked them. I sprinkled powdered sugar over the whole thing, and voila. A wedding rice-ball cake. Anyone want to try it?"

Zoë held up her hand. "Wait. Dylan and I need to cut the cake!"

Angelina frowned. "I think it will fall apart if you try to cut it."

Dylan found a small knife. "Angelina and Nick. Thank you. This is great. We'll cut just the top ball. Gently. Someone take our pictures, okay?"

Zoë and Dylan pulled off the top rice-ball, cut into it, and fed each other bites. Zoë shoved a piece at Dylan, most of which fell apart and landed on the floor. Boots had it gone in seconds. Nick took their picture with his cell.

Angelina's creation was truly delicious but, I couldn't stop feeling guilty. There were people starving on the beach.

Makala stood and announced she was going to make a butterfly mobile out of the butterfly pictures and a coat hanger, and give it to the bride and groom. She hung her head. "I really wanted it for myself, but it is Zoë and Dylan's wedding, so I'm going to give it to them."

While everyone chuckled, Dylan thanked her and suggested they share it. Makala's face broke into a grin.

I excused myself and went to the girls' cabin to find something to give the happy couple. I had some jewelry, but nothing as grand as what Zoë had found on the yacht in Grays Harbor. My clothes wouldn't fit Zoë. I rifled through my small supply of stuff, and then found it. The perfect gift. I wrapped it in a pillowcase and handed it to Dylan.

He unwrapped the pillowcase gently and looked down at my gift for a long while. Zoë picked it up and scowled.

"Turn it around," the wedding party cried.

Zoë turned a framed picture around so the group could see it. It was a photo of Dylan, Cole, and me when the boys were around eight and I was six. Mom had shoved it into one of the bags of clothes she'd packed for me.

"Sis. I don't know what to say." Dylan kept his head lowered.

"Cole would want you to be happy. This is from both of us."

Dylan gave me a hug, and hurried up top.

"Dylan, where are you going?" Zoë cried.

"He's checking to make sure the boat's okay." I held up my glass of water. "I want to make a toast." I gave the first of many toasts to the beautiful bride and when Dylan returned, the happy couple.

Zoë beamed all evening.

Dylan and I exchanged worried glances.

Chapter Twenty-Four

The exhausted crew finally went to bed. I'd never stayed up alone on deck before, but promised everyone I would be fine. I'd wake Nick and Angelina when I got too tired. I watched for some sign from the beach. Maybe Takumi would set off a flare or wave a torch around. But there was nothing. And no text messages.

It didn't make any sense that we were getting our messages and he wasn't. Takumi was even closer to the cell tower and should have great reception. But, for whatever reason, he didn't. Or, maybe he didn't want to communicate with me. Maybe he had changed his mind and had chosen Kat. Maybe he hadn't known how to tell me, so he just didn't.

And what was the deal with Zoë? I'd just thought she was self-centered. What if she really couldn't deal with the way the world had changed? What if she was really pregnant?

My thoughts kept me wide awake. I fed the fire, stayed wrapped in a blanket, and every hour walked around the boat checking to make sure we weren't about to crash into anything.

Around midnight, the military scavengers finally headed back to the base. I wondered what treasures remained on some of the big ships. A find of toilet paper would be huge. I decided to talk to the crew about boarding one of the ships before we left the area.

Off our bow, a short ways away, a huge cruise ship floated. It was over twenty stories tall and the size of a city block. It would be a good place to search for supplies, even though the military had been all over it. I studied the huge boat closely, trying to find a way for us to get on board. It seemed to be listing hard to one side. I hadn't noticed that before, but then, I'd been busy.

Suddenly, I heard the creak and groan of bending metal. The entire cruise ship shook, and then crashed with an enormous splash onto its side. The splash created huge waves. And the waves were headed right at us.

"Wave! Hold on," I yelled to the sleeping crew, and turned the wheel to aim *Whistler* into the waves. But without the sails or power, the boat didn't respond. I braced myself. Dylan, Angelina, and Nick raced up on deck.

"What's going…?" Dylan stared at the approaching ten-foot wave.

I gestured. "That cruise ship just flipped over." The first wave hit us from the side. We rocked so hard I had to hold on tight to keep from falling off.

Whistler righted herself and we braced for the second wave. As the wave grew near, the cruise ship shuddered, then sank, stern first, into the sea. The sea above the ship began to fill with bubbles. Frothy water churned and fizzed.

A second wave hit. Dylan and Nick wrapped their arms around the mast as they worked to raise the sail. The third wave headed toward us was much smaller. With just a little of our sail up, I was able to turn *Whistler* into it.

Nick and Dylan hurried to pull up and out our sails. I checked the boats that were still scattered around in the bay, searching for any that were listing hard. We watched the air bubbles spread over the sea. Dylan and Nick finally had both the main sail and the jib up. They were securing the lines and facing away from where we were headed.

A life raft that had come off the cruise ship bounced over the water where the ship had gone down. Suddenly, it sank in the frothy water the sunken cruise ship had created.

Angelina grabbed my shoulder. "Did you see that? The little boat just disappeared in the bubbles."

"Ready to come about!" I screamed.

"What?" Dylan dropped the line he held and stared at me.

"Bring the main in. We have to get away. Boats are sinking in the bubbles." I nodded at the churning water.

Nick ran to the stern to grab the jib line. Dylan held his hands on his hips. "We need to head into the waves."

"No! The waves are not our biggest problem. The sea is full of air. Everything in it sinks. Watch."

A tugboat that had been floating close by the cruise ship drifted near to the churning water. Suddenly it disappeared beneath the surface. Just like the life raft had.

Dylan gasped and brought in the main.

We were only about a hundred feet from the bubbling sea. I spun the wheel. Dylan let out the main. The sail luffed.

Dylan screamed. "Turn us!"

I shoved the wheel around as far as I could. "There isn't enough wind."

"Do something!" Nick yelled.

We watched a small pleasure boat sink in the froth. We were fifty feet away.

Whistler was still floating towards it.

A gust of wind hit the boat. For a moment, the sail filled and we heeled over. I yelled as I gripped the wheel to keep from falling.

Then the wind died.

A tugboat, dead ahead, sank in the air bubbles.

Another blast of wind overpowered the sails. *Whistler* spun around. We were finally moving away from the bubbles.

"That was close." My legs felt like rubber and I plopped down. Angelina took the wheel.

We left the bay and entered the open waters. A steady wind filled the sails and we picked up speed.

We were headed away from Santa Barbara… and Takumi.

"I'll go down and check on Makala." Angelina squeezed my shoulder.

"Get some rest. I'll take over," Nick told Dylan and me.

Dylan tried to argue with him, but Nick kept reminding Dylan that it was his wedding night. Dylan hadn't slept for days either.

I left the boys and crept below.

Angelina stood in the doorway of the girls' cabin. "Makala didn't even wake up. I'll stay on deck and help Nick."

I nodded and climbed next to Makala, and Boots came and snuggled. I buried my face in my pillow and let the tears flow.

We'd left Takumi behind. I'd never see my grandma again. My best friend from home was trapped in the snow. Cole was dead. And there was nothing I could do to make any of it better.

It was still dark, when I woke up to still-rough seas. Makala sucked her thumb and rolled back and forth with the waves. I checked my cell and saw I no longer had service.

Unable to sleep, I put my phone away, and waited for morning.

Chapter Twenty-Five

I don't know how long I lay there, trying to force sleep to come. I couldn't keep going without it. But Dylan was yelling up on deck and he sounded upset. I groaned and wondered, "What now?"

I rubbed my eyes and felt around on the bed. Somehow Makala and Boots had left the cabin. I hadn't heard them, so I must have gotten at least some sleep.

Nick called out, "Twenty-three feet."

"Drop anchor," Dylan ordered.

The boat shuddered and I heard a splash. We'd returned to the island of Santa Cruz. I hopped out of bed and climbed up top. The tacky wedding decorations were gone. The only reminder of the wedding fiasco was Zoë. She wore a sheer white nightgown under her heavy jacket. I couldn't believe she'd actually stolen a nightgown from the yacht in Grays Harbor.

I joined the rest of the crew, who were staring out at the long beach dotted with kayaks, rowboats, and half a dozen tents.

Were my parents in one of the tents? My heart thumped in my chest.

"Good. You're finally awake," Dylan grinned. "Want to go ashore and find Mom and Dad?"

"I'll get a jacket," I said and headed below to check my cell. Still no service. The time was eight a.m. Early, but not too early… I was surprised the people onshore weren't up and out of their tents already. I shrugged. Maybe they were on island time.

At the last minute, I grabbed one of the water bottles we kept refilling and a leftover rice ball. Dylan rowed ashore while I ate. I jumped out of the dinghy and held onto the line while Dylan climbed out and pulled the dinghy a ways up the beach.

"It's strange everyone is still asleep." I tied the line to a beach log.

"Maybe they partied late last night." Dylan glanced nervously around at the tents.

We hadn't talked about it, but I knew he was as worried about seeing our parents as I was. There was no good way to tell them Cole was gone.

I took a deep breath and walked toward the closest tent. Flies on the beach were horrible and grew worse as I neared the small dome. I slapped the canvas door and a swarm of flies flew out. That was gross. So was the terrible smell. I held my nose.

"Hello!" I called. "Hate to wake you. We're looking for our parents."

There was no response. I pounded on the tent again. Dylan and I exchanged looks. He leaned down and opened the flap.

"Oh, God!" He turned and vomited in the rocky sand.

I held my nose and peeked inside. Two people were lying on top of sleeping bags. They were covered in flies. At first I couldn't tell if they were male or female. As I moved closer, I could see that one was a man, the other was a woman.

Were they our mom and dad?

"Mom?" I squeaked and entered the tent. A fly crawled out of the mouth of the male. I shuddered and swatted at the flies. They flew up and into my face. I screamed, closed my eyes and covered my nose and mouth.

Before the flies could settle back down, I knelt beside the woman. Her hair was long and dark. Nothing like my mother's.

"Toni! Get out of there. They might be contagious!" Dylan screamed.

If they were, it was already too late for me. I found a towel and covered the woman's face. I threw a sweatshirt over the guy. As I backed out, the flies returned.

Dylan grabbed my arm.

"Maybe you should keep away from me too," I told him. "I might be contagious now."

"You're right. But it's probably too late for me as well."

I collapsed on the log we'd tied the dinghy to and smashed three flies between my hands. "Dylan?"

"What?" Dylan stood staring out at *Whistler*.

"Nobody has come out of any of the tents." I scanned the beach.

"I know." Dylan joined me on the log. Gentle waves lapped at the shore. Our boat glistened in the morning light.

We had five tents left to investigate.

The excitement we'd felt earlier turned to dread as we approached each tent. The next two tents held dead young men. None of the bodies had any wounds I could see, although I wasn't willing to touch them or look under their clothing. In one of the tents, the guy had been sick. There was vomit around the bed. But the young couple and the other guy just seemed to have died in their sleep.

Who would we find in the last three tents? Is this how we'd see our parents—dead and covered in flies? I started to shake. Then I heard a noise. I grabbed Dylan's arm. "Listen!"

We squinted at the tent we were about to investigate. Then I heard it again. A moan. Dylan and I looked at one another. Someone was still alive. I ran to the tent. "Mom!" I prayed as I threw back the flap

The flies were almost as thick as they had been in the other tents. Although this was one of the smaller tents, there were four people in it. Two children and two adults. None of them were my parents.

The man opened his eyes, stared at us for a moment, and mouthed, "Water."

I scanned the others. One of the kids moved. At least two people were still alive. I ran to the dinghy, grabbed my water bottle, and hurried back.

"What's going on?" Angelina called out from *Whistler*'s deck.

"What are you doing?" Zoë sounded annoyed.

I gestured toward the tents. "The people in those tents are dead, but we just found a family. At least two are still alive."

"I'm coming ashore," Zoë yelled.

"No. Stay back. Let us check things out." I entered the tent. Dylan held the flap open.

"Small sips," I told the man as I held the bottle up to his lips.

He took a drink and fell back on the sleeping bag. "My family…" he gasped.

I carefully climbed over arms and legs and went to the child that had been moving. I propped her up. Her eyes rolled back in her head.

"Here," I whispered. "Water. I have water." When she didn't respond, I poured a tiny bit into her mouth. She coughed and most of the water dribbled down her chin.

"Come on!" I begged. "Wake up. Drink."

She choked again but opened her mouth. I poured a tiny bit in. This time she swallowed it. I tried again. Just a little. She swallowed again. Four more times I got her to take small sips. Finally, I laid her back down.

A woman lying next to her was not moving. I started to check her out when I heard a faint whimper. I stepped over the woman to a toddler who was curled up next to her. His eyes stayed closed when I picked him up and carried him outside. I poured a little water into his mouth like I had the little girl. He made a gurgling sound, but swallowed it. I took off my coat and laid him on it.

Dylan and I pulled the father out of the tent and into the fresh air. I leaned him against a log while Dylan went back for the girl. He laid her on the rocky sand next to her dad.

I took turns giving them all sips of water until my bottle was empty.

"I need more water. I'll be back," I told the man.

"There's no water," he said in a raspy voice, and grabbed my hand. "Don't go."

"We have water on our boat." I stood. "I'll be back."

"I'll go," Dylan offered.

I nodded and walked with him toward the dinghy.

"What about the mom?" I whispered to Dylan when we were far enough away I didn't think the dad could hear.

He grimaced. "Dead."

"And the rest of the tents?"

He shook his head.

My hand flew to my mouth. "Are Mom and—"

"They aren't here. There's another couple. They're dead too."

"We have to stay away from *Whistler* until we find out what killed all these people. We can't take an illness back to them," I whispered.

"Dylan!" Zoë yelled. "You get back here."

"But…!" Dylan whispered to me as he held his hand up to Zoë.

"No buts. Have them throw supplies at you, or better yet, float them in one of the plastic bins. We are going to be here a while helping this family and we can't be around anyone until we are sure we aren't contagious."

"Damn!" Dylan headed for the dinghy.

Dylan and Zoë had a heated discussion while he rowed to *Whistler*. She insisted we needed her help. Dylan argued it was too risky and reminded her that she was pregnant. I went back to the family lying on the beach. Both the kids were asleep or passed out. The father mumbled something I couldn't make out.

I kneeled beside him.

"Wife?" he croaked.

"She didn't make it. I'm so sorry."

He closed his eyes and his body convulsed. "My fault," he moaned.

I decided to give him a few moments alone and went back to their tent. I tried to ignore the flies and dead body and started pulling out duffels and sleeping bags.

"Toni, what are you doing? Get out of the tents," Zoë screamed across the water.

I turned to her. Dylan was floating in the dinghy a short ways off the stern. Nick was tossing water bottles into the dinghy. Zoë and Angelina were on the swim platform filling a plastic bin with stuff.

"Zoë, I've already been exposed. Quit yelling." I hurried with my arms full of supplies back to the dad.

I put a life jacket behind his head as a pillow. He stared into space.

"Look," I told him as I unzipped the sleeping bag and covered him. "You have two kids that need you. I know this is incredibly hard. I just lost loved ones too. But you can't fall apart. They're just kids and you're all they have."

He inhaled deeply and for the first time seemed to notice his children. I pulled the sides of the sleeping bag out and moved the kids on top of the bag that covered him. He continued to silently cry. The toddler whimpered. The little girl opened her eyes.

Dylan returned with the water bottles. He handed one to the man. I was glad to see he had the strength to lift the bottle to his mouth, but I had to stop him when he began to guzzle it.

"It will all come back up if you drink too fast." I pulled the bottle back.

"I'll go slowly…" he gasped.

"Okay then." I gave it back.

He took a long swig, sat the water down beside him, and closed his eyes. Dylan grabbed it before it tipped over and screwed the lid back on.

I placed another life jacket under the little girl's head and drizzled water into her mouth. This time it went down smoothly. I held the toddler on my lap and gave him a little at a time.

I laid the toddler back down and covered each of the kids with smaller sleeping bags. Both the kids, and finally the father, fell asleep.

Dylan gestured for me to follow him. He perched on the edge of the dinghy and I joined him.

"How long are you planning to nurse this family back to health?" he asked.

"Dylan!"

"Mom and Dad might be in the next harbor. And didn't you text Takumi that you'd be right back? We're wasting time."

Part of me knew he was right. I glanced at the tents and then at the family that was barely alive. "We don't know what happened here. If we're contagious we can't go anywhere anyway. We have to help this little family recover and maybe do something with the dead bodies."

"Dead bodies! We are not touching them." Dylan stood and began to pace. "We've already taken a big risk. Look around. There is death and disease in every tent. We need to get away from here as fast as we can."

"The dad seems to be getting stronger. I bet he'll be able to talk soon. Once we learn what happened, we'll know how to deal with it. Can you just relax until then?"

Dylan stared back at *Whistler* and Zoë. "No. I wish we'd never stopped here."

He rowed to the boat three times for supplies. Each time I was sure Zoë would come back with him, but she didn't. It gave me a small amount of pleasure to know she actually listened to him.

We spent the morning giving water to the family and preparing our campsite. Dylan brought back a tent for us and I gathered firewood. There weren't any trees around, and surprisingly, very little debris on the beach. I gathered mud-covered dead shrubs, but knew they would burn up quickly. The toddler started moving around and began to whimper. The man was awake and watching us, but didn't react to his son. The toddler's cries grew stronger and louder. The dad didn't seem to notice. After about ten minutes of constant crying I couldn't stand it.

"Your son needs you." I stood over the dad with my hands on my hips.

"Mother," the man whispered. "Needs mother."

"You are mom and dad now." I picked up the little guy and laid him on the man's chest. "Comfort him." I walked away.

The toddler's cries stopped for a little while, then started back up. I tore branches off the dead brush I'd gathered and pretended to ignore the pitiful cries. Finally, it stopped. I watched the man massaging his son's back. The toddler had his thumb in his mouth.

It was a start.

Chapter Twenty-Six

Zoë's high-pitched voice echoed across the water. "Soup's ready."

Dylan headed for the dinghy.

"Let me go this time." I ran past him.

It felt wonderful to be back on the water. The gentle waves comforted me. I felt clean and safer. I wondered how I'd manage to sleep with dead bodies all around me. And flies? I shuddered. I would never go off and leave the young family helpless, but I understood Dylan's desire to flee.

"Where's Dylan?" Zoë called to me as I rowed.

Boots yipped. He was excited to see me.

"Quiet," Zoë yelled and clapped her hands at the little dog. Boots put his tail between his legs and ran to Makala.

"Don't talk that way to Boots!" Makala comforted the quivering dog.

I spun the dinghy around. My back was to *Whistler* as I rowed. Dylan was building a fire pit with some large rocks. If I could see him, so could Zoë.

"I need to talk to Dylan!" Zoë's shrill voice had gotten louder.

I dipped the oars in the water. "Talk to him, then. We can hear you loud and clear from the beach."

"You are so mean!" Zoë cried. "This is my honeymoon, and I'm not with my husband. He won't let me go ashore."

The dinghy bounced on a wave. "Believe me, you are better off on *Whistler*. There are dead bodies and so many flies it's just... He's trying to protect you, and the baby."

"But what if he gets sick?"

I stopped rowing and floated around so I could face her. Angelina and Nick joined Makala and Zoë on the stern. "We're helping a father and his two kids. They seem to be getting stronger. Once we learn what happened, we'll know what to do. Dylan and I both want off that beach badly."

I shoved a plastic storage bin toward the swim-platform. "You mentioned soup?"

Angelina stepped to the rail. "Since the family was so dehydrated, Zoë thought they might need salt to retain water. She suggested we make a salty soup. We used part sea water, some seaweed for vitamins, and a whitefish that Makala caught."

"Makala caught a fish?" I grinned at her.

Makala smiled shyly and nodded her head.

Angelina winked. "She did. And it was a big one too."

"Sounds yummy." The fish soup reminded me of something Takumi would make. I pulled out my phone to see if he'd sent a message. My cell battery had died.

The crew floated the bin out to me. A small wave rocked it. I worried it would tip and spill the soup, but soon I had the bin securely onboard the dinghy. I unloaded the kettle, the utensils, and a bottle of gin.

"Gin?" I stared back at Angelina.

"Pour it over your hands to disinfect them," she said.

I laid my cell in the bottom of the bin and shoved it back toward *Whistler*.

"Please charge my phone the next time you have power. And if I get a message, read it to me." I watched the crew as I rowed with my back to the beach. Makala kept waving at me.

Nick fished the bin out of the sea. "We're short on water. We need to leave tomorrow to find some."

I steadied the pot as a wave rocked the little boat. "The dad is almost ready to talk. Hopefully we can go with you."

"Are you feeling okay?" Angelina asked.

"I'm fine. But I hate being around all this death. It's so sad. And the bodies are just… rotting. We should bury them, but I'm afraid to touch them."

"What about burning them. Tents and all?" Angelina suggested.

"Will the canvas burn?" I turned to see how close to the beach I was.

"I've heard of tents catching on fire, especially if the tent is old. The newer ones have fire retardant built into the canvas, but they'll burn if the fire is hot enough," Nick said.

"I saw you gathering dried brush. Maybe if you put some kindling inside the tent, and piled more on top, you could get a blaze going," Angelina suggested.

Dylan had been listening to our conversation and called out, "Remember when you gave away two containers of gas to those Coast Guard dudes? If we had that gas, we could make a really hot fire."

Dylan was right, but I had no regrets. The gas I gave to the desperate sailors might have saved their lives. The people in the tents on shore were already dead.

"What about a burial at sea?" Nick suggested.

"We'd have to get them out of the tents and onto a boat. I like the fire idea. No touching allowed, but at least we'd be stopping the flies and risk of disease." I hopped out of the dinghy and sat the soup pot on the beach. Dylan secured the little boat.

"What do you think?" I asked him.

He shrugged. "I'm not sure it will work, but it's better than doing nothing. What if we wait until low tide and drag the tents to the shoreline? Fire them each up as best we can, and then let the tide take what's left out to sea."

It wasn't a great plan, but it was something we could handle. I would sleep better at night knowing we'd given the people who'd died some kind of closure. I picked up the pot and headed up the beach.

The dad was helping his daughter drink from a bottle of water when I showed up with the soup. Four empty water bottles lay in the sand. That seemed like a good sign. The toddler stared up at me, his eyes huge and questioning.

"Anyone hungry?" I showed them the pot of soup.

"She's not doing well," the dad croaked as he laid his daughter back on the edge of his sleeping bag. She groaned and closed her eyes.

I poured a little soup into a plastic cup. It was still hot and the cup warmed my hand. "Maybe this will help. Zoë, my brother's wife, was a sports medicine student. She said you all need salt to help you rehydrate. She and my friends made a salty fish soup for you."

The man pushed himself up and took the cup. He glanced down at it and made a face.

"The green stuff is seaweed. My boyfriend says it's full of all kinds of good stuff. It takes a little getting used to, but grows on you after a while."

The man took a sip, looked up at me, and mouthed: "Thank you." He turned on his side, raised his daughter's head, and fed her. The toddler held his arms up to me. I scooped him up and held him on my lap. After a moment, he struggled to get back to his dad, but stopped when I showed him the soup. He hungrily ate almost a half a cup.

The act of eating wore them all out. I covered the family back up and sat with Dylan while we had our lunch and planned the rest of the day.

The tide was still coming in. We spent our time gathering as much dry brush and wood as we could find. The larger pieces Dylan threw into the campfire pit he'd built for us to light at night. Soon we had a six-foot high pile of dried brush.

Dylan and I took turns forcing the family to drink small amounts of water as often as we could. There was no one on *Whistler*'s deck most of the afternoon. I guessed they were napping.

When the tide began to turn, Dylan and I decided it was time to talk to the dad. He had been growing stronger by the hour. The toddler was still weak, but alert. The little girl worried me.

The dad was sitting up watching us as we approached. Dylan blurted out, "We need to know what happened here."

The man nodded. "Can you take me to the bathroom first?" His voice was weak, but stronger than it had been. And if he had to go to the bathroom, didn't that mean he was doing well?

Dylan propped him up and took him away. I kneeled to check on the kids. The little girl was asleep and felt hot. The toddler grinned at me. The dad asked Dylan to stop at his tent on their way back, then crawled into his tent by himself. When he opened the flap, a swarm of flies escaped. I covered the kids and my face with blankets.

The dad was in the tent for a long time. Finally, he emerged with a pillowcase full of the family's belongings, and handed the bag to Dylan. When he was settled in, I asked, "How did all these people die?"

He spoke in a soft whisper. Dylan and I had to lean close to him to hear.

"My name is Greg." He laid his hand on top of his children's heads. "This is Beth and Byron. Our family's from Santa Barbara. We went to the mountains to be safe from the tsunami, and came back when it was over. Our home was destroyed." He laid his head on the log behind him. I handed him one of the last of the water bottles, and he took a big swig.

Greg scooted forward and continued. "We ended up in one of the camps. There wasn't enough water or food. And it was dangerous. A group of us joined together to protect ourselves. We talked about getting away."

He took a deep breath. "Most of us had gone on day trips to Santa Cruz Island. We knew it had water. We searched the California shoreline for broken and abandoned boats and kayaks, saved as much water and food as we could, and headed out. We figured we could make it over here in one long day. Two, at the most. But a storm hit."

"Oh no!" I groaned.

He lay back on the log. "We tied our kayaks and boats together and rode it out. We arrived here four days later. We ran out of food and water on day two."

"Were any of you sick? I hear there's sickness in the camps." Dylan stared down at Beth.

"No. I don't think so. Some got seasick. They grew weak faster than the rest of us and were the first to die."

"That had to be horrible." I scooted down in the sand beside Byron.

His head drooped. "We'd become close friends."

Dylan began to pace again. "So you made it to the island. What happened then?"

Greg narrowed his eyes at Dylan. "We came ashore at the first land we found. I still don't know the name of this beach. A couple of us were strong enough to go and look for water. But there wasn't any. By the time we figured it out, we were too weak to row away."

I took his hand.

"My wife refused to eat or drink early on. She gave the kids and me her rations. She didn't make it, but her sacrifice…" He stared at his kids.

A tear rolled down his cheek. "Beth needs a doctor and Byron needs his mom. I don't know what to do."

I patted Greg's shoulder and stood. Dylan and I moved to the receding water's edge.

I whispered in Dylan's ear. "We need to tell him our plan to burn the tents. He should have some say. His wife is one of the dead. The rest were his friends. The good news is, if they all died from dehydration, they weren't contagious."

"If he's telling the truth." Dylan scowled.

I took a step back. "Why would you say that?"

"He's not stupid. He knows that we won't take them with us if they're sick."

"Stop it, Dylan. The man just lost almost everything. We need to burn the bodies and get his daughter some help."

"After we look for our mom and dad."

I sighed. "First things first."

Greg was appalled at our plan to burn the tents with the bodies, but finally agreed if we would let him bury his wife. I wasn't sure how we would manage that, but we agreed.

We ate the last of the fish soup for dinner. It had been cold for hours, but was still filling. The conversation had been too much for Greg. He barely managed to feed the kids and change his son's diaper before he fell asleep.

Dylan and I put on winter gloves and covered our noses and mouths with scarves Zoë had sent over. We pushed, pulled, and dragged the tents down to the shoreline. We had waited all day for low tide, and now that it was here, we were racing the clock. Halfway through the process, I started to limp. My injured ankle was hurting, but there was no time to baby it. I kept going.

Finally we had all the tents lined up, except for the one with Greg's wife in it.

We ran back and forth from the pile of dried brush to the tents. At first we threw the branches into the tents, then tried to pile them on top. But everything rolled off the rounded roofs. Finally, we unhooked the poles that held the domes up. When the tents collapsed, we had a place to pile more sticks and twigs.

Greg woke up and watched us. So did the crew from *Whistler*.

"Okay, it's time," I told Dylan.

Dylan searched his pocket for matches, but came up empty. I reached into the bag of supplies Greg had brought out of his tent and found a stick lighter.

"Wait!" Angelina cried from *Whistler*. "We should at least know their names. We need to report their deaths."

To whom, I wondered. But Dylan and I turned to Greg.

He pointed at the tent farthest away. "Susan and Bill Barnes."

One by one, Greg told us the names of the campers. Dylan called them out to Zoe, who wrote them down in dad's logbook. Dylan lit the dried twigs inside the tents first, then those on top. Slowly, every tent burst into flames, although some smoked more than others.

Angelina read a short verse from her Bible for every name. Nick sang, *Amazing Grace.*

Soon the shore was ablaze and Whistler's crew grew silent. I leaned on Dylan as the fires raged on. I wanted to cry, but somehow couldn't. Dylan was tense and fidgety. Greg cradled Byron in his arms and shed enough tears for all of us.

It was dark and cold when the fires finally died out. Dylan and I found a sandy hill a short ways from the campsite, and began digging with the small shovel we'd gotten off the boat. We made great progress at first, but then hit a hard rocky layer. The grave wasn't as deep at it should have been, but it would have to do.

Greg laid his sleeping son down and pulled his wife's body, wrapped in a sleeping bag, out of the tent. "Her name was Beverly," he mumbled. He insisted on carrying Beverly to her grave. Dylan steadied him from behind and twice had to help him up when he fell.

We gave Greg and his deceased wife some time alone. He knelt beside the grave, sobbed, and told her how sorry he was. Alone with his sleeping sister, Byron woke up and began to wail. I ran to him. Dylan went to the shore to check on the burning tents.

I handed Byron to Greg when I felt it was time and began shoveling the sandy dirt over the top of

Beverly's body. Dylan showed up and took over. When the grave was filled in, Dylan brought the rocks he'd used to make a fire pit and stacked them on top of the mound of dirt.

We left Greg and Byron at the gravesite. Beth slept through it all.

Dylan headed for the shoreline. He gestured back at Beth. "She's sick."

I shrugged. "Maybe she just got really dehydrated."

"You and I are out of here first thing in the morning."

"We can't leave them here. They'll die."

"If we take her with us, she could make us all sick." Dylan kneeled and washed his hands, using sand as soap.

"She doesn't have diarrhea. That's the kind of sickness everyone on shore had." I poured gin over his wet fingers.

Dylan reached for the bottle. I held it behind my back.

He glared at me. "What if we tow them behind us in the dinghy? We have to find water before we head to the mainland anyway, and Zoë could treat her from a distance. With a little medicine, food, and water, maybe she'll get better on her own."

I exhaled with relief. It wasn't a perfect solution, but it was something.

Chapter Twenty-Seven

Dylan was gone when I awoke. I'd slept surprisingly well on the hard sand, but then it was also the first full night of rest I'd gotten in days.

I peered out from the tent flap and found Dylan building a fire. Greg perched on the log he'd been leaning against the day before. There was no sign of the children. All but one of the tents we'd burned had washed away. We'd have to drag the last one back down into the water. That wouldn't be fun.

The morning air had a chill to it and the clouds seemed darker than normal. I wrapped my sleeping bag around my shoulders and joined the guys.

"How are the kids doing?" I plopped down next to Greg.

He hung his head and mumbled something I couldn't hear.

"Sorry?" I faced him.

He raised his bloodshot eyes. "Byron is okay. Beth isn't doing as well. But she woke up and went to the bathroom this morning."

"She can pee? That's good, right?"

His head drooped. "Her skin feels hot and she keeps asking for her mother."

I glanced at Dylan. His lips were pursed.

"You're going to leave us here, aren't you?" Greg said softly.

I shook my head. "No. But as long as Beth has a fever, we can't let you onboard our boat."

"So you're going to stay?"

"No. We have to leave. Our boat is out of fresh water now, too. But, we can tow you in our dinghy. It's large. We have extra blankets and even a tarp. And we have some medicine onboard. As soon as Beth's fever is gone, you can get on our boat."

Greg stared at *Whistler*. "You have a blue sailboat."

His statement caught me off guard. "We do. It's my family's boat. Dylan's my brother."

Greg nodded. "There was a couple who traveled with us. They were looking for a blue sailboat."

Dylan stopped feeding the fire and stared at Greg.

"Do you remember their names?" I croaked.

"Debbie and Alan. They rode bikes all the way from Seattle."

I began to tremble. Dylan closed the distance between us in seconds. "What happened to them? Where are they?"

"You're their kids, aren't you?" Greg said. "You look like your mother."

Dylan was ready to pounce. I pulled him down beside me. "Please. Tell us where they are."

"I don't know where they are. They didn't come with us into the bay because there wasn't a blue sailboat or people around. They were looking for the boat or people who might have seen their children. They decided to keep going along the coast."

"Were they healthy? Did they say which bay they were headed to?" Dylan's eyes narrowed.

"They were dehydrated and exhausted like the rest of us, but otherwise, fine. They didn't say which harbor they were going to."

"Were they heading North or South?" I asked.

"North."

"Why didn't you tell us this earlier?" Dylan gritted his teeth.

"I was pretty out of it yesterday. It wasn't until this morning that I realized your boat was blue." Greg hung his head

Dylan hopped up.

I grabbed his shoulder.

He shook it off. "We have to go. If you want to leave with us, you ride in the dinghy. Come or not. Your choice."

Greg turned and faced the hill where his wife was buried.

"Your children need a future," I said, and headed to my tent.

****

It took us less than an hour to load the dinghy, with Greg, the kids, and our gear. He insisted on tying his rowboat behind the dinghy with his camping gear. We attached a couple of kayaks that had belonged to the dead campers behind his boat to put onboard *Whistler* later. We only had one kayak left.

Nick held up his hand to stop us as we neared the sailboat. "Guys, we're a little worried here."

Dylan swung the dinghy around so he could see Nick. "Worried? About what?"

Nick gestured at the shore. "A lot of people died there. We don't want you exposing us. Zoë's pregnant and Makala is just a child."

"Greg and his kids are going to stay in the dinghy," Dylan said.

Nick busied himself straightening the sail lines. "Yeah. But, we think you and Toni should stay on the dinghy too."

Dylan almost dropped his oars in the water. "You're kidding. You're telling us we can't get aboard *our own* sailboat."

Nick turned to face us. "I'm asking you to not put us at risk."

I grabbed the sides of the dinghy. "Nick. We told you. They all died from dehydration."

"They're dead. You aren't doctors."

"So, how long do you expect us to stay in the dinghy?" Dylan snarled.

Angelina and Nick studied one another. "Until the little girl is better or we get to the next anchorage. You can go ashore and camp," Angelina said.

"Wow. Nice of you." Dylan turned the dinghy back around and continued rowing.

A cold wind came up. The water in the bay became choppy. The ocean would be even rougher. We were in for a miserable time. Greg slid down on the floor of the dinghy and held his children close.

Dylan threw a line and Nick tied the dinghy a short distance behind *Whistler*. We brought the kayaks around and Nick and Angelina hauled them onboard.

"Are you really going to make us do this?" Dylan snarled as Nick raised the sails.

Nick nodded. "We don't have a choice."

Zoë joined Angelina and Nick on the stern. Boots and Makala were surprisingly absent.

"Honey," Zoë began. "I'm sorry. But it was my idea. The little girl has a fever and must be sick. If the antibiotics make her fever go away, then we know we can cure whatever illness she has. We have to protect our baby. It's not just all about you and me anymore, you know."

Zoë had banned us from our boat. Zoë!

****

Nick, Angelina, and Zoë handled the sailboat well without us. I wasn't sure how I felt about that, but soon we were out of the bay and sailing along the coast. The clouds grew darker and a drizzling rain began to fall.

We were moving at a fast pace. I hated to slow down our progress, but we were getting soaked.

"Take the boat into the wind," I yelled at Nick. "We need the sail cover."

When the boat slowed, we pulled up close to the swim step. Angelina and Zoë threw raingear and the canvas sail cover at us. We moved Greg and the kids to the bow and tied the canvas over the top of the dinghy. We couldn't see a thing huddled under the dark fabric, but we were dry.

The air grew stale, and when little Byron had a dirty diaper, unbearable. We had to throw off the canvas for a few minutes to keep from getting sick. But Greg rinsed the diaper out in the sea and soon the motion of the waves lured the children back to sleep.

I startled awake when Nick yelled, "Drop anchor." Dylan and I yanked back the cover. The rain had stopped, although the air was still chilly. When my eyes adjusted, I scanned around the narrow inlet we had entered. Off the port side, a stream of water poured out of a cave and splashed down the side of the cliff. It was lovely—and had to be fresh water.

The entire bay was surrounded by steep cliffs that rose to what seemed like a hundred feet from the sea above us. The bay itself was only slightly wider than *Whistler* was long. I couldn't believe Nick had brought us to an inlet that was so tight.

Dylan scowled with concern. "Nick, what the hell? Why'd you bring us in here?"

Angelina was behind the wheel. Nick counted the marks on the anchor chain as he lowered the anchor. The sails were down. The wind was blocked by the high cliffs anyway.

"Because of the beautiful waterfall," Zoë said, and grinned.

"Are you crazy?" Dylan swiveled from side to side. "There's not enough room to turn around in here."

"Just back out," Nick shrugged.

"Back out?" Dylan screamed. "We can't sail backwards. And we're almost out of gas. I don't know how the engine started last time. We were running on fumes."

Nick's face fell. "I didn't... We saw the waterfall and thought... I've seen sailboats bring the boom all the way around."

"You idiot! You've been on *Whistler* for over three weeks now. Our boom doesn't do that!"

Nick went silent. The stern began to swing toward a sharp rock jutting off the side of the cliff.

"Get us out of here. Now! Try the engine. Angelina, put it in reverse. Nick, pull the anchor up as *Whistler* starts to back up. Don't wait for the anchor to be up all the way. If there is any gas left, there's not much."

Nick ran to get the key. Angelina stood behind the wheel. Nick turned the key. There was a clicking noise, then nothing. He tried again. There was a puff of exhaust out the stern. The engine rumbled for a second, then died. By the fifth try, there wasn't even the clicking noise. Not only were we out of gas, the starter battery was dead too.

"We're trapped." Dylan slammed his fist on the dinghy. The toddler began to cry. I felt like joining him.

"Angelina, find the boat hook and keep *Whistler* off the rocks," Dylan yelled. "Zoë, lift the storage hatch and pull out the stern tie ropes. We need two lines."

"What's a stern tie rope?" Zoë peered down in the deep storage locker

"It's a colorful nylon rope. Like a water-ski rope."

"Is this it?" Zoë held up a reel of red, blue, and yellow line.

"Yes. Did you find two?"

Zoë laid the line down and dove head first in the locker. After what seemed like forever, she appeared with a tangled ball of the same colored line.

"Nick, help me," Angelina yelled as *Whistler*'s stern headed for the cliff face.

Nick grabbed an oar and joined her. Together they managed to stop the boat from smashing on the rocky wall.

Dylan gestured for me to follow him and yelled at Zoë. "Okay. Fasten one end of the line to the port stern cleat, and hand that line down to us."

"Which side is port?" Zoë turned from side to side.

"The side farthest from the cliff." Dylan stood and pointed. "Greg, get ready to fend off the dinghy too." Dylan and I climbed over all our gear, and jumped into Greg's rowboat.

We rowed alongside. Zoë threw me the wheel of colorful lines. One end was tied to *Whistler*. I slowly let the line out as Dylan rowed toward the cliff.

"Why are we doing this? We have to find Mom and Dad. Takumi is waiting. We can't stay here," I said through clenched teeth.

"If we don't stern tie, *Whistler* will be smashed on the cliff. We don't have our other anchor. If we had it, we could just throw it off the stern. But we let it go, remember?" He took the line and began climbing the cliff. From a distance, it appeared to go straight up, but close in, there were a number of boulders that stuck out. About twenty feet up, two hardy trees hung on with deep roots. Dylan wrapped the line around one of the trees, and pulled hard.

Whistler's stern slowly moved back to the center of the bay. Dylan climbed back into the rowboat and handed me the spool of line. I kept the line tight and fed it out a little at a time as Dylan pulled us hand over hand along the end of the line. There was about fifteen feet of slack line left when we made it back. Nick secured this end onto *Whistler*, too.

Zoë and Angelina were frantically untangling the second line. We floated and waited. Byron woke up and began to wail. His cries echoed in the tight little bay. I was happy to see Greg care for him.

"What are we going to do?" I studied the bay. It was only slightly wider than *Whistler* was long.

"I don't know. Even if we manage to turn the boat, the cliffs block the wind. I don't know how they managed to sail in this far." Dylan spoke loudly, not caring if everyone heard him. "We can try towing it with the dinghy and the rowboat. But I think we'll need help."

At long last, the line was untangled. Dylan rowed to the waterfall side of the bay. This time, Dylan found a log held fast beneath a pile of rocks to wrap the line around.

There was about ten feet of line in reserve when I handed it back to Nick.

"Won't we get hung up when the tide goes down?" Nick asked me. He and Dylan were avoiding looking at one another.

"We'll leave some slack, and let the line out or bring it in, according to the tides. Kinda like going through the Ballard locks. It's good we have extra line. We'll need it as the tides change," I told him.

Angelina tilted her head back and stared up at the falls. "I'm ready to go explore. Do you think there is another way to get up there?"

I followed her gaze up to the cave the water poured out of. It had a fairly wide opening. The water ran in a trough in the middle of the cave. Clear fresh water splashed down into the sea and I wondered if my parents had found this water. Takumi would have loved the waterfall. I sighed and reached for the cell I no longer carried.

Chapter Twenty-Eight

Dylan and I kept a close eye on *Whistler* to make sure the anchor held and she was secure in the tight inlet. Nick and the girls left the deck and went below.

"What are we going to do now?" I asked.

Dylan stared up at the cliff. "If Zoë won't let us onboard *Whistler*, I'm thinking of climbing up there, and checking out the cave. There might be a spot where we can spend the night. At least we'd be on land. Loading the water tanks is going to take most of the day, and I refuse to spend the night in this dinghy."

"And then?"

"In the morning we tow *Whistler* out. Backwards!"

"With the rowboats? Will that even work?" I stared at our boat.

"They used to tow the ancient sailing ships with row boats. They had more men than we have, and it was slow going, but they managed."

"They did? Really?" I craned my neck to better see the cave. "Okay, then. I'm going up there with you."

"But—"

"I'm a high diver, remember? Heights don't bother me, and if you can climb the wall, so can I. Besides, I don't want to sit around in the dinghy all day just collecting water."

Nick appeared on deck with Makala and a fishing pole. Without a word to us, they hurried away to the bow. Boots merrily followed.

Dylan elbowed me. "Tell Nick to fill the water tanks."

"Tell him yourself." I hunted through my bag for my sneakers.

Dylan sighed. "Hey, Nick. We need to fill the tanks with fresh water. Will you do that while Toni and I check out the cave?"

Nick stood with his back to us. He slowly turned and nodded. "As soon as Makala and I catch something. We're out of food, too."

Angelina brought up a large blackened pot. "We have rice. It's cold, but better than nothing. I'll help Nick collect water." She scooped the rice into soup bowls and floated the bowls over to us in the bottom of a bin.

Zoë appeared and worked on starting a fire in the cockpit barbecue. While we ate, Dylan told Greg our plan.

We asked Angelina to dig out an old rope Dad stored at the bottom of the storage locker. I tied the ends together to make two very long lines. Dylan took one line, while I grabbed the other. We wrapped the lines around our waists and climbed into Greg's small rowboat.

"Dylan," Zoë yelled. "We need firewood. If you find some up there, bring it down." Her voice echoed off the sheer walls.

I wondered how she thought we'd be able to climb down the cliff with an armful of wood.

"Throw me my backpack," Dylan said.

Zoë tossed the gear to Dylan but missed the rowboat. Dylan had to fish his pack out of the sea and put it on his back. Water dripped down his legs as he tied the rowboat off, then started climbing the cliff. I followed close behind him. The first half of the ascent was slow, but not too difficult. The higher we went, the steeper and harder it became. Wind and water had smoothed over much of the upper cliff's surface.

Dylan clung to an uncomfortable looking perch and called to me. "There's nowhere to go from here. Nothing to hold onto. I'm coming down."

Zoë yelled, "Careful, darling. Our baby needs a daddy."

I rolled my eyes and moved to a little ledge that jetted out. Dylan angled down and away from the falls, then tried going back up.

I watched his technique for a while and placed my hands and feet exactly where he did. But after a few minutes, I realized I had to find my own way. His arms and legs were much longer than mine.

The hardest part of the climb was moving horizontally toward the cave. I searched for a hold and wedged my foot into a small crack in the wall. I reached to grip onto a jagged rock, placed my foot on a point that stuck out from the cliff, and stretched out for the next handhold. When I neared the cave opening, Dylan leaned down and hoisted me up.

It took a few moments for my eyes to adjust to the dim light in the cave. It was too dark to see far and I wished we'd brought a flashlight. The ground was flat and smooth. A small stream meandered the floor of the cavern and trickled over the cave's opening to form the waterfall. There was room to stand on both sides of the stream. A number of stone outcroppings and ledges lined the walls of the cave, some big enough to lie down on.

With running water and places to sleep, the cave would make a great place to stay. I was sorry we hadn't found it earlier.

Dylan took a few steps towards the rear of the cave. "It goes back quite a ways, but it's too dark to see."

“I’ll have someone send up a couple of lights.” I tied one end of the rope to my waist and threw the other over the lip of the cave. It landed a few yards away from *Whistler*. “Angelina, Zoë, Nick. Tie a couple of flashlights or the lantern onto the rope, will you? The cave is awesome, but dark.”

Nick kayaked to the line. “I had to get into our stash of batteries to make the spotlight work.” He tied a black bucket to the rope I’d lowered, dropped the lights in it, and yelled at me to pull the bucket up.

Dylan picked up the spotlight and led the way. It was the same light we’d used to search the water for Cole. If Dylan remembered, he didn’t say.

I followed close behind with a little crank lantern. We hadn’t gone far when the opening narrowed to only a few feet above the stream. Dylan stepped down into the cool water and I followed. We had to stoop low, but after a foot or so, we entered a huge cavern. Dylan shined the light on the stalactites that hung from the ceiling. A small pool of water had formed off to the left. What appeared to be ancient drawings of animals decorated the wall to the right. The stream came out of a small opening at the rear of the cavern, but the opening was too tight for us to climb through.

“Guess this is far as we go,” Dylan sighed.

I cranked the handle of my lantern until the light was bright, and stepped over to the drawings. A stick figure of a man with a spear was hunting a heard of small deer. I turned to the side. In the corner next to the drawings, three bare trees, almost ten feet high, stood. I pushed on the one closest to me and it wiggled. The trees had been cut down and wedged into the rocks in the cavern by people at some time.

The leafless branches cast eerie shadows against the walls, and I shivered.

"Dylan, I have an idea." I spun to face him.

Dylan was on his hands and knees with the spotlight aimed into the tight opening at the rear of the cavern. "What?" He stuck his head into the hole.

"The trees. I'm pretty sure they're longer than the cave's opening is wide. If we drag one of the trees to the mouth of the cave, we could place it across the opening. We could secure our ropes to the log to help us ascend. We could even tie the camping chair on the lines and hoist our gear and Beth up, if Greg and the kids want to join us."

Dylan mumbled something about not being able to see a thing.

"Were you listening to me?" I shoved the tallest tree. It fell over with a crash.

"Toni!" Dylan leapt up and bumped his head.

I grimaced. "You okay?"

"What was that?" He rubbed his scalp and scanned the cavern.

I showed him the trees and repeated my idea. He moved beside me and lifted one end of the tree that had fallen.

"Jeez! It's heavy," he groaned.

"But that's good. It's strong. And we don't need to carry it. We could float it."

A smile broke across Dylan's face. "I have an even better idea. Do we still have that enormous piece of fishing net you and Takumi found when you rescued Boots?"

I thought for a moment. "We stowed it under the v-berth."

"What if we tied the net to the log and hung it from the mouth of the cave… We could climb up and down the net instead of the cliff. We could even take the branches off the trees and weave them in and out of the net to make footholds."

"That's a great idea." I looked around. "This is a cool place."

"It is. But don't tell Nick."

I grinned. "You're mean."

"Me? They're the ones who won't let us get on our own boat. I think we should set up the net ladder. It wouldn't take long, and we need the extra storage space on *Whistler*. By the time we're done, maybe Beth will be better. At least we'll all have a great place to sleep tonight."

"And bathe." I knelt and let the pure clean fresh water drip between my fingers.

We got the small hatchet from *Whistler* and chopped the branches off the tree. Then we tied a rope around the log and rolled it into the stream. Dylan pushed the front of the log with his foot to keep it going. When we were close to the cave opening, Dylan jumped in and hoisted the front of the log up and out of the water. Together we rolled the log across to the cave. The log stuck out more than two feet on both sides of the mouth of the cave.

"Is that enough to hold it in place?" I asked.

"Looks like it," Dylan said. "But just to be sure, let's get another log."

The second tree was even longer. We tied the two logs together and placed them back down across the opening.

We lowered the remaining rope and yelled at *Whistler* for the net. I wrapped the top of the net around both logs, and wove my line through the net and around the logs. I dropped the edge of the net in the stream and secured it on the bottom with boulders. The net wouldn't stop an adult, but it might keep one of the kids from being swept off the cliff.

Then we dropped the net down the face of the cliff. On our first try, we'd centered the net too much. Part of the net disappeared in the waterfall. We hauled it back up and moved it over.

When we dropped the net again, it fell perfectly down the side of the cliff and just barely touched the sea.

We had a ladder to our home for the next day or so. Dylan and I argued about who should go first. I won.

As we rowed back, everyone, even Greg, fired questions at us about our cave.

Our cave. The thought made me smile. It truly was the first place we'd found since the tsunami that felt like it could be a home. We couldn't stay until Dylan and I found our parents, and I talked to Takumi, but we could come back. When I asked how the fishing had gone, Nick and Makala held up three fish and a lobster.

"Wow. Which one did you catch?" I asked Makala.

"The big one." Makala pointed. "Can we have a fish picnic in your cave?"

"Sorry. Zoë said we have to stay away from you."

"Why? I want to see your cave." Makala pouted.

Zoë stood on the stern of *Whistler*. "What was it like?"

I told her about the pool of water and the drawings on the wall.

She folded her arms. "Did you find firewood? It's cold down here."

The cave had actually been warm, I realized, as icy sea water splashed my leg. We'd left the tree branches in a pile. I waited for Dylan to offer go back up for them, but he didn't.

We scrambled onto the rowboat and began rowing back to the dinghy. Little Byron was busy pretending he was fishing. He'd toss a line into the water and quickly pull it out, flipping drops of water across the dinghy.

He was cheerful and appeared completely recovered. Beth was even sitting up, awake. Her cheeks were a little red, but she seemed better. Greg however, was agitated.

"Is everything okay?" I got aboard the dinghy and pulled my sleeping bag up and over my lap.

"I want you to help us get up to the cave. It has water and would be a great shelter. Once we're settled, you can leave and go find your family."

Dylan and I looked at one another. "We can't abandon you here. How would you hunt or fish for food? You couldn't go off and leave the kids. The cave is great, but not a safe place for a toddler."

"Beth is six years old. She can keep an eye on Byron if I have to go out for a little while. They would be safer up in a cave than back at the camps of Santa Barbara. I won't take them back there." Greg inhaled and closed his eyes for a moment. "My wife sacrificed her life to get away from the disease and criminals in the camps."

"We won't make you go back to the camps. We promise. But there are good people here on the island that you could join up with. You need help with the kids."

"Forget it, then. I'll get them up there by myself. We're safer alone."

"Does Beth still have a fever?" Zoë had been listening.

Greg felt his daughter's forehead. "I don't have a thermometer. She feels cooler. The pills you gave us seem to be working."

Zoë floated the thermometer over to us. Angelina was piling some small pieces of wood in the barbeque. Nick was cleaning the fish.

"I'm sooo hungry," Makala complained.

"We'll have dinner as soon as I get the fire going." Angelina blew and sparks flew. "Nick kayaked all the way out of the mouth of the bay to find this wood, but it won't last. How long are we going to stay here?" She stared at Dylan.

"We need our water tanks full. Doesn't sound like you guys got that done," Dylan said as he tidied the lines. Dylan and Nick still avoided one another.

"While you were off playing Dora the Explorer, Angelina and I made three trips to the falls. But then I had to search for fire wood so we could cook your dinner." Nick concentrated on the fire.

"Whatever!" Dylan said. "Send me over one of the kayaks. While you're fixing dinner, I'm going to make a quick trip out of the bay and see if there are any settlements close by. We could use some help towing *Whistler* in the morning and I want to ask around about our parents. I won't be gone long."

"Fine." Nick tossed a bottle of water he'd refilled into the kayak, and then floated the kayak to Dylan.

Greg placed the thermometer under Beth's tongue and we waited. He read the results and showed the thermometer to me. Beth still had a slight fever, ninety-nine point four, but that was much lower than it had been.

"The medicine is working," I told Zoë.

"She still has a slight fever."

"Ninety-nine point four isn't much of a fever," I mumbled as I picked up Byron and rocked him.

Greg touched my shoulder. "I want to check out the cave. Will you watch my kids for a little while?"

Byron was asleep and Beth was easy. "Okay. Take your shoes off to climb the net. Works better. I'll watch the kids, but don't be gone too long."

Beth scooted over to me and asked me about my family. I offered to tell her a story instead. Makala sat on the stern of Whistler, wrapped in a blanket, and listened. I told them both Makala's favorite story about a little mermaid. Byron woke up and cried when he realized his father was gone. Beth tried to comfort him, but he wouldn't stop whimpering.

Makala began singing: "Twinkle, twinkle, little star." Byron finally stopped fussing to listen. Beth joined in the song. I stared up at the darkening sky. For the first time in weeks, I had a glimpse of a star between the breaks in the clouds. Then it was gone.

Chapter Twenty-Nine

Greg came back from the cave energized. He grabbed Beth and hugged her so tight she squealed. The dinghy rocked back and forth. "You should see it, Beth. It's everything your mom and I hoped to find on the island. I wish she…" He turned away and stared up at the waterfall.

"All right," Nick said from Whistler's stern. "I've heard enough about this cave. Zoë, Beth's fever is going down. Let's call her good. I want to see it too."

Angelina smiled. Makala jumped up and down. "Can we go, Sissy?"

Zoë shook her head. "If you all get sick, don't blame me."

"Either the antibiotics worked, or she got better by herself. It doesn't matter. You said if her fever went down, we'd all be safe. She's better. Don't you want to check it out? Toni said there's a fresh water pool. We can take a bath!" Angelina grinned at Makala. Zoë's eyes got huge. "I didn't think about that. Was it a hot springs?"

I shrugged. "No, it's cool, but not cold. Just imagine. Fresh water. No salt drying on your hair or skin."

"Okay, then. I agree." Zoë grinned. "The little girl is well, and Toni and Dylan can get back on *Whistler*."

****

We ate fish and boiled seaweed, then organized ourselves for the short climb up to the cave. I reminded everyone who was climbing to go barefooted and headed up first with my shoes and supplies in my pack. Angelina followed me. Nick carried Makala on his back and then went back for Beth.

Greg insisted he could put Byron in his pack. When he got to the top, I took Byron from him. Zoë came last. Her backpack was stuffed to overflowing.

Boots barked and barked from the closet on *Whistler*. We'd agreed he'd be safer on the boat, but he wasn't happy.

I turned on the spot light and gave a tour. The children had to be held when we stepped into the stream to enter the large cavern. Everyone was fascinated by the art on the wall and the hanging stalactites.

Greg held Beth's hand while she led him around and shined her flashlight. "Here, Daddy. We should sleep here." She climbed up on a slightly raised area, where the last of the dead trees remained wedged upright in the rocks. "We can hang our clothes on the tree and see, there's just a little light coming from the cave opening." She smiled.

It was the first time I'd seen her smile. Maybe Greg was right. Maybe they would be fine alone.

"Okay. Everyone out. I want to take a bath!" Zoë laid her bag down at the side of the pool.

I shook my head. "Nick, why don't you help Greg carry the rest of his gear … We'll watch the kids and wash up."

"I'm not taking a bath with all of you!" Zoë cried.

"Leave your underwear on. It's just like wearing a swimsuit anyway." I swung Byron up in the air. He giggled.

Zoë frowned. "But, then it's not a bath."

I started taking off Byron's clothes. His little bottom was red and he needed a bath more than all of us. Beth watched him while I undressed, then I carried him into the pool with me. At first he was startled, then he splashed and laughed. Byron's joy was all it took to get everyone in the water.

Zoë climbed in the water then opened her backpack. She pulled out a couple of towels, some lotion, and a huge bar of designer soap.

"Soap!" Angelina cried. "You've had soap all this time."

"Zoë!" I glared at her.

"Don't '*Zoë'* me. I am having a baby. I need to keep clean. I've been saving this soap for childbirth. It is a dangerous time for women, you know."

"Hand it over," I demanded.

"No, I brought a knife. I'll give you each a little sliver of soap. And that's it."

"You're giving the bar to me to wash Byron with. Then you can do your slicing thing."

"Fine," Zoë scowled, but passed me the bar. After a while she even offered us one of her towels and a cap full of shampoo. But she had to let us know that she'd brought the second towel to dry her hair. It would be a sacrifice, but she would try to make do with just one.

Angelina and I dried the kids off first and she held Byron for me while I dressed. Angelina was great with him. He adored her right from the beginning. I noticed Zoë watching us with the toddler, but she didn't offer to help.

I searched through Greg's gear for clean baby clothes, or at least a clean diaper. I even found some baby ointment for his bottom. There was a bag of dirty diapers and I thought about Beth's idea of hanging them on the tree to dry. It took a while for the little girls to act comfortable with one another, but they were soon chatting away. When the girls finished getting dressed they headed for the back corner of the cave.

Makala said she wanted to see the animals again. Angelina and I found a blanket and laid Byron down to dress him. He started to fuss and Angelina held a musical toy near his face to distract him. I put the ointment on his sore bottom. I wasn't sure how to use his cloth diapers, but Angelina knew. She showed me how to Velcro the diaper into the plastic liner. The cleanest clothes I found for Byron smelt sour, but at least they were dry.

Greg and Nick returned with the gear and asked if they could enter the cavern.

"I'm not dressed yet," Zoë yelled as she rubbed lotion over her flat stomach.

"Fine, we have one more load to bring up. And then we should go down and start collecting water," Nick said.

"We'll be ready," I told him although I hated the thought of leaving the cozy cave.

While Zoë was busy getting dressed I stole her bottle of shampoo and started washing Byron's diapers. The water slowly drained from the pool and entered the stream. I hoped Nick wasn't at the bottom of the falls filling a tub with the water we'd bathed and washed diapers in.

Zoë was furious with me when she saw me using her shampoo, but I didn't care. Soon all the diapers were at least somewhat clean. I was spreading the diapers over the tree to dry when the guys came back.

"Are you dressed yet?" Nick called to us through the cave opening.

Zoë was tying her damp hair up on her head. "Almost!" She stepped into her pants. "Okay. You can come in, now."

Nick carried a large load in fount of him as he entered. Greg followed close behind.

"Daddy, Daddy, Daddy!" Byron cried.

Greg took him from Angelina and sniffed his head. "He smells great. Thank you, girls." He glanced around the cavern. "Where's Beth?"

We spun in a slow circle, looking for the girls.

"Makala?" Angelina cried.

"Beth? Where's my daughter?" Greg yelled.

I took a couple of steps back, and stumbled into the pool. "They were right over there!" I gestured at the drawings on the back wall of the cave and stepped out of the water.

We stared at the tiny opening near the picture. The one Dylan had bashed his head looking into.

"No!" I gasped. "They wouldn't go in there." I desperately searched. "They have to be here. They must be hiding. Makala, Beth, come out. This isn't funny."

We listened, but there was nothing.

Angelina ran to the cave opening and yelled for Makala.

"You said you'd watch her," Greg yelled, and his fingers formed a fist.

Nick grabbed Greg's shoulder as he moved towards me.

"Hush," Angelina said. "I think I heard them."

We all leaned toward the tight opening. Angelina called to them again. We waited.

Angelina turned around. Her eyes were huge. "I heard them. They're in there. We have to go after them." She started clawing at the edges of the opening. A small bit of rock crumbled away.

"Help me!" she screamed.

Greg ran over to the tree, knocked the diapers to the ground, and dragged it to where we stood.

"Mommy!" We heard one of the girls cry from deep inside the passageway.

How far in where they? I couldn't tell. "Hurry!" I yelled and then remembered Byron. Where was he?

Again I scanned the cavern for a missing child. I was breathing so fast, I felt faint. But Byron was okay. Zoë sat on a giant boulder with Byron on her knee. She was bouncing him up and down, then made a face, and turned away when he spit up on her shoulder.

Nick helped Greg lift the end of the log up and wedge it into the opening. "On three, shove the log to the side. Maybe we can use it as a lever and dislodge some of the rocks."

We tried the log from all angles. The rock edges crumbled, but not enough to make the gap in the rock wall big enough for any of us to climb into.

Nick was about to strike at the cave with the hatchet we'd used to cut the limbs off the tree when Dylan began calling to us.

He entered the cavern and stood with his hands on his hips. "Why isn't anyone guarding *Whistler*?"

I pointed to the narrow crack in the cave wall. "Makala and Beth snuck into the passage behind the cave. Now they're lost in there. And the opening's too small for us to climb into."

Dylan ran to the narrow slit in the wall. "Jeez, how did they get in there? I would think it was too small for even them."

Both girls screamed from deep inside the passageway.

"Girls, talk to me. What's going on?" Greg yelled.

"Have them follow your voice," Dylan suggested. "Keep talking to them."

"Beth, come this way. Follow my voice. Keep coming."

"We can't see!" Beth cried. "The flashlight's broken. Daddy. I'm scared."

Greg's face filled with panic.

Angelina grabbed the hatchet from Nick and struck at the opening. Small chips of rock fell away. She struck again and again. When she grew tired, Nick took over.

"You're going to be okay. Don't move. Just stay where you are. We'll get you out of there!" Greg screamed.

"I don't know what to do!" I clung to Dylan's arm. "I was supposed to be watching them. It's my fault."

"We'll get them out. Everyone calm down. Toni, you're the smallest. Keep trying to climb in." Dylan pushed me forward.

I tried to squeeze through the gap, but the opening was still too small.

Then, in the distance, I heard the roar of an engine. We all paused and turned toward the mouth of the cave. A motorboat was in our tiny bay, heading towards us.

"*Whistler*!" Dylan hissed. "Nobody's onboard."

Chapter Thirty

Dylan headed for the mouth of the cavern.

"Forget your boat," Greg said and grabbed Dylan's arm. "You're going to stay and help me get my daughter out of there."

Below on *Whistler*, Boots began barking again. His yips became frantic growls, as the sound of a large power boat grew closer.

Boots! I waved my arms to get everyone's attention. "I have an idea. Boots is small. We can send him to find the girls and lead them out. I could even tape a small flashlight to his back so the girls will have light again."

Angelina and Nick looked at one another.

Nick nodded. "It's worth a try. He isn't the smartest dog, though."

"How can you say that? He loves Makala. And he's a dog. He can follow her scent." My hands were on my hips.

"Sissy!" Makala screamed from deep within the cliff.

Angelina took the hatchet from Nick. "Go. Get Boots." She swung and chipped away a tiny bit more off the rocks.

Dylan left the cave seconds ahead of me. I stripped off my clothing as I ran. It would be faster to dive off the cliff than to climb down and row back to *Whistler* like Dylan would do.

I stood on the cliff's ledge. Halfway down the long narrow inlet, a large silver boat was cruising our way, but at a cautious speed. I searched for what appeared to be the deepest water below me. A clock began ticking in my head. I couldn't worry about protecting *Whistler*. I had to get Boots up to the cave. Dylan would have to keep whoever was on that silver boat off of *Whistler* by himself.

I took a calming breath. Just like the time I rescued Takumi and Kat, I couldn't be sure what was below the water. I remembered the seaweed that had almost drowned me, and jumped instead of diving. The water was much colder than I'd expected and I kicked hard for the surface. This time, nothing caught my legs and I swam fast, toward our boat.

Boots' barking grew frantic. As I pulled myself up out of the water, I wanted to yell at him to calm down, but I was out of breath.

I stumbled to my cabin and grabbed Angelina's backpack. I pulled on a pair of pants and an old swim team sweatshirt and began to thaw. I left my feet bare for the climb back.

The silver boat was now close enough I could hear voices coming from it. Dylan was still paddling his kayak back to *Whistler*. I raced past the closet where Boots whined and found Angelina's pistol in the captain's desk. My hands were shaking as I searched the silverware drawer for the bullets. I dropped as many on the floor as I managed to get into the gun.

"Toni," Dylan finally called out from the stern.

I took the stairs two at a time. I placed the loaded gun on the captain's seat. Dylan handed me the dinghy line.

The silver boat was slowing to a stop right off our stern.

"Greetings, *Whistler*," a gray-haired old man in a military uniform yelled to us.

"The gun's on the seat cushion. It's loaded," I whispered to Dylan as I tied the dinghy off and ran to get Boots.

Dylan hurried up onto *Whistler*'s deck. "That's close enough." Dylan leaned against the rail and aimed the gun at the man in uniform.

The old man chuckled. "Just as feisty as ever, I see."

His voice sounded familiar. I lowered Boots into the rowboat, looked up, and studied the gray-haired man.

"You're Toni, aren't you?" He smiled down at me.

Dylan cocked the gun.

"I'm Commander Wilson, formally of the U.S. Coast Guard. Now with the United States Combined Forces." He smoothed his blue and red uniform jacket. "You, young lady, saved my life and the lives of the men in my lifeboat. Do you recall this incident?"

I smiled back, then climbed aboard the dinghy. "You're the… Of course I remember. Right after the tsunami. You and the guys in your raft were injured and out of fuel and water. We gave you some."

"As I recall, you were the one who argued on our behalf. Every man on that raft is alive today because of you."

"I'm glad." I picked up the oars.

"As am I. Most of the men that were on that raft are stationed now in Santa Barbara. When they told me you were somewhere on this island, I had to come and thank you in person."

I paused. "You heard I was here?"

The Commander turned to the man next to him. "Sergeant, please escort our guests to the forward deck."

A sliding door off the port side opened. Takumi and Jervis stepped to the rail and made their way to stand next to the Commander.

"Takumi! Jervis!" I screamed, started to stand, and almost tipped the rowboat over.

"Toni, are you all right? Why did you leave?" Takumi moved to the rail. His hair was cut very short and he wore blue pants and a red jacket I'd never seen before. He looked cute, but not like my Takumi.

"We waited, but you didn't show up on the beach." I started rowing back to the cave. Dread weighed me down. Why was he here? Did he just come to say good-bye? Was he going to tell me that he was staying with Kat?

I sped up and wished I wasn't facing him.

"Wait! Where are you going now?" Takumi's voce grew louder. "When *Whistler* left, I went crazy. I thought you'd be right back. When you weren't I tried to find a boat. Then I ran into Jervis."

"Hi, Dylan. Hi, Toni." Jervis grinned and waved. Two little girls, one around six, the other eight, ran to his side.

I was still processing what Takumi had said, but managed to smile back. "Jervis! You found your family." I turned around to check how close I was to the climbing net. There was still about a hundred feet to go.

Jervis's grin faded. "Well, not all. Mom and the girls made it from Disneyland to the military base on foot. Along the way, they all got dehydrated and sick. The medics were able to help my sisters, but there was nothing they could do for my mom. She died before I found them."

"Oh, Jervis. I'm so sorry," I said.

Jervis cleared his throat. “Commander Wilson has been trying to locate our dad for us. All we know is that he is stationed at one of the border camps.”

“So, you told the commander about *Whistler*?” Dylan waved the gun in the air.

“I did. Then he told me the story of almost dying in his raft after the tsunami. I remembered him and here we are.”

I kept rowing. “I’m sorry. I can’t talk right now. Makala and another little girl are lost in that cave.” I gestured with my paddle.

Dylan paced from one side of the stern to the other. The commander spoke quietly to a young soldier who stood next to him. The soldier hurried away and returned with a young woman dressed in the same blue and red uniform he wore.

“Toni and Dylan, this is our technology specialist, Sergeant Livingston. Please explain in detail the emergency situation you are facing.”

I told her how the little girls had climbed through the narrow crack at the rear of the cave. I explained how close Boots and Makala were, and that I was sending him in after her. I’d thought about strapping a flashlight to his back but was open to suggestions.

The woman nodded. “I can stick a small wireless device on Boots’ collar. It has a speaker-phone and can light up the cave. I’ll track the dog on a monitor, and if he becomes confused or lost, I can track him on GPS.”

“Perfect,” I said. “But we are running out of time. If you want me to row back and pick you up, you have to be on *Whistler* when I get there.”

Both Jervis and Takumi offered to carry Boots and the equipment up to the cave. “Hurry!” I spun the boat around.

The gangplank lowered towards *Whistler*'s deck.

Dylan pulled out his gun. "Only Jervis, his sisters, and Takumi can come aboard."

Takumi scowled, ran onboard, and down to the swim step. "Knock it off, Dylan."

Jervis held his sister's hands and helped them across. "Dylan, you gonna take on the entire U.S. Military? They went out of their way to help us find you."

"I'll need to set up the monitor in the cave," Sargent Livingston said. "The signal will get lost in the rocks."

"Permission granted, Sergeant." The commander turned to Dylan. "Son, I applaud your vigilance. But, on my honor, we are only here to help." The Commander motioned for the woman to follow Jervis.

Dylan sighed and put the gun in his waistband.

The girl winked at him as she walked the plank. "Hope you put the safety on, Rambo."

Dylan pulled the gun out of his pants and set the safety.

I made it back to *Whistler* and threw the line to Takumi. As soon as he climbed into the rowboat, he pulled me into his arms and hugged me. "I've been so worried."

I didn't hug him back.

Takumi held me at arm's length. His forehead creased and he seemed confused.

Boots whined and jumped at him. I scooped the little dog up and moved to the bow. Takumi tipped his head and stared at me.

"Hmmm. Didn't you say we had to hurry?" Sergeant Livingston jumped into the dinghy and handed the monitor to Takumi.

Jervis' stared down at us. His sisters begged to go with him. He argued that he would be right back. The youngest girl started to cry.

"Jervis, stay with your sisters and get them settled. We'll let you know if the plan doesn't work and we need to dig out the tunnel." His sisters were stressed and we had to leave.

"But Makala…" He stared up at the cave.

"We have lots of help. Your sisters need you more." Takumi handed me the monitor and started rowing.

Jervis' brow wrinkled as he hugged his sisters to his side and watched us row away.

"How's Kat's dad?" I held Boots in my arms and had to force myself not to scream, "Faster, faster."

Takumi leaned into the oars, rowing with all his might. "He's okay, now. He had surgery and almost didn't make it. Kat begged me not to leave until he recovered. Now, he and Kat are going to stay on at the base with the medical personnel."

My face burned as he talked on about Kat, but I my gritted my teeth, and tried to focus on the girls trapped in the cave.

Angelina was singing with Makala and Beth to calm them when we arrived. Nick and Angelina were angry I'd been gone so long, and then shocked to see Takumi. We quickly told Angelina and Nick about Jervis and the military vessel. The sergeant set up the monitor, put the device on Boots, and yelled at the girls to call his name.

Both Makala and Beth called to Boots. When we lowered him onto the floor of the passageway beyond the cavern, he sniffed the ground once, and took off. We lost him from view a couple of times, but then watched on the monitor as he ran right to the girls. They were huddled together and tears streaked their faces, but Boots soon washed them away.

The Sergeant instructed the girls to follow Boots, and we all called to him. Twice he ran ahead of the girls. They screamed when they were left in the dark. The Sergeant told Beth to take the device off Boots and hold it in front of her like a flashlight. The girls followed Boots, and the Sergeant's instructions, back to us.

Angelina pulled Makala out first. I don't know who was sobbing harder.

Greg held Beth in his arms. "Are you okay? Are you okay?" he asked her again and again as tears streaked his cheeks.

I thanked the Sergeant and she began to pack up her gear.

From inside the cave, Boots yipped. We'd forgotten him. His floppy ears came into view as he tried to leap out of the deep gap.

Takumi reached down and lifted him out. His tail wagged as he welcomed Takumi back, then ran to Angelina and Makala, and barked some more. He knew he'd been the hero.

Chapter Thirty-One

Greg insisted on remaining with his kids in the cave for the night. We gave him our crank lantern, one of our flashlights, and he moved to the part of the cave closest to the opening. "It's too dark in the rear cave and I don't want to go through this again."

"I won't go into that black hole, ever again," Beth promised. We grinned and told Greg to lower the bucket, and we'd send up some fish and rice for his dinner.

While we rowed back to *Whistler*, the commander spoke to us from the deck of his ship. "So, how are you guys going to get your boat out of here?" He surveyed the narrow inlet.

Dylan paused rowing. "I kayaked to a settlement about a mile to the north. I told the settlers that if they came here and helped us tow the boat out of the bay, they could explore an awesome freshwater cave. A couple of people said they'd be here in the morning." Dylan stared up at the cave. "Greg, the father of the two kids, won't be happy with visitors—especially if they decide to stay—but in the long run, he can use some support."

"I see," the commander said and rubbed his chin.

Dylan picked up the oars and continued rowing. "Toni, I didn't get a chance to talk to you. Mom and Dad had been there. At the settlement I kayaked to. They stayed for a couple of days, resting up after the rough crossing."

I bolted up in my seat. "How were they? Did anyone know where they were headed?"

"The people I talked to said they were okay. Still looking for us. They'd heard from some guy in Santa

Barbara that a blue sailboat was headed for the border. Shortly after Mom and Dad arrived on the island a large custom sailboat named *Carolina* anchored off the beach. I guess most of its crew decided to stay on the island. Mom and Dad offered to crew, and the captain was happy to have them. The boat was headed for Tijuana."

"No!" My knees started to buckle. "We were so close. It's not fair."

Takumi wrapped his arm around me. I'd missed having him to lean on.

The commander stared at Dylan and me. "With your permission, captains, I'd like to anchor in this bay for the night. When we are secured, you and all your crew are invited onboard for dinner. What do you say?"

I sniffed. "That would be nice."

Takumi and I sat on the bow of *Whistler*, watching the clouds darken. Night finally arrived. He reached for my hand. I pulled it away and pretended to smooth my hair.

"Toni! You can't be angry. You left *me* behind."

I could see why Takumi might think that, but I'd imagined him with Kat too many times to just forgive him for taking off with her. I stared for a long moment at a seagull as it circled a log and landed with a squawk.

When I turned back, I told him about the sharks and the messages we'd gotten from our parents. "We waited all day and into the night for you to show up on the beach. You didn't. Just before dawn, a huge cruise ship sank. One by one the boats around us started disappearing into the bubbly water too. We put up the sails and barely got away. Once we were a safe distance away, well, we decided to keep going and find our parents before they moved on."

I walked to the rail. Takumi followed. The seagull cried out again.

I absent-mindedly watched the bird. "I honestly thought we'd find our parents and come straight back. In the text they sent, they said they were right over here. But at the first camp we sailed to, we found tent after tent of dead bodies."

"Dead bodies?"

"Dylan and I were terrified that we'd find our parents dead and covered in flies. It was awful." I shuddered. "And then Zoë wouldn't let us back on board."

"Zoë? Zoë wouldn't let you or Dylan…?"

"Nope. She said we were contagious. Nick sailed us into this bay. We didn't see where we were going until it was too late."

Takumi glanced around at the cliffs that pinned us in. "I wondered why you sailed in here."

I looked into his eyes. "We always planned to go back for you."

"I hoped it was something like that. Not that I hoped you'd find dead bodies. I'm so sorry."

Tears welled in my eyes. "My parents were right next door." I turned to face the mouth of the bay. "They were at a settlement a short ways east of here. We just missed them. Now, they're sailing to Tijuana."

"At least you know your parents are still alive and where they're headed."

I sniffed. "Did you ever hear from your family?"

Takumi shook his head and gripped the rail.

I reached out and touched his arm. "So what are you going to do now?"

"What do you mean?" Takumi asked.

"Well, are you going back to the base or…?"

He gently turned my face to his. "I plan to go wherever you go. That has always been my plan."

"But what about …?" I couldn't look him in the eye.

"Toni! Do you want me to leave?" Takumi whispered.

I'd been afraid for days that I was losing him. Now I was pushing him away. What was wrong with me? "No. I want you to stay," I said in a small voice.

"Then come here." Takumi wrapped me in his arms. I melted into him as the tears I'd held back for days flowed down my cheeks. He slowly kissed the fear and horror I'd kept hidden deep inside me, away.

"I missed you." I pulled him down onto the deck with me. Our kisses deepened until there was only the two of us.

"Time for dinner," Zoë's shrill voice called out.

I moaned as the real world intruded on us, again. We kissed once more, then our breathing slowed to normal, and we sat up.

Zoë stood on the stern dressed in a long, glittery gown. We stared at her and burst out laughing. The more the world around us changed, the more Zoë stayed the same. In a strange way, it was comforting.

*** *

Dinner was fabulous. The cook prepared real hamburgers and crunchy French fries. There was even cheese and fresh tomatoes. And ketchup. I didn't realize how much I'd missed ketchup until that meal. I forced myself to eat slowly and not gorge myself. But I still managed two hamburgers and three helpings of fries.

Dylan attended, although he arranged so one of our crew was always on board *Whistler*. Zoë beamed with the compliments the Commander gave her on her dress.

When Makala saw Jervis, she started to run to him, then stopped and stared at his sisters. Jervis kneeled and opened his arms.

Makala wrapped her arms around his neck. "Where'd you been?" she asked.

We laughed, and for a moment it felt like old times.

Jervis introduced us to his little sisters, Rebecca, and Naomi. They were as small as Jervis was large. Their eyes were huge and dark in their thin faces and they were too quiet. I could tell by the way Jervis watched them that he was concerned.

Makala glared every time one of the girls spoke to Jervis. His sisters scowled at the way Makala clung to him.

Angelina and Nick took Makala back to *Whistler* right after dinner. She was exhausted and we worried she'd fall apart and say something awful to one of Jervis' sisters.

Towards the end of the evening, the commander stood and turned to Dylan. "Young man, I know you have rowers coming to tow your boat out of the inlet, but may I make a suggestion?"

Dylan smiled through clenched teeth.

"You are all exhausted. Why don't you stay put for a week. Resupply your boat with wood, water, and whatever food you can find. I wish I could share more of what we have, but supplies are running low, and there are so many people in need."

"No! We need to follow after our parents," I cried.

Jervis took a sip of his soda. "I need to check the border camps for my dad."

I'll put a call out to the border patrols to be on the lookout for a sailboat named *Carolina.* The patrols can tell your parents where you're going. What is your next destination?"

Dylan narrowed his eyes at me. I didn't know what he was trying to tell me, so I let him do the talking.

Dylan stood. "We'll sail to Tijuana. If our parents could just stay there until we arrive, that'd be awesome."

"Works for me, too." Jervis nodded.

The commander nodded. "Okay, I'll tell the patrols to pass on the information. It would take you most of a week to tow this boat with your rowboats, anyway. And you would wear yourselves out even more. My crew and I will be honored to return in seven days and tow you out to the sea with the *Silver Rose*." He placed his hand over his heart. "My men and I owe you our life. It is our privilege to help you."

****

Dylan finally stowed the gun when the *Silver Rose* motored out of the bay the next morning, then went to bed.

Takumi and I snuggled together on *Whistler*'s deck, wrapped in a sleeping bag.

"Want to go up to the cave later? You didn't really get a chance to check it out. We could even camp up there if you'd like." I was thrilled to have Jervis and his sisters on board, but it did make the boat crowded.

"I'd like that." Takumi nuzzled my neck. "But no place is better than where I am with you."

"Does that even make sense?' I snickered.

"Think about it."

We watched a seagull drop a shell onto a rock ledge. The shell exploded and the seagull landed and ate his breakfast.

“Why didn’t you text me back when you were at the base? I texted and texted you,” I asked.

“My battery died and I forgot to bring my charger. Before we left to find you, one of the soldiers let me use his. I finally saw your messages, but when I texted you, you didn’t respond.”

I laid my head on his shoulder. “We lost service as soon as we got to the island.”

Takumi checked his phone. “You’re right.”

“I wish you’d had a chance to meet my parents.” Takumi studied his feet.

“Me too.” I turned his face to mine. “We’ll find my parents and then a make a new life.”

“Do you think they’ll like me?”

“They’ll love you. I’ve been thinking. Maybe when it’s all over, we should come back here.” I glanced up at the cave.

“Really? I thought we were headed to Mexico or maybe even further south.” Takumi thought for a moment. “We should camp in the cave, then. Test it out.”

“A whole week in one place. I can’t believe it.” I squeezed Takumi’s hand.

“I almost forgot. I brought you gifts.”

“You did?” I grinned.

Takumi left and came back with a burlap bag.

I smiled as I pulled out six rolls of toilet paper and stacked them beside me. “Nice!”

Then came two plain wrapped bars of soap. I inhaled the flowery aroma and told him about the soap Zoë had been hoarding. He shook his head and laughed.

The next item was a brand new tube of toothpaste. I solemnly promised to save it for special occasions.

But, as I dug deep, I realized he’d saved the best gift for last.

A very large bottle of ketchup.

"Wow! This is awesome. How did you know?" I read the label. It was a brand I'd never heard of.

"I saw you drowning everything in ketchup last night and begged a bottle from the cook."

I chuckled and put the bottle down. "Ketchup. I love it."

"I'm glad. Wonder how it tastes on seaweed…?"

I wrinkled my nose.

Takumi kissed my forehead. "I missed your funny expressions."

"Really? Kat didn't make silly faces at you?"

Takumi froze and stared into my eyes. "Yours is the only silly face I love."

My heart swelled with joy.

I pulled the sleeping bag up around us.

We still had a long ways to go, but with Takumi onboard, I could survive anything this messed up, crazy world threw at me.

For now however, I was going to relax, bathe three times a day, and enjoy just being in this beautiful place.

The End

www.brendabeem.com

Author's Note

Thank you for reading *Beached*. I do hope you enjoyed it. Word of mouth is so important to the success of any novel. I would be very grateful if you'd tell your friends and family about the Knockdown Series, and take a moment to post reviews on Amazon and Goodreads. Reviews only need to be a couple of sentences.

For updates on the series, or survival tips (should a mega tsunami be headed your way), visit my website: http://www.brendabeem.com

I love to hear from my readers. You can email me at brenda@brendabeem.com or friend me on Facebook.

Evernight Teen ®

www.evernightteen.com

Made in the USA
Charleston, SC
10 November 2015